Beachbound

OTHER TITLES BY JUNIE COFFEY

Sunbaked

Beachbound

Junie Coffey

LAKE UNION
PUBLISHING

Published by Lake Union Publishing, Seattle

www.apub.com

Amazon, the Amazon logo, and Lake Union Publishing are trademarks of Amazon.com, Inc., or its affiliates.

ISBN-13: 9781542046459
ISBN-10: 1542046459

Cover design by Danielle Christopher

Printed in the United States of America

Beachbound

1

Nina woke up with a loud banging reverberating through her skull. She rubbed her eyes and sat up, trying to get her bearings. It took her a moment to realize that she was on the faded chintz sofa in the cottage she had recently bought on the island of Pineapple Cay. She was still wearing her black silk party dress from the night before. She gingerly held the sides of her head with her fingertips and looked out the window at the beach. The sun was already high in the sky. The tide was out. Fronds of coconut palms swayed in a gentle breeze. With great physical effort, Nina shifted her gaze from the vista of white sand, palm trees, and turquoise water that constituted her backyard to survey her surroundings.

The room was a mess. Half the contents of her bookcase were scattered across the floor. A trail of wet towels led from the bathroom to the bedroom door. There was a half-eaten birthday cake on the kitchen table, the candles melted all the way down into pink wax puddles on the creamy-white icing. Next to the cake sat Ted Matthews's battered wide-brimmed khaki hat—the one she rarely saw him without. Nina's eyes widened, and she was suddenly jolted fully awake. What happened last night? Had Ted been there? Ted Matthews, the handsome neighbor who owned the fishing lodge on the point up the beach from her. Ted Matthews, with whom she had only recently shared a knee-wobbling kiss after many days of meaningful looks. Surely she would remember that.

Nina stood up cautiously and tiptoed across the room to her half-closed bedroom door. She paused for a second, listening for the sounds of Ted's breathing. Nothing. Then she heard the rustling of sheets as someone rolled over in bed. She pushed the door open with the tip of her finger and peeked in. Danish Jensen, her mailman/yoga instructor/bartender, lay sprawled across her bed sound asleep, wearing only his boxer shorts. Nina closed the door quickly and silently, then stood in the small hallway in her bare feet and wrinkled party dress while she tried to figure out what was going on and what she should do now.

She wasn't aware that the loud pounding in her head had stopped until it started again. This time it was not coming from inside her head, but from the front door. Through the sheer curtain covering the window in the door, she could see the tall, rangy outline of Deputy Superintendent John "Blue" Roker, the Pineapple Cay chief of police. He appeared to have a constable in tow.

Nina hesitated, then crossed the varnished pine floor to the door. *He must be here about Les.* Les was her recently arrived neighbor. The neighbor with the hot tub. The one with whom she had recently had words. But the look on Blue's face as she opened the door was far too serious for his visit to be about Les.

"Morning, Nina," said the ever-polite Blue Roker. He had the good looks of a movie star, tall with searingly blue eyes that contrasted with his smooth brown skin. He was not the chatty type, and this trait combined with his height gave him an intimidating presence. He'd been unfailingly courteous to Nina since she'd moved to Pineapple Cay a month and a half ago, but she still found him a little unnerving at close range.

"Hello, Blue," said Nina, careful not to stare directly into his eyes for too long. Her voice was a bit scratchy, it seemed.

"May we come in?" he asked, taking off his hat. His deputy did the same. She became very aware of the holstered gun on Blue's hip.

"Of course," said Nina, stepping aside to let the police officers enter. They made their way into the house's common area—an open living room/dining room/kitchen that ran the length of the cottage facing the beach and the Caribbean Sea.

"Please, sit down," said Nina, gesturing to the sofa and the matching chair beside it. She prayed that Danish would not choose this moment to make his appearance. She watched them sit, and the younger officer extracted a notebook and pencil from his pocket. They both studied her without speaking.

Trying to fill the silence, she asked, "Would you like tea or coffee?"

The constable opened his mouth to speak, but Blue cut him off. "No, thank you."

Nina watched Blue methodically sweeping the room with his eyes, logging the pile of books, the wet towels on the floor, the collapsed birthday cake, and Ted's hat on the table. His eyes rested on the hat for a couple of seconds and then flitted briefly to the bedroom door before he returned his gaze to Nina. She sat uncomfortably on a wooden kitchen chair. His gaze drifted over her mussed hair, bare feet, and disheveled dress, and then he glanced over to the high-heeled shoes discarded by the back door that led out onto the veranda. The shoes. Right. Nina wiggled her toes and felt sand between them.

"Nina, I have to ask you a few questions," said Blue. This was beginning to sound serious.

"OK," said Nina. "What's going on?"

"Are you a close friend of professor Philip Putzel?" asked Blue.

Philip. Nina almost laughed.

"No. I wouldn't say that, exactly," she replied. "He's the head of the department at the college in New York where I taught before moving here. I know him quite well, I guess, as a colleague. I sort of worked for him—or more precisely, under him. I was a junior instructor. He's a full professor with tenure. Untouchable." Blue looked at her intently as she spoke. The constable made a note in his notebook.

"Philip Putzel was attacked last night," said Blue evenly. "Someone tried to kill him and came very close to succeeding."

Nina breathed in sharply and covered her mouth with her hand.

Blue continued, his eyes fixed on hers. "He was found unconscious this morning by a hotel guest on the beach at the Plantation Inn. His injuries indicate foul play. You had dinner with him there last night, is that correct?"

That's right. The banquet. They had all been seated together around a candlelit table, the warm night air floating in through the open windows. Nina was seated with Philip on one side and Philip's ex-wife Sylvia on the other. Victor and Razor Hudson were there, and so was Philip's research assistant, Bridget. Bubba Delancy and his wife, the owners of Delancy's Distillery, had joined them. Nina recalled the moon on the water and the glittering lights from Bubba's yacht moored out in the cove. There had been a piano player dressed in a white dinner jacket playing old jazz standards in the bar. She remembered taking a sip of her wine as she settled into her seat, finally relaxing after the busy weeks of planning the symposium. The setting was magical, and the evening was unfolding nicely. She'd done her job well. And now someone had tried to murder Philip Putzel. A dead conference delegate would not be a sign of a successful event.

"Yes, I was there," said Nina. "Philip gave the keynote speech at the dinner last night. We were all there. It was meant to be a highlight of the conference. What happened? Is he all right? Do you need his wife's contact information?"

Nina glanced around for the three-ring binder in which she'd been keeping all the bits of paper related to organizing the conference. She felt slightly nauseous from the combination of her hangover and the shock of hearing about Philip. She was even woozier when she realized her binder was in the bedroom; getting it would mean opening the bedroom door. She sat for a moment, trying to take it in.

"I can't believe it. What happened? He was fine at dinner. Well, I mean he was in good health and content with the way things were going. He gave his speech, the dinner party broke up, and the last I saw him, he was regaling someone with a story in the bar, looking like he was having a good time."

Then another horrifying thought dawned on her.

"Wait a minute, Blue. You're not thinking I tried to kill him, are you?" She stared at him incredulously, temporarily immune to his mesmerizing gaze.

He looked at her without speaking for a second, rubbing his temples with the tips of his fingers.

"I'm asking for your assistance in solving this crime, and in preventing a second attempt on Philip Putzel's life. He's here on Pineapple Cay as a result of his connection with you. As far as we know, he has no other ties to the island of any kind. This is the first attempted homicide on Pineapple Cay in over twenty years. Therefore, I consider it unlikely that the perpetrator is a member of the local criminal class. They generally confine their activities to petty theft, small-time smuggling, and poaching. Whatever light you might be able to shed on the circumstances surrounding the events of last night would be very much appreciated."

"So, I'm a *person of interest*, assisting the police with their inquiries," said Nina matter-of-factly. She felt a bit insulted. "I didn't have to *kill* Philip Putzel to get away from his petty feuds and drama, Blue. I moved to a beautiful tropical island a thousand miles away."

"And shortly after you relocate, he also arrives; then, within forty-eight hours, someone tries to kill him. What feuds did you need to get away from?" asked Blue.

"Well, none in particular. He wasn't a factor in my moving to Pineapple Cay. I hardly ever think about him, to be honest, and I'm sure he thinks of me even less. He just isn't one of my favorite people. Unfortunately, he rubs a lot of people the wrong way, I'm afraid you'll discover. That doesn't mean I'm glad someone tried to kill him. Obviously."

Blue sighed. "Nina, look. I know you didn't try to kill him, all right? But I need a lead, and we're losing valuable time. We're a small detachment on a small island. I've grounded flights at the airport temporarily while we check out all arriving or departing passengers, and I have officers watching the marina and marine traffic, but as time passes, the attacker's trail will go cold. He or she could be anywhere on that big, wide ocean in no time flat. Worse, I have a terrible feeling that the perpetrator is still hiding somewhere on the island, watching and waiting for the opportunity to try again—and even more determined to succeed the next time. Whoever did this meant business, but the physical evidence at the crime scene is, so far, inconclusive. I need a motive. That's where I need your help. Who might want him dead? You know these people, don't you?"

"There are about fifty participants in the conference. I don't know all of them, and neither would Philip, but I have their names. I know the group seated at my table last night, some better than others. They would also be the people who know Philip best. Offhand, I'd say that most—if not all—of them have, at some point, been victims of Philip's breathtakingly callous treatment of anyone he feels is beneath him. Which is to say, pretty much everyone. It was some speech he gave last night. Ripped open a few festering wounds. But I can't really see any of them as a murderer. They're a bunch of book-toting college professors!"

"You might be surprised what your otherwise average human being is capable of doing on an otherwise average day," said Blue. "Let's start with the people who sat with Professor Putzel at dinner last night, then." He turned to the constable. "Mandy, will you please go get us some coffee? I think we're going to need it."

"Yes, sir." The younger officer started to rise. Nina thought of Danish slumbering in the bedroom a few feet away, and she jumped to her feet.

"Blue, I just woke up, and I think I'd be a lot more use to you if I could take a quick shower and change my clothes. I promise to be in your office in twenty minutes. If I'm not, you can always arrest me."

Blue hesitated for a moment, glancing at the bedroom door. Maybe he was weighing the odds of her harboring a murderer in her boudoir against a reasonable request to bathe. Maybe he was just wondering if his friend Ted was in there.

"Of course. We'll wait outside and give you a lift to the station. I appreciate your cooperation," he said. Blue rose, and his constable followed him out the door to a red Jeep with a police insignia on the door.

Nina saw a woman walking her dog on the opposite side of the street, her head swiveling to take it all in. *Great,* thought Nina. *The Pineapple Cay bush telegraph has been activated.*

As a rule, not much happened in the quaint village of Coconut Cove, population three thousand. The police chief's Jeep parked in front of Miss Rose's cottage, so recently bought by that lady from New York, would be a juicy tidbit to chew over down at Carrie's beauty salon this morning.

Nina showered as quickly as she could, letting the warm water run over her tender skull and wake her foggy brain. Wrapped in a towel, she stepped over the debris scattered across the living room floor, opened the door to the veranda quietly, and went out to snatch a clean pair of jeans and a pink flannel shirt off the clothesline. The air smelled sweet and soft, and the blue sky was dotted with puffy white clouds. She glanced up the beach to the point as she gathered her clothes. There was no movement in front of the fishing lodge. Only the roofs of the guest cottages and the main lodge were visible above the fringe of palms and casuarina pines that lined the sandy beach. The four or five outboard motorboats that were usually pulled up onto the sand in the evenings and on windy days were gone. It must be business as usual today at Matthews Bonefish Lodge.

Inside, she tiptoed past her bedroom door and slid on her flip-flops. She'd have to get to the bottom of the Danish issue later, when Blue Roker wasn't parked in front of her house. She shut the front door gently behind her. No one bothered to lock their doors on Pineapple Cay. That was how rare crime of any sort was.

As Nina approached the police Jeep, the constable hopped out of the passenger seat and held the door open for her. She slid in front beside Blue, and the constable shut the door behind her without speaking. Blue turned the key in the ignition, glancing into the rearview mirror as he pulled away from the curb. Nina looked back to see the constable still standing on the sidewalk in front of her house.

She turned to Blue. "So, you're watching my house? Is he waiting until we're out of sight to go rummaging through my underwear drawer looking for a smoking gun or a bloody knife? Or maybe there's a to-do list stuck to the fridge door with 'Kill Philip Putzel' written on it?"

Blue sighed again. "Right now, and until we can complete a thorough search of the inn and interview all the guests and staff, the only lead I have is you," he said without taking his eyes off the road. "It's possible the assailant has ties to both of you and will seek you out."

"Great!" said Nina, alarmed. "Now you think some incompetent but frustrated murderer is going to turn up at my house?"

"I just have to cover all the bases," said Blue. "And for the record, you need a search warrant authorized by a judge to examine the contents of someone's drawers."

Nina snorted. The situation was so surreal she felt giddy. Blue didn't seem to notice that he'd made a junior high school joke. She wondered if she was still a little drunk. Punch-drunk, maybe.

Blue glanced over at her, his eyes hidden behind police issue mirrored shades. "Also, for the record, you need to be a police officer to execute a search warrant and to examine another individual's property."

Was he alluding to her past exploits as an amateur sleuth on Pineapple Cay? She waited for him to continue, but he had reverted to his strong, silent-type mode. Apparently, she would have to wait until they were at the station to find out more about Philip.

Nina echoed Blue's sigh and rolled down the window, resting her head against the frame and letting the soft, fragrant breeze soothe her temples. She watched the scenery roll slowly by. Nina's house was on the edge of town; to drive to the police station, they passed through neighborhoods of candy-colored cottages tucked in behind white picket fences and stone walls draped in cascades of pink-and-purple bougainvillea.

The speed limit in the village was twenty miles per hour, and the golf carts that made up most of the local traffic topped out at fifteen miles per hour. Nina could sense rather than see the impatience building in Blue as they crawled along behind a banana-yellow golf cart rental driven by a pair of tourists in matching beige shorts, red T-shirts, and bright-white sneakers. They both had their eyes on the prettily painted clapboard cottages and tidy flower gardens that lined both sides of the narrow lane. The woman touched the man's shoulder and pointed to a hummingbird feeder hung from the eaves of a deep veranda. He pulled the cart over to the side of the road, digging out his camera with one hand as he went. Blue swerved out and around them.

As they rolled through the small commercial district with its row of shops and striped awnings shading the sidewalks in front, Nina mulled over the chain of events that had seemingly culminated in Philip Putzel's near demise here in this sleepy island paradise.

2

It had all started a couple of weeks ago. Nina had just returned to Pineapple Cay after a two-week magazine assignment on an island farther south. The assignment had involved trekking across the densely forested interior of the island alongside an actor famous for his portrayal of Mafia gangsters in movies, and a naturalist revered for rescuing orphaned animals and nursing them back to health at her wildlife refuge. The idea was that the gentle, animal-loving naturalist would help the tough, hard-drinking actor get in touch with his never-before-revealed feminine, nurturing side, and he would teach her a few street smarts that might come in handy in the jungle. The editor was counting on the inevitable clash of personalities to generate some entertaining anecdotes over the ten-day trek across the island, which Nina would be on hand to record and then write about.

Instead, the actor and the naturalist started a torrid affair on day two of the trek. Instead of oohing and aahing over the wonders of nature, they spent a lot of time in a flimsy nylon tent while Nina and a grumpy Norwegian magazine photographer sat uncomfortably by the campfire a few feet away, with nothing to say to each other. The expedition ended a week later at a luxury hotel on the coast with a waitress dumping a platter of curried rice over the photographer's head, and the naturalist and the actor spending the night in the local drunk tank after driving a motorcycle across the golf course. The next morning they had a noisy breakup in the town square's bustling farmer's market; the naturalist hurled large quantities of tropical fruit at the actor—and Nina had to pay for all of it, since no one else was on hand.

Although it was unlikely that the article would ever appear in the magazine after the actor's publicist and the naturalist's PR firm got involved, Nina was happy for the work. She had taken a leave of absence from her teaching job in New York when she moved to Pineapple Cay, and she needed the money. It was pretty easy work, as far as work went. Just a few blisters from her new hiking boots. Still, she was happy to be back home in her little yellow cottage on the beach in Coconut Cove.

The morning after her return, Nina made herself a cup of coffee and carried it out onto the veranda. The day was fresh, and the water was mirror smooth. She sat on the steps with her feet in the night-cooled, soft white sand and let her eyes wander up the beach to the fishing lodge on the point. She could just make out the roof of Ted's hilltop cabin nestled above the main lodge and the guest cottages. She wondered when and if they'd ever have the dinner date he'd proposed just before he'd left to take some clients fishing in the cays for a week. Her last-minute writing assignment had popped up before he'd come back, and now he'd gone off-island to some big fishing and hunting expo up north to promote his business—this was according to Nina's friend Pansy, who'd picked her up at the airport last night.

The gentle surf broke on the beach with a soothing *shush*. Out on the horizon, a cargo ship inched along in the seam of brightening sky where the sea met the air. Nina was thinking about Ted's slow smile and long eyelashes when her morning reverie was broken by the tinny sound of a portable stereo. It sounded like 1980s muscle rock. Maybe AC/DC. Holding her warm coffee cup in two hands, she looked around, trying to locate the source of the music. It wasn't coming from the direction of the lodge. Ted owned the long swath of vacant, treed waterfront between her house and his lodge, and the beach was empty. She looked in the other direction. About fifty feet away, through a graceful stand of coconut palms, was a low-slung periwinkle-blue bungalow with a wide deck facing the beach. She hadn't seen any sign of life there since she'd moved to Pineapple Cay. Assuming that it was a vacation home owned by someone off-island, she'd pretty much forgotten she even had a neighbor.

It looked like the owners were back in residence. The house was definitely the source of the blaring music. As Nina watched, a man emerged from the house and stood at the edge of the deck facing the beach. He stretched his arms above his head in a sort of salute-to-the-sun yoga pose. It appeared that he was naked. What Nina had first thought was a dirty white bathing suit was actually his pale, skinny bare bottom, contrasted against his thin, tanned, and very hairy legs. He thrust his head back and gave a loud Tarzan yell, then sprinted across the sand and threw himself into the surf. He thrashed around in the water, chugging back and forth in front of his bungalow in a lazy back crawl, singing along to the music blaring from his stereo, which Nina now saw was positioned on the deck.

Nina took a sip of her coffee and watched him. Drinking her morning coffee on the veranda was one of her favorite parts of the day. But at least for today, it seemed her peaceful interlude of solitude was over. So much for listening to the gentle lapping of the waves and the birds singing, and to watching the fishing boats head out before the low-grade bustle of a day on Pineapple Cay began. She began to get up, but then she thought better of it. As much as she wanted to get away from the noise, she was afraid that if her neighbor saw her he would think she was spying on his skinny-dip. So, she stayed put, sipping her coffee and looking out at the horizon, glancing over at him surreptitiously every few seconds. After several minutes, the man emerged from the water and strolled leisurely back to his deck, where he slipped into his hot tub with a sigh of pleasure that Nina could hear from her own porch. When his eyes closed, Nina quietly went inside.

She spent the next few hours putting the finishing touches on the never-to-be-published magazine article about the actor and the naturalist. Maybe her neighbor was just glad to be back in the islands and was celebrating the first day of his vacation in paradise, she thought. She put it out of her mind.

It happened again the next morning. And the next. Only the musical selections varied. On day two, it was Neil Diamond singing "Sweet Caroline," a song Nina liked under ordinary circumstances—which these were decidedly not. On day three, it was Duran Duran's "Hungry Like the Wolf," and Nina had had enough. She walked down the short, sandy path that wound through a shady stand of coconut palms and banks of cocoplum bushes to the beach in front of her cottage, and then she walked down the strand until she was standing in front of her neighbor's deck. The music was blaring, but he was nowhere in sight.

"Hello!" she called, trying to make herself heard above the volume of the stereo. She definitely wanted to avoid his naked entrance onto the deck.

No response. She tried again.

"Hey! It's your neighbor from next door! May I talk to you for a minute?"

After a couple of seconds, he emerged from the dark interior of the bungalow. Mercifully, he was wearing a pair of flowered surf jams, with a pair of enormous headphones around his neck like a necklace. He had a can of beer in his hand and took a slug as he moseyed down the steps and across the sand to where she stood.

"Hey, man," he said.

Thin and wiry, he had brown hair styled in a boyish bowl cut that flopped around his face as he strolled across the sand toward her. She swiftly categorized him as a frat boy taking full advantage of his mom and dad's beach house for a few days. As he came closer and halted in front of her, he pulled his sunglasses off, leaving them dangling around his neck on a strap along with the headphones. She realized then that he was considerably older than she had guessed. Under his youthful, glossy locks, his face was beginning to soften and sag. Midforties, she decided. A beach bum gone to seed. A beach bum with an accountant's haircut. A closet conformist trying to pretend he was a laid-back man of the world. Some unresolved issues from his adolescence, if she had to guess. She sighed quietly and stuck out her hand.

"Hello. I'm Nina, your neighbor from over there." She gestured toward her yellow cottage, its covered veranda visible through the trees.

"Yeah. I saw you swimming the other day. Nice polka-dot bikini."

Nina cringed inside.

He reached out casually and slapped the palm of her hand with his own, sliding his hand across hers and hooking her fingertips in his before releasing them. She guessed it was some kind of pseudo-island greeting.

"The name's Les. Pleased to meet you," he said, not so surreptitiously sliding his eyes down to her bosom and back to her face.

Nina resisted the urge to cross her arms over her chest, and stuffed her fists in the pockets of her shorts instead.

"Hello, Les. I moved in about a month ago, and I've never seen any lights at your place until day before yesterday. Are you just here on holiday?" she asked hopefully.

"No, man," said Les. "This is my crib. I'm a professional gambler. I was away on business for a few months. Playing the cruise ships, Monte Carlo, Vegas. I just got back."

Nina was well aware.

"Really. You're a professional gambler," she repeated, skeptically.

"Yeah, man. I'm not one of those high rollers, but I make a comfortable living. The rest of the time, I enjoy the fruits of my labors." He gestured to his hot tub, a big and shiny propane barbecue, a Sea-Doo parked around the side of the house, and then to the whole beach.

"If you're a professional gambler, wouldn't it make more sense to live on an island with a casino?" asked Nina. Even she knew how unlikely it was that he'd see her point and put his house up for sale immediately.

"Ever hear of the saying 'Don't shit where you sit'?" he asked. "I like to keep my private life separate from my professional life. My job requires constant diligence. I can never let down my guard. Here, I can be myself. Let it all hang out. Woo-hoo!" he yelled, throwing his empty beer can up onto his deck, where it landed in the hot tub.

Clearly, her new neighbor was a charmer.

"Yes," said Nina, wondering how to broach the subject of his music in a way that would get the result she desired. "That's sort of what I wanted to talk to you about. Maybe you don't realize it, but I can hear your music all the way over at my place. It's pretty loud, especially for first thing in the morning. I mean, Duran Duran can be a bit hard on the head before you've had your first cup of coffee, right?" She smiled to lessen the sting in her words.

"I'm playing it *ironically*," he said. "That's what makes it good. Maybe if you tried listening to it that way, it would solve your little problem."

"I doubt it. And I don't think you can listen to eighties music *ironically*," said Nina. "Fifties rock and roll and seventies disco, maybe. But not the eighties. And not the sixties, either, for that matter. The music was too earnest. Or too jaded. Something, anyway, that makes it difficult to listen to *ironically*."

"Ah, I think I will have to disagree with you there." Les scrutinized her. "Man, you've built a lot of mental cages for someone who lives in a shack on the beach. I thought you'd be cool."

"My house isn't a shack!" said Nina, her hands going to her hips. "My point is, your music is too loud. Could you please turn it down?"

Les didn't answer, just looked down the beach toward the town wharf without making eye contact with her. He was singing the chorus to "Hungry Like the Wolf" under his breath and throwing a few furtive dance moves.

"Another thing," said Nina, exasperated. "The nudity. I do not wish to see your naked form while I drink my coffee, all right? I see you own a bathing suit. Could you please do me the courtesy of wearing it when you are out and about, at least during daylight hours?"

"Hey, man," said Les, finally looking her in the eye. "Don't cramp my style. I'm on a journey on a road that has no map. Blowing with the breeze. I need to feel the ocean air on my skin. It makes me feel alive! A fully self-actualized human being living in the here and now!" He ran his hands over his scrawny bare chest in an offputtingly sensual manner.

"No, no, no!" said Nina, shaking her head. "We already have one of those here." An image of a saronged Danish Jensen in the lotus position on her veranda, a doobie drooping from the corner of his mouth, flitted through her mind. "The free-spirit position on Pineapple Cay has been filled! Can't you express your individuality in a way that does not require me to see your bare bum at breakfast?" she said.

"Man, you're uptight. When I saw you the other day I was thinking that it might be fun if we hooked up, us being neighbors here on this patch of paradise and all, but your vibe is stressing me out. I think I'm going to have to take a pass. See you around." Before she could reply, he clamped his headphones over his ears, turned, and ambled away toward his pleasure palace. Why was he even wearing headphones? Duran Duran was still belting it out from the deck.

Nina sighed and strolled back to her own cottage. That had not gone as planned. Inside, she finished her coffee and perused the local paper at her kitchen table. She would stop in at the police station when she was in town that morning and file a complaint about noise pollution. There had to be some bylaw he was breaking.

The ringing of the telephone startled her—it happened so rarely. People had a tendency to just show up on your doorstep on Pineapple

Cay. It was Philip Putzel, from the college in New York where—until a month ago—she had taught.

"Nina. Good. You're there. Listen, there's something I want you to do for me."

His voice boomed down the line. No time wasted on "Hello, how are you?" He had her on speakerphone, as was his habit. He was probably puttering around his study watering his orchids or looking for a book in his floor-to-ceiling mahogany bookcases. He liked to give the impression—or maybe he really believed—that he had far too many important things to do to give someone his full attention on the phone.

"Hi, Philip," Nina replied, and waited for his request. She was technically on leave from her job and not required to do anything he asked. However, as head of her department, Philip had approved her sudden request for a leave of absence and even arranged for her to teach some online courses from her base on Pineapple Cay. She felt she owed him one.

"Right. Look. We've hit a snag with the Delancy Symposium. It's scheduled to take place two weeks from now at a resort hotel in Jamaica. The manager just called to say that she's had to cancel our reservation. Apparently, a soccer team staying there won a trophy and trashed the hotel. All the other hotels in town are already booked up. I had Wendy check, first thing. The point is, we need a new conference venue. Preferably one with palm trees and a pool, because that's the photograph in the bloody conference brochure. I've got fifty distinguished delegates arriving from across the country, and from Europe, India, Australia, and God knows where else, and nowhere to put them. Naturally I thought of you, lolling on the beach down there. Why should you have all the fun while we're suffering up here in the city? Ha ha."

It was very unlikely that Philip was suffering, thought Nina. He had a young wife and a new baby, a huge office with a window, a full-time assistant, a big fat salary, and a gorgeous apartment in Manhattan where he never had to lift a finger, thanks to a live-in housekeeper. He was still talking.

"What I want to do is move the conference to your island. What's it called again? Pineapple Cay? Ha ha." His indulgent laugh was meant to signify the frivolous nature of the major life change she'd made in leaving New York.

"Wendy can take care of the airline tickets and travel visas from up here. My assistant, Bridget, will take care of the program and delegate registration when we arrive onsite. What I need you to do is line up a venue, take care of the menu, and maybe plan a few excursions for the conference participants. You don't mind, do you?"

"Philip," said Nina, "I'd like to help you, but you know, there's only one inn on this island, and it only has thirty rooms. They're usually booked months in advance. The main island might be more feasible."

"No, I want something unique. This is an important event. A lot is riding on its success. I'll leave it with you, shall I? Wendy will be in touch about a contract. Ciao." He hung up.

An important event? Nina thought. It was just a conference on tourism—how people spend their leisure time and the things they get up to when they are on vacation. An annual occasion for a group of academics to travel to some scenic location, listen to a few presentations, and argue a few points to death, then get drunk, overshare, and behave badly. It was not a meeting of the United Nations Security Council on nuclear disarmament. What he meant was that it was an important event *for his career.*

Although as far as academic conferences went, Nina had to concede that this one was a big deal. Attendance was by invitation only, and Philip had pulled off a coup in being asked to host it this year. He'd even managed to have the event's title changed from the Wheat Treats Conference to the more refined-sounding Delancy Symposium by replacing the previous sponsor, a breakfast-cereal manufacturer, with Delancy's Distillery—purveyors of fine Caribbean rum. In a final master stroke, Philip had pushed his pet topic as the theme of the con-ference—Travelers and Tourists: Unpacking the Beach Vacation—to justify scheduling himself as the keynote speaker due to his status as a leading scholar in the field.

Well, at least I'll get paid for my time, thought Nina. She wasn't in a position to turn down a paying gig. She might as well walk over to the Plantation Inn to confirm they were fully booked before calling Philip back to rain on his parade.

～

The Plantation Inn was a gracefully restored eighteenth-century manor house on the grounds of a former pineapple plantation at the southern edge of the village. It was surrounded by landscaped flower gardens and shade trees, with a row of guest bungalows tucked discreetly in among the coconut palms and flowering shrubs that fronted a pristine swath of beach. Modern creature comforts and amusements like tennis courts, a tiled swimming pool, and a spa had been added while preserving the property's historic character.

Nina crunched up the long gravel drive in her sandals and sundress. The canopy of banyan trees lining the drive provided welcome shade from the midmorning sun. She skirted the stone fountain in front of the entrance and went up the steps and through the open doors into the lobby of the main building. A breeze wafted through the spacious hall. The French doors that opened to the ocean had been flung wide, and the sea sparkled at the foot of a lush green lawn. From the side veranda, Nina could hear the gentle murmur of conversation and clinking of china as vacationers enjoyed a late breakfast. The lobby was casually chic, with highly polished wide-plank wood floors, whitewashed walls, antique carved-wood furniture, and original artwork. In the corners, low sofas and chairs were grouped around teak coffee tables topped with artfully arranged bowls of tropical fruit and a selection of glossy magazines. Wide-paddle fans turned slowly in the white coffered ceiling.

"Miss Spark. What a pleasant surprise!" Michel, the owner of the inn, approached Nina from the direction of the reception desk, where he had been in conversation with an employee. As usual, he was casually but elegantly dressed. Today he was wearing a dark-blue linen shirt, white linen trousers, and the type of leather sandals that only European men could really wear with flare. His silver hair was closely cropped, and his face was tanned. He smiled knowingly.

"Ah, mademoiselle. I hear you have been very adventurous! I nipped down to Martinique for a decent cup of coffee, and while I am away two or three days, you and young Mr. Jensen managed to rid our island of some nasty pests. I must remember to stay on your good side. How are you?" He took her hand, kissed it, and released it, making it seem the most natural gesture in the world. He was referring to the Tiffany Bassett affair, in which Nina and her friends Danish and Pansy had recovered a valuable emerald that had gone missing, among other things. Their interference hadn't been appreciated by everyone, particularly not Blue Roker.

Nina smiled uncomfortably and jumped straight into Philip's conundrum. "Hi, Michel. I'm fine, thank you. Well, actually, I have a problem. I'm looking for a place to hold a weeklong conference beginning two weeks from today. Meeting rooms, accommodations for fifty delegates, and a banquet . . ."

Michel stared at her for a couple of seconds. She didn't know him well enough to know if he was going to laugh in her face or get angry at such an absurd request, and she braced herself for either response.

"This is unbelievable. You will not believe it. Josie has just now informed me that the romantic wedding on the beach that we had booked for the week in question has been canceled. It seems the bride and groom are no longer simpatico. So unfortunate. Alas, they must forfeit their deposit for arrangements already made that cannot be undone at this late date. The rooms that were to be the setting for a celebration will now be empty, and the ten cases of Châteauneuf-du-Pape in my wine cellar are in danger of going undrunk. The family had reserved the whole inn for this grand affair. It seems that you might once again cure a headache for me, Miss Spark!"

He flashed his widest charming-host smile.

"We can accommodate as many of your delegates as will fit in our thirty rooms. And Madame Gallagher can no doubt help you secure additional accommodation in the private rental villas adjacent to the inn. At this time of year, there are usually one or two vacancies. And should you or any of your guests feel moved to matrimony, we have already made arrangements with the local justice of the peace." He chuckled at his joke. "Josie will be delighted to work out the details with you."

He looked toward the reception desk and raised two fingers. Josie immediately stopped typing at the computer and walked briskly toward them. Michel turned to Nina again.

"It is a little early in the day for champagne, but won't you please join me for cocktails in the bar some evening very soon? I should like to raise a glass in your honor."

"That would be very nice, thank you," said Nina.

"*Magnifique.* I shall look forward to hearing all about your escapades," said Michel. "*Maintenant*, if you will please excuse me, I must get back to my duties."

He smiled, bowed slightly, and turned away from Nina to greet a well-dressed couple who had been waiting patiently nearby to speak to him.

Nina could not believe her good fortune—or rather, Philip's good fortune. The inn was an ideal setting for any event. Over the next hour, she worked out the major details with Josie, including deciding to serve the planned wedding-supper menu at the opening banquet. Nina reasoned that whatever dishes she could come up with were bound to be inferior to the menu the would-be bride had labored over for six months. So, a choice of lobster or jerk chicken it was, with the coconut wedding cake to be transformed into dainty cupcakes.

She made a mental note to talk to her friend Pansy, the local real estate agent, about villa rentals, feeling slightly uneasy at how smoothly everything was coming together. Surely, she wasn't going to get off that easy. When did that ever happen in real life? But this is Pineapple Cay, she reminded herself. The rules that governed her former life in New York no longer applied.

She set off down the driveway toward the police station in the village to deal with the Les issue. Time to nip that situation in the bud.

The police station was a sky-blue stucco building on the waterfront in the very center of the village. It stood next to the colonial-era pink stucco government building. A narrow lane between them ended at the police dock and the municipal wharf, where the mail boat called every Friday, and the local fishermen came and went, cleaning their catch and gathering to shoot the breeze on lazy afternoons.

In front of the pink-and-blue official buildings was a small grassy park with a bandstand, and on the opposite side of this village green was the main commercial district of Coconut Cove. It consisted of a couple of blocks of tidy, gaily painted storefronts catering to locals, tourists, and a steady flow of yacht cruisers sailing through the cays.

Nina entered the police station through the open arched entryway. She shivered at the immediate change in temperature, from the intense heat of the midday sun to the cool, cement-walled interior of the building. From the street, the police station was a grand colonial edifice. Inside, however, the decor was modern institutional, with baby-blue cement block walls in need of a fresh coat of paint, and a row of plastic stacking chairs set against a wall facing a laminate-topped counter.

Nina approached the counter. The open office area on the other side was empty of any sign of life other than a large buzzing insect lazily whacking itself against the windowpane over and over again, trying to

22

escape. It was lunchtime, and all three of the metal desks visible were vacant. She heard a filing cabinet slam shut in the enclosed office at the back, and a couple of seconds later, Deputy Superintendent Blue Roker emerged from his office gripping a folder in one hand. He saw her and strode toward the counter with the smooth, relaxed lope that homegrown Pineapple Cayers seemed to have perfected by the time they were three or four years old.

"Good afternoon, Nina. How is it? What can I do for you?" he asked.

"Hello, Blue. Deputy Superintendent Roker. Yes. I would like to register a complaint about noise pollution and public nudity, please. Maybe those are two separate complaints."

Blue looked at her for a moment without speaking, his mouth a straight line. Then he opened the heavy metal door in the wall beside the counter and gestured for her to come inside. She followed him to his private office at the back of the building. Although she'd only been a resident of Pineapple Cay for about a month, she'd already been in this office twice—twice more than she'd ever been in a police station up to that point in her life.

It looked pretty much the same as the last time. A big window overlooked the police dock, with a view of the harbor and the low, shimmering white-sand hump of Star Cay on the horizon about a mile offshore. The top of the sagging bookcase under the window was covered with stacks of files and reports, their pages curling and faded from the sun and humidity. Blue's desk was bare except for a computer, an overflowing in-and-out tray, and a framed photograph facing the desk chair. That was new, noted Nina. On the wall behind Blue's desk were his diplomas from the University of the West Indies and the police academy, plus a nautical map of Pineapple Cay showing the string of small cays trailing off its southern tip that composed Diamond Cays National Park.

Blue gestured for her to take a seat in the chair in front of his desk and dropped into another chair on the opposite side. He sat back, his hands gripping the armrests.

"All right. What happened?" he asked.

Nina squirmed a little in her seat and took a deep breath.

"You must know my neighbor Les. The professional gambler." She watched him closely and waited for him to react, to show some interest in this possible vector for the spread of vice on Pineapple Cay that lived next door to her. Blue sat stone-faced and silent, with his startling blue eyes fixed on her, waiting for her to continue.

"Well, he's playing his music too loud and frolicking in the nude on the beach in front of his house—which is more or less in front of my house—and on his deck, where I can still see him, roaming all around, cooking steaks on his barbecue, climbing in and out of his hot tub, *dancing*. I want him to stop. I've asked him politely, but he is . . . noncompliant."

"You'd have to turn your head about seventy degrees to the left to see him on his deck from your veranda, wouldn't you?" asked Blue with a hint of skepticism in his blue eyes.

It threw Nina off for a second, but she forged ahead.

"Does it matter?" she asked. "What if some impressionable young girls walked by on the beach when he was out there doing alfresco yoga? They'd be scarred for life. And his stereo. It's like a tinny little bee buzzing in my ear all the time. And let's just say his taste in music leaves a lot to be desired."

Blue took a deep breath and let it out slowly. "Nina, I'm sure it's irritating. I understand. I also like peace and quiet. And solitude. But unfortunately, from what you've described, no law has been broken. The village council set the noise threshold at one hundred ten decibels. That's as loud as a Jet Ski or a table saw, because those boys like their toys."

24

"Can't you get an officer to go talk to him? If you could just stare at him for a few seconds, it might do the trick."

"Nina, if I went personally to investigate every single complaint about a bothersome neighbor in this village, I wouldn't have time for anything else. This island is full of little old ladies who think it's their duty to keep their fellow residents on the straight and narrow. Example: 'I saw so-and-so's boy litter a candy wrapper on Water Street just now. What're you going to do about it?' or 'My neighbor has painted his house a bilious shade of green that offends my eyes and clashes with my much more tastefully painted house. That must be against the law.'"

He stood and walked around his desk, putting his hands in his pockets, then sat on the edge of the desk in front of her.

"In fact, one of our most dedicated members of the unofficial neighborhood watch was in here a couple of weeks ago, complaining about the dead plants in your window boxes, citing the unsightly premises bylaw. Should I have gone to see you about it?"

Nina huffed and stood, drawing herself up to her full height in front of him. "I've tried everything with those plants. Water, compost, flower food. And still they die. Also, I'm sorry, but did you call me an *old lady*? Just for future reference, I'm thirty-six years old. You've got at least five years on me, Blue. And I'm not a busybody with my nose in everyone else's business."

Blue raised his eyebrows slightly, reminding Nina that he, unlike Michel, did not find her amateur sleuthing all that amusing.

"I'm not," said Nina. "That was a one-off. I'm not a killjoy. I like music. I enjoy the odd skinny-dip under the cover of darkness."

Blue raised his eyebrows again.

"But Les's taste in music is appalling, and his naturalist lifestyle is infringing on my rights as a member of the clothes-wearing community." She paused, then put her hands on her hips. "Which one of those print dress–wearing gossips ratted me out, may I ask?" she asked.

Blue sighed. "All right, look. I'll send an officer over to ask Les to keep the volume down. I can't do much more than that." He stood and walked to the door, holding it open for her. "Try spraying your hibiscus with a solution of iron chelate. The soil might be lacking in iron."

Nina had forgotten that Blue was a flower gardener. It was his chosen form of stress relief, according to Danish. Blue was waiting for Nina to pass through the door in front of him. She could feel his eyes on her back as they crossed the outer office to the front counter. The room was still empty. He unlocked the metal door to the waiting room and held it open for her. She turned to face him again.

"OK. Thanks, Blue. I appreciate it."

"Pleasure. Have a good day." He forced a half smile and strolled leisurely back to his office, disappearing inside. Nina wondered what he did in there when he wasn't out cruising around in the police boat looking for smugglers and poachers in the cays. And whose photograph had recently appeared on the corner of his desk? Maybe she *was* becoming a busybody. She slipped on her sunglasses and stepped out into the brilliant sunshine.

Across the sunburned grass of the village square, the shops along Water Street, Coconut Cove's main drag, were now bustling with customers. The weekly mail boat had just arrived and tied up at the municipal wharf. A steady stream of beat-up pickup trucks and men straining under wheelbarrow-loads full of goods passed up and down the lane. Residents from around the island were arriving in town for their weekly shopping expeditions. The sidewalk tables under the awning in front of the bakery were fully occupied with tourists—maybe yachties in for some R & R and to resupply, or people renting the vacation villas scattered along the island's beaches.

Nina glanced down at her watch. It was past noon. Time to meet Pansy at The Redoubt and then head down-island to their friend Veronica's farm for lunch. Veronica also owned The Redoubt, and since Nina's arrival on Pineapple Cay, the three had regularly lunched together.

Nina crossed the park to Water Street and headed down the sidewalk to The Redoubt. Pansy's shiny turquoise golf cart with its Pineapple Cay Real Estate logo on the door was parked out front, under the shade of a mango tree. Nina smiled and pushed open the restaurant's heavy wooden door. Pansy was a cold-weather refugee from Winnipeg, and one of the sweetest, kindest people Nina had ever met. She and her husband, Andrew, lived in Coconut Cove with their two children, both still in elementary school. Veronica was a local Pineapple Cayer and one of the island's leading entrepreneurs, proprietor of the hot spot on the waterfront and of Smooth Harbour Farm, an operation that supplied not only her own restaurant with fresh produce but the Plantation Inn as well. She was easygoing and straight-talking, and she laughed a lot. She had twenty years on Nina and Pansy, but she was fitter than either of them. Veronica ran six miles at dawn, five days a week, and had the muscles to prove it.

The Redoubt was busy with the regular lunch crowd of holidaymakers and locals. Reggae seeped from the sound system, its beat steady under the buzz of conversation. The wood-paneled walls were festooned with fishing nets and buoys and old black-and-white photographs of Pineapple Cay from the days when tall-masted wooden schooners filled the harbor. Glass doors opened onto the deck, which extended out over the water on heavy wooden pilings. The picnic tables on the deck were filled with laughing, sunburned vacationers and locals Nina recognized from around town. Veronica had a good thing going here, night and day.

"Hi, Nina!" Pansy waved at her from a stool at the bar. A little shorter and rounder than Nina, Pansy had long red hair with bangs and a smile that lit up the room. She loved shiny things, and today she was wearing silver sandals bejeweled with blue cut-glass stones. Nina slipped into the seat beside her.

"Hi, Pansy. All set?" asked Nina.

"Yes. Maybe I'll just run to the loo first," she said, jumping down from her stool.

"Nina. Just the person I wanted to see." It was Danish, popping up from behind the bar with a white dish towel over his shoulder. He ran a hand through his thick dark hair, causing it to stick straight up in stiff hanks, one longish piece flopping down over his left eye. He leaned forward on the bar. His arms were deeply tanned, and both wrists were wrapped in faded cotton friendship bracelets and leather laces strung with silver beads.

"I've got a win-win, limited-time-offer business proposition for you," he said to Nina. "I'll stop by later to give you the details."

"What kind of business proposition?" Nina asked warily. Danish was a hardworking guy, but based on past experience, she wasn't sure how far he bought into reality.

Danish glanced around.

"I can't talk about it now. Just keep an open mind," he said.

"I don't think I'm interested, Danish. I'm not exactly a big-time investor, you know," said Nina. "Right now, I'm just looking for a bit of peace and quiet." Danish dropped down onto his elbows and looked deeply into her eyes, giving her a serious look. She figured he must have practiced in front of the mirror at home.

"Nina, everybody dies. Not everybody lives. I'm offering you a chance to live a little. I'm not looking for a cash buy-in. I have another role in mind for you."

"That sounds ominous. We'll see. Probably not, but I am curious to know what you would consider a sound business venture."

Pansy was back, so Nina waved goodbye to Danish, and the two of them went outside to the golf cart. They motored out of the village heading south, past clapboard cottages behind white picket fences, past the lemon-yellow primary school and the pristine whitewashed church next door, its steeple piercing the cloudless cobalt-blue sky. Nina craned her neck for glimpses of turquoise water between the buildings and palm trees on their right. Having grown up in a cold climate, it still gave her a thrill to see it. As they left the village behind, they entered a stretch of the road where the crowns of tall mango, banyan, and coconut palm trees arched over the road, creating a green, sun-dappled tunnel. There was no other traffic.

After a while, Nina turned to Pansy. "Pansy, what do you know about Les, the professional gambler who lives next door to me?"

Pansy grinned and glanced over at Nina, her eyes twinkling. "Oh, is old Les back on the island? He's pretty harmless, I think. Not a gangster or anything. Just a full-time playboy. More of a trustafarian than a Rastafarian or a wage-earning professional gambler, I'd say. As I recall, his mother is a rather well-off pillar of the community somewhere in Connecticut, and he gets a regular allowance. In a small town, you hear these intimate details about people you hardly know. I don't even recall where I heard that."

"Hmm," said Nina. "Did Miss Rose ever complain about his music or his habit of walking around in the nude?"

"What?" asked Pansy, giggling. Ribbons of dark-red hair fluttered wildly around her face in the breeze. "Is that what he's up to these days? Miss Rose never mentioned any noise. She was pretty hard of hearing the last few years. Couldn't see that well, either, come to think of it. She wore glasses with very thick lenses."

"That explains a lot," said Nina. "I don't know if it's me or if it's him, but he's really getting under my skin. I think it's him."

"Did you talk to him?" asked Pansy.

"Yes," replied Nina. "He told me that Duran Duran was vital to his fulfillment as a human being and that I needed to loosen up. He also told me that I'd messed up my chances with him because I'm too uptight. Darn."

Pansy laughed. "Oh, that's too bad, Nina." She paused for a second, her head cocked to one side. "Sometimes I feel a bit sorry for Les, even though he can be an annoying know-it-all. It always seems like he's trying to prove something, even when no one is really paying much attention."

They had arrived at the turnoff to the dirt road that led to Veronica's farm. Pansy slowed down to slalom around the potholes. In a couple of minutes they crested a low rise, and the orderly rows of Veronica's orange and mango groves, her greenhouses, and the vibrant green squares of her herb and vegetable gardens lay spread out before them. Among the gardens and orchards stood a white clapboard farmhouse with a wraparound porch. The backdrop to the whole spread was the sapphire-blue Atlantic Ocean, its surface whipped up to frothy whitecaps. As they rolled to a stop at the front door of the farmhouse, Nina could hear the thunder of the waves crashing against the beach below the cliffs that formed the back perimeter of the farm.

Nina unfolded herself from the golf cart and stretched her arms above her head, taking a deep breath of the fresh sea air. The sun warmed her shoulders and back like a deep muscle massage. A couple of dogs lay stretched out on the veranda in front of the screen door, snoozing in the midday heat. They barely opened their eyes as Pansy and Nina stepped over them. Delicious smells wafted out to meet them.

"*Mmm.* Smells like Veronica baked a key lime pie. Yum," said Pansy.

Nina pulled open the screen door and called out, "Hello! We're here, and we've brought wine!" They followed the divinely mingled smells of lime and curry to the kitchen. Veronica was standing at the stove, stirring something in a tall copper-bottomed pot. Her long, cornrowed, silver-streaked black hair was pulled back in a ponytail at the nape of her neck, revealing dangling gold medallion earrings. Her fingertips flashed pink polish, which matched the fuchsia silk blouse she wore. Veronica was by far the most glamorous farmer Nina had ever met.

The style of her kitchen, however, was homey comfort. A square wooden table stood in the middle of the room. It was surrounded by four chairs and topped with a checked blue-and-white tablecloth and a mason jar filled with blossoms. Nina opened the fridge and put the wine in to chill.

"Hello, ladies! How is it?" sang Veronica. "I made curried sweet potato–coconut soup. Let's go out to the garden and pick some salad greens to go with it." She turned down the heat under the pot, passed them each a basket of the type made by local women and sold in the market, and pushed open the back door to the porch. It was furnished with a couple of white wicker chaise longues with faded cushions angled toward the water view. Sheets and towels snapped in the breeze on a clothesline that ran between a porch post and the corner of an outbuilding off to the side. A few steps away was Veronica's kitchen garden.

"Oh, these tomatoes are looking good. Let's have some of these," Veronica said, plucking plump red, yellow, and orange cherry tomatoes from waist-high plants neatly staked along one side of the vegetable patch. "Pansy, cut some of that coriander and dill, eh? Nina, there is arugula, green-leaf lettuce, and some spinach in that row next to you. That'll make a nice mix."

Nina tiptoed carefully between the orderly rows of plants and bent down to pinch off a basketful of leaves of different shades of green. They carried their baskets back into the kitchen, where Nina washed the tomatoes and greens and made the salad while Veronica mixed a dressing and Pansy gathered dishes and utensils.

They ate outside at a table under the shade of an ancient mango tree. The wine was cold and crisp, the curried soup delicious, and the company entertaining. Nina felt the wine warm her brain and a sense of well-being envelop her.

"So, Veronica, you know everything that happens on this island. What do you know about Les Jones?" asked Pansy. "Nina says he's back."

Veronica snorted and shook her head slowly, then took a sip of her wine.

"That boy arrived in Coconut Cove with a big wad of cash four, five years ago. He tore down the little chattel house next door to Rose's place—your place now," she said, smiling at Nina, "and hired the Johnson brothers to build him that bungalow. Paid for the whole thing in twenty-dollar bills, Joe Johnson told me."

"Why cash?" asked Nina. "And how did he come by enough of it to build a house?"

"Well, he tells everyone he meets at The Redoubt that he's a professional card player. Who knows? He disappears for months at a time, and then suddenly he's back, in the bar every night, telling stories about the night he fleeced a Saudi prince in an all-night poker game in Macau, et cetera. The young college girls on spring holiday eat it up, hanging on his every word. Baffling to me, but then I'm not twenty years old anymore, thanks to God."

They all chuckled at that.

"Funny thing," continued Veronica. "Leslie always comes in alone. Doesn't always leave alone, but I don't know anyone on the island who would say they know him well."

"There was that girl who came here on holiday and caused a scene in The Redoubt one night, remember, Veronica?" said Pansy. "She poured a pitcher of beer over Les's head and told him off. Something about how she'd thought he was a real man, but he was just an overgrown teenager."

"Yes, I remember," nodded Veronica. "Some women take men far too seriously. Like they're some form of mystical creature. The best approach is to take them at face value. Literally. What they're thinking is usually written all over their faces."

Nina thought of her conversation with Blue earlier that day. His laser gaze and the photo on his desk that she hadn't had a chance to sneak a peek at.

"What about Blue?" asked Nina. "What does his face say?"

Pansy giggled. Veronica raised an eyebrow and looked at Nina for a moment before replying.

"Ah, well. Blue," Veronica said. She took a sip of her wine. "He might be a special case. That one has got the stone-faced look down pat."

"What's his story?" asked Nina. "Did you know him growing up?

"I used to babysit him when he was little. His parents were very strict. Devout. Like his sister, Agatha. He was a quiet kid. Read a lot. Had a pet lizard, I remember. His parents sent him away to high school to some cousins up north, and I didn't see much of him for ten years. He'd changed quite a bit by the time he came home." She laughed lightly.

"Does he have a girlfriend?" asked Pansy.

"I heard rumors about someone he'd met in college, but he came back here on his own, must be close to fifteen years ago now. He doesn't talk much about his private life," said Veronica. "He comes and goes a lot to the main island. It's possible he has someone over there, but he's never told me, and I've never asked."

"And what about you, Veronica?" asked Nina. "What's the story? I imagine men throw themselves at your feet on a weekly basis. Successful businesswoman. Amazing cook. As fit as an Olympian, and all-around fabulous. Where are you stashing them?"

Veronica chuckled and shook her head.

"In my experience, men are an unsubtle flavoring to life. If you aren't careful, they can overpower the dish," she said. "I got married right out of high school. Just like the rest of the girls in my class. Had my babies boom, boom, boom. One right after the other. Next time I looked up, my babies were in high school themselves, and their daddy was living on the main island with his new girlfriend. That was just fine with me. I was thirty-six years old when I signed the lease for the restaurant. All on my own. My granny left me this farm shortly after that, and I haven't had any regrets. Like my granddaddy used to say, 'Don't look back—something might be gaining on you.'" She threw her head back and laughed.

3

The next two weeks were busy for Nina. She made several trips to the Plantation Inn and a flurry of calls to New York to finalize arrangements for the conference. In between, she nursed the flowers in her window boxes with the medicine Blue had recommended. The cottage she had bought off the Internet in the middle of the night less than two months ago felt more like home every day, but it still needed some fixing up. She devoted one morning to painting her bedroom walls robin's-egg blue, and the next to covering the bathroom with a nice leaf-green on the walls and fresh white trim. The following day she started the daunting task of sanding the pine floorboards down so that she could varnish them. At least she'd have muscle tone in her arms when her renovations were finally done, she told herself.

As she had every day since she moved to Pineapple Cay, Nina made a point of stopping whatever she was doing in the late afternoon. She'd peel off her sweaty work clothes, put on her bathing suit, and take a dip in the sea in front of her cottage. The silky water felt exquisite on her tired muscles as she took a few strokes back and forth, then lay on her back in the water, facing the beach. She looked with satisfaction and contentment at her sweet yellow cottage set in a grove of tall, graceful palm trees. Her own piece of paradise. After her swim, she took a warm shower, put on her favorite soft flannel shirt and jeans, mixed herself an exotic cocktail from the tropical drinks recipe book her friend Louise had given her as a going-away gift, and sat on her veranda watching the sun sink into the sea. As she did every evening, she let her eyes drift up toward the fishing lodge and watched the skiffs come back from a day on the flats. Half a dozen vacationing sport fishermen and their guides would unload their gear from the boats and head up the path to the lodge for dinner, their laughter and banter floating down the beach to her ears. She looked for Ted's distinctive wide-brimmed hat among them, but he wasn't there. He must still be away, she concluded.

On the day before the Delancy Symposium was due to begin, Nina woke early. She stretched as she lay in bed, gazing out at the morning sunlight filtering through the green fronds of the trees outside her window. The birds were singing with purpose. Philip and the first batch of delegates would be arriving midmorning, but she had a bit of time to enjoy the peace before heading out to the airport. She hopped out of bed with a plan for a healthy mango-banana smoothie and yoga on the veranda. Part of her new island regime, starting today.

A few minutes later, Nina pushed open the screen door and stepped outside. She breathed in the soft sea air and let it out slowly. She looked left. All was quiet at Villa Van Halen. The only sounds were the wind chimes she'd hung from the eaves of her cottage and the slow, steady *shushing* of the surf. The hammock she had hung between two coconut palm trees swayed invitingly in the light breeze. She decided to take her smoothie and stretch out there with a new mystery novel for a while after she'd done her exercises. What better way to spend a quiet Sunday morning? Feeling virtuous for getting up so early to exercise, and at peace with the universe, Nina sighed with contentment and unfurled her new yoga mat. She led off with a Sun Salutation. Inhale. Exhale. Stretch. Inhale. Exhale. Stretch. She was in the middle of a Downward-Facing Dog when the peace was shattered by the enervating whine of a two-stroke engine.

"You have *got* to be kidding me," Nina muttered. She heaved herself upright, slipped on her flip-flops, and stalked toward the buzz, her yoga bliss evaporating with each step. The noise was coming from the street side of the periwinkle-blue bungalow. She rounded the side of the building, and there was Les aiming a Weedwacker at the thin fringe of grass along the base of the bungalow's foundation. He was wearing a pair of white tennis shorts, unlaced work boots on his bare feet, and no shirt. A bulbous pair of orange ear protectors and electric-blue wraparound sunglasses completed the ensemble.

"Hey!" said Nina, as loudly as she dared at eight o'clock on a Sunday morning. He didn't react. She marched over and stood right beside him with her hands on her hips, waiting for him to notice her.

"Hey, Les!" she said again, waving her hand in front of his face. He peered at her through the yellow lenses of his sunglasses. They made him look like a space alien. He didn't seem too surprised to see her. He leisurely turned off the Weedwacker and pulled off the ear protectors, leaving them hanging around his neck. He looked at her expectantly.

"It's a bit early for motorized yard work, don't you think, Les?" she asked, her hands still on her hips and her eyebrows raised in exaggerated disbelief.

"Actually, this is the perfect time of day for lawn maintenance," he said. "The dew has burned off, but it's not too hot yet for manual labor."

"It's Sunday morning. Maybe you forgot?" said Nina.

"Oh, I'm sorry. Are you a church lady? I guess not, though, or you would be there right now and not lounging around the house in that stretchy getup," said Les with a fake puzzled expression on his face.

"I know you're not from Pineapple Cay, but here, Sunday is a day of rest and peace and quiet. It's bad form to mow your lawn on a Sunday morning. I'm sure your mother told you that, even where you're from. Connecticut, is it?"

"Well, I guess we don't move in the same circles, milady, because my old man always said that the best time to get your work done was right now."

Nina rolled her eyes.

"Forgive me if I look a tad surprised," she said. "I had no idea you had such an impressive work ethic, what with all the lounging in the hot tub and beer drinking that seem to take up most of your time."

"Baby, take it from me. You have no idea what I get done in a day. It would make your head spin," said Les. He leaned the Weedwacker against the house and did a few back arches.

Nina averted her eyes from his thin, hairy stomach, with its unappealing sheen of oily perspiration. He straightened up again and grabbed the Weedwacker in one hand.

"Well, the moment has passed. I'm no longer in the mood." He started to walk away, but then he stopped and turned back to face her.

"Oh yeah. I didn't want to make it a thing, but since we're on the topic of neighborliness, could you please do something about your shaggy grass and the dead plants in your window boxes? It's bad feng shui to foul your own nest like that, and I don't want any of those negative vibes drifting over here onto my sanctuary."

Nina looked over at her own front yard. He had a point. Her lawn looked like it had a bad haircut, with long tufts sticking up here and there. She'd cut it with a machete and had missed a few spots. It pained her to look at the window boxes she had so lovingly scraped, painted, and planted, now sparsely filled with limp, desiccated stalks.

"Yes, well . . . ," she said, trying to think of a good retort.

"Later," Les said, and walked away before she had a chance to reply. He went into his house. Nina stood there for a moment, watching his screen door slap shut behind him. She was too agitated to go back to her yoga or to lie in the hammock. Just what exactly did he do in there all day when he wasn't parading around on his deck? He never had any visitors that she had seen, and as far as she could tell, he never went anywhere. His late-model red sports car with the spoiler on the back (of course) was always under the carport.

Nina went inside her cottage, poured herself a glass of orange juice, and brought it out onto the veranda. She ignored the vista of turquoise water, white sand, and palm trees and trained her eyes on Les's bungalow, looking for any movement. Nothing.

"What're you looking at?" asked a voice very close behind her. She jumped. It was Danish, with a glass of orange juice in one hand and the last banana muffin from the jar on her kitchen counter in the other.

"Jeez, Danish! You almost gave me a heart attack!"

"I knocked, but there was no answer," he said. Nina turned back to Les's house, and they stood together watching the blue bungalow in silence for a few seconds.

"Nina, you're obsessed with Les. What gives? Do you have the hots for him? What about Ted? What about Roker? I guess it must be true what they say about older women."

"And what is that, Danish?" she said, still watching for signs of life next door. "Wait! I think I just saw something move in front of the window."

"Well, if you really want to see inside, we need to get closer." He hopped off the veranda and strode toward Les's house. Nina hesitated for a moment, then tiptoed after him. As they got close to the house, they heard the Bee Gees warbling away on Les's stereo. They crept to a window and peeked in. It was dark inside, and it took a few seconds for Nina's eyes to adjust to the gloom. They were looking into the kitchen through the window above the sink. It was surprisingly tidy. A few dishes were drying on a tea towel spread on the counter. The light on the coffee maker was on, and a stream of steaming brown liquid was dripping into the glass pot. Beyond the kitchen was an open living area, sparsely furnished with a rattan love seat and two rattan chairs, all upholstered with pastel-flowered cushions. Sheer navy-blue curtains were drawn over the sliding glass patio doors, adding to the gloom. Les was sitting at a desk that was pushed against the far wall and typing on a keyboard, three computer monitors arrayed in front of him. One displayed a map, one showed what looked like news headlines, and the third displayed a document that was unreadable from their vantage point.

"What's he doing?" whispered Nina. "Is he playing video games? I knew it! He's just the type who would move to a tropical island and then sit in the dark playing video games all day."

"Boy, you sure are grumpy today," said Danish, glancing at her. "I've never seen that game before. Looks sort of complicated."

Les pushed back his chair and stood up, coffee cup in hand. He was headed for the kitchen.

"Quick! Let's go!" hissed Nina. They scuttled back to her veranda. Nina glanced back at Les's house as she hopped up onto the porch. Les was standing at his kitchen window with his coffee cup in his hand, staring out at her. They locked eyes for a long second, then he turned and walked back into the gloom of his darkened living room.

Nina followed Danish into her cottage.

"That was a bad idea. I still don't know what he's up to, and he caught us snooping. Anyway, I have to get ready to go to the airport now, Danish," she said.

"No prob. I just stopped by to run my idea by you, but it's so good it'll keep. See you at The Redoubt later?" he said, heading for the front door, where his red postal cart waited at the curb.

"I'll have to see how things go," she replied.

Nina strolled over to the Plantation Inn to catch a ride to the airport in the inn's passenger van. The Pineapple Cay Airport was a low-key affair—an airport terminal about the size of a large garden shed painted a cheery yellow, dwarfed by a giant sign reading WELCOME TO PINEAPPLE CAY mounted on its roof. The runway was only long enough for puddle jumpers, and the two regularly scheduled daily flights from the main island deposited sunseekers and locals in small batches of no more than twenty at a time. A row of private four- and six-seater planes stood on the concrete apron by the terminal building. They belonged to wealthy expat residents and to a couple of charter pilots based out of Pineapple Cay.

Attached to the terminal was a covered patio furnished with benches. A few people had already gathered to meet the incoming flight. Nina watched the plane descend from the cloudless blue sky and roll to a stop in front of the building. The local ground crew leisurely rolled the air stairs and then a baggage cart out onto the tarmac. A few minutes later, the door of the plane popped open, dispensing a couple of dozen stiff-legged passengers onto the pavement. Nina picked Philip out immediately. He was wearing a tropical-weight beige suit with a straw fedora, a bulging leather briefcase over his shoulder. He strode purposefully toward the covered patio, overtaking several of his fellow passengers. When he was about thirty feet away, he spotted Nina on the other side of the chain-link fence and called to her, startling the elderly lady in front of him with his booming voice.

"Excellent! Nina. You're here. Not a bad flight. Where do I collect my bag? These small airports in the out islands. Always a bit chaotic." He spoke as he edged through the crowd, drawing a few sideways glances from the locals.

"Hello, Philip. Welcome to Pineapple Cay," said Nina. "The baggage will be on the cart behind you in a few minutes."

As they waited for their turn at the luggage cart, Nina became aware of a tall young woman standing beside Philip. She was clutching a large canvas satchel in front of her and smiling at Nina expectantly. Nina looked at Philip, who was oblivious, riffling through the inner pocket of his jacket for something, then back at the young woman. She didn't seem to be going anywhere, so Nina stuck out her hand.

"Hi, I'm Nina Spark. Welcome to Pineapple Cay. Are you here for the Delancy Symposium?" The young woman smiled, shook Nina's hand, and opened her mouth to speak. Philip broke in.

"Oh yes. Nina, this is Bridget Neary, my research assistant. She's here in a support capacity, to help with registration, coordination of the panel discussions, that sort of thing. If you would be so good as to find a room for her in the overflow accommodation you outlined in your e-mail."

Although Philip always implored his staff to "*Please* call me Philip," he made sure they never forgot their place. Nina smiled at Bridget.

"Pleased to meet you, Bridget. I saw your name in the program." The young woman beamed at Nina and again opened her mouth to speak, but she was interrupted by Philip, who had grabbed his bag from the trolley and was on the move.

"Which way to the taxi, Nina? I'd like to get settled in and go over the program before the rest of the delegates arrive this afternoon." He charged ahead through the small cluster of arriving passengers and greeters, holding his leather briefcase up in front of him to clear a path.

Bridget fell into step beside Nina. "Wow! This island is so beautiful. I can't believe the color of the water! I've never been this far south before. It was so great of Philip to bring me. You live here, right? That must be fantastic! Oh, look. There's Sylvia. I wonder how she got here. I didn't see her on the plane."

Philip had clearly not managed to cow the poor girl into silence. Nina followed Bridget's eyes to a petite woman standing beside the Plantation Inn van. She wore a sleek black dress and sky-high red heels, and she was scrolling through her phone messages. She was in her midfifties, with a sophisticated upsweep of salt-and-pepper hair, bright-red nail polish, and lipstick that matched her shoes and nails. Sylvia Putzel-Cross. Philip's first ex-wife was herself a distinguished professor at a university in Chicago. While Philip had embraced the tweedy-professor stereotype, Sylvia was the complete opposite: she always dressed impeccably in crisp designer ensembles. Nina had met her a few times over the years and could never fathom that Sylvia and Philip had been a couple, let alone had two children together. The only thing they seemed to have in common was ambition.

Sylvia looked up as they approached.

"Philip. Hello, Bridget. You're looking well. And Nina, how are you? I thought you were mad when I heard you'd given up Manhattan for an island with a population of five thousand fishermen and no Starbucks, but it is quite charming." She offered her cheek to Nina for air-kisses.

"Hello, Sylvia, my dear," said Philip. "How did you get here? One is tempted to make a little joke about a flying broomstick, just to keep up appearances. Ha ha."

Sylvia raised her chin and glanced at Philip briefly before scanning the line of waiting taxis, vans, and golf carts through narrowed eyes.

"Bush league, Philip. How disappointing. A pimple-faced ninth grader could have done better." She turned to address Nina.

"I flew in to the main island last night. Thought I'd treat myself to dinner at Wave, since I'd heard such wonderful things about their new chef. It was marvelous. Ran into Oprah there. Hadn't seen her in months, so we had a lovely catch-up. Also met a charming pilot in the bar, who dropped me here this morning on his way to Havana. Oh, what a glorious day to be in the islands again! Shall we?"

"I've got to meet a few more people coming in on a charter flight," said Nina. "Enjoy your afternoon at the inn. I hear the porches on the guest bungalows have hammocks. I'll come find you for predinner drinks on the veranda later."

She remembered that Bridget was staying at the rental villa next door to the inn. Some delegates were sharing suites at the inn, and Pansy had lined up the villa for the overflow at a reduced rate. "Bridget, the driver will drop you at your villa. I toured it yesterday. It's gorgeous. It's got a hot tub on the roof! The housekeeper left some snacks in the fridge for you and your housemates. Have a great time!"

Bridget smiled and nodded vigorously.

"Right, then, Nina. We'll need to meet to go over details later," said Philip as he jumped into the front passenger seat of the van. Bridget and Sylvia climbed in back with a few other guests, and the van pulled away.

Nina headed back to the arrivals area to wait for the charter plane. It was just taxiing down the runway toward the terminal. When it stopped, the pilot jumped out and opened the door for his two passengers. The trio chatted as they ambled across the hot tarmac to the covered patio. The tallest among them, a man in his fifties wearing horn-rimmed glasses, waved at Nina. It was Victor Ross, whom Nina had gotten to know at conferences they'd both attended over the years. She'd last seen him at the Wheat Treats Conference at the airport Hilton in Cincinnati last year. His traveling companion was a shorter, younger man in tight-legged hipster khakis and an olive-green T-shirt with a bar code across the chest.

The pilot veered off into the terminal building to deal with his paperwork, and Victor and the other man passed through the chain-link fence to where Nina waited.

"Hello, Nina!" said Victor, bending down to kiss her on the cheek. "Lovely to see you. I must say, Pineapple Cay is a much more attractive setting for a dronefest than the Cincinnati airport Hilton. Well done."

"Hi, Victor. I'm really glad you could come," Nina said, then turned to his companion with a welcoming smile. The man stuck out his hand.

"Hello. Razor Hudson. I missed the last conference. I was doing fieldwork on tourist interaction with service workers in a fast-food restaurant on the motel strip in Fort Lauderdale. I went undercover on the milk-shake machine for three months. Pretty intense. I lost ten pounds. Then I got deep into the intersection between political protest and surfer culture in Wisconsin, thanks to a buddy of mine up there. So, not really much time for conferences. Nice to meet you, though."

"Welcome to Pineapple Cay," said Nina. "Is there surfer culture in Wisconsin? That's pretty far from the ocean, isn't it?"

"That's the thing. People have all these stereotypes about surfing, but it's pretty progressive, politically." Razor leaned toward Nina as he spoke, gesturing with his hands. Nina wasn't quite following his argument, but she smiled and nodded.

"Well, I for one would like to ponder that idea while sipping a refreshing cocktail beside the Caribbean Sea," said Victor. "Any chance of that, Nina?"

"Of course," she replied, glancing at her watch. It was only ten o'clock in the morning. But in London, where Victor lived, it was midafternoon. "You must both be tired. Let's get a taxi, and I'll take you to the inn."

Nina led Victor and Razor out front and hailed a cab. She left them at the Plantation Inn to settle in and headed back to her cottage. She was running out of clean clothes to wear, so she stuffed most of her limited wardrobe into her duffel, along with her sheets and towels. She heaved the bag onto her shoulder, slipped her sandals on, and headed into the village where there was a Laundromat at the marina. While she waited for the washing machine to do its thing, she wandered down the block to The Redoubt. She had a sudden craving for a grilled cheese on coconut bread and sweet-potato fries topped with a dollop of curried mayonnaise.

Nina pushed open the wooden door from the street and glanced around the nearly empty restaurant. It wasn't quite lunchtime, and even the stragglers from the breakfast crowd had cleared out by now.

There were just a couple of regulars stationed on their stools at the bar and two tables of sunburned vacationers. South Korean pop music was banging away on the sound system, meaning two things: Danish was working, and Veronica was out.

Nina gritted her teeth as the repetitive beat and chirpy vocals tracked her steps toward the bar. She passed a bewildered-looking white-haired foursome in golf togs who looked like they might be about to bolt and veered toward the jukebox, pulling from her pocket the half roll of quarters she'd brought for the coin-operated washing machine. The jukebox would automatically shut off the sound system, so she quickly flipped through the selections and fed some quarters into the slot. A couple of seconds later, sweet calypso filled the air. Nina relaxed. She glanced over at the golfers. They were settling back in their seats and opening their menus, chatting among themselves. Nina strolled over to the bar. She slid onto a stool where she could catch the breeze coming through the open doors to the deck and picked up the local paper someone had left behind.

A few moments later, Danish emerged from the kitchen.

"Great! You're here. Let's talk business," he said.

"Oh, Danish, not now, OK? I've got to focus on the conference for the next few days. That's how I'm paying the bills. I really don't have time for anything else right now. I'll have a grilled cheese with sweet-potato fries on the side, please."

"OK, sure. How about tonight, then? I'll come by and give you the skinny. Eight o'clock?"

"It's Sunday night. Aren't you and Alice heading over to Star Cay for the beach barbecue, as usual?" asked Nina.

"I don't know what Alice's plans for the evening are, but just hear me out," he said. The cook started ringing the bell insistently in the kitchen. Like maybe he was continuing a heated conversation he and Danish had been having behind the kitchen doors.

"That's my pickup," said Danish. "Just keep an open mind. I'll be right back." He disappeared through the swinging doors into the kitchen. Nina was surprised. Danish's number one priority since she'd known him was Alice. Strange that he didn't seem concerned where she'd be tonight. Nina shrugged and turned her attention to the classifieds, her favorite part of the paper.

> For sale: wedding dress, only worn twice, and one ticket to the Super Bowl.

There's a story there, Nina thought. A shadow fell across the page in front of her.

"Listen, Danish, I'm really sorry, but could you sell your wares elsewhere? If I win the lottery, I'll let you know. Now you're standing in my light. I'm trying to read Dear Auntie, and I really need to know what the proper Thanksgiving dinner etiquette is when your ex-husband's brother marries your sister, whose boss is your new boyfriend."

"I apologize. I didn't know you had a sister. But I'm glad to hear you aren't interested in Danish Jensen's wares."

Nina looked up quickly. It was Ted. Her stomach did a little flip. It had been more than a month since she'd seen him—a month since their first, only, and very memorable kiss. He slid onto the stool next to her and faced her with an amused smile on his face. He took off the battered wide-brimmed khaki hat that she'd rarely seen him without and ran his fingers through his dirty-blond hair. Then he leaned one elbow on the bar and caught and held her gaze with his warm, brown eyes.

"How are you, Nina?" he asked.

He was tall and tanned from spending his days outdoors, and there were pleasant laugh lines at the corners of his eyes. As usual, he wore a dark khaki shirt, light khaki shorts, and sand-colored boots.

Gold-rimmed aviator sunglasses hung on a strap around his neck. She swallowed.

"I'm great, thanks. How was your trip? Pansy said you went up north to some hunting-and-fishing shows."

"I just got back this morning. I went to check on the lodge and then stopped at your place on my way back into town. There was no answer at your door, so I thought you might still be off-island. I'm glad to see I was mistaken. We had dinner plans that went awry."

Just what she liked in a man—persistence without being creepy.

"I got back a couple of weeks ago. So, how did your shows go?" she asked.

"It was a good trip, business-wise. Five shows in four states in six days. I got to spend all day talking about my favorite subject—fishing—with what must've been a thousand folks. And I've got most of next season fully booked. I can't complain. But I think I've seen enough hockey arenas, convention centers, and motel rooms to do me for a while. I stopped off to see my folks in Florida on the way home. That was good. But I'm glad to be back."

Nina smiled at him, and he smiled back. They sat looking at each other for a moment without speaking. The silence lengthened. It was probably her turn to speak. She trawled desperately through her brain, searching for something intelligent to say.

"It is good to be back," she finally said. "I was away, too. There's a nudist living next door to me now."

"I'm assuming you don't mean me or Cheryl," he said, smiling. Cheryl managed the daily operations of the fishing lodge for Ted. "Are you talking about Leslie Jones? Haven't seen him around in a while. Thought maybe the novelty had worn off and he'd moved back to the States."

"No. Apparently he was away gambling—which, according to him, is his *job*."

"That rings a bell. I think he told me something like that in here one night. So, how was your trip?"

"Well, let's just say I didn't learn as much about the spotted tree frog as I'd hoped from my expert guide, but I did hear all about how the digital camera has ruined the professional photography industry and how Norway has the only national soccer team that's never lost a match to the mighty Brazilians. Anyway, the scenery was amazing."

Ted chuckled. After a brief pause, he said, "So, are you still up for dinner?"

"I'd love to have dinner with you," she replied. "But I'm going to be pretty busy for the next week with a conference I've been organizing. It begins tomorrow." He sat back and looked at her pensively.

Oh no, he thinks I'm blowing him off.

She quickly added, "I'm free tonight, though, if you aren't too busy at the lodge."

He smiled. "Great. They can manage without me for one more night, I'm sure. I'll pick you up at seven. I'd like to hear more about your trip." He stood up. "I'd better go get a few things done between now and then."

He leaned down and kissed her lightly on the cheek. "I'll see you tonight."

She watched him walk out the door.

"Well, well, well. You and old Ted." Danish had materialized in front of her bearing her grilled cheese sandwich with a side of fries.

"It's just dinner. No big deal," she said with a shrug, dipping a sweet-potato fry in the dab of curried-mayonnaise dressing on the side of her plate.

"Ah, I beg to differ. He just kissed you, and you let him."

"He's a gentleman. That's what gentlemen do. Very gallant."

"He was marking his territory. That's what he was doing. Been there, done that."

"Not quite like that, I'm guessing."

"My point exactly."

He headed over to the table of golfers to take their dessert order. Nina ate her lunch and read the paper. As she stood to leave, she noticed Ted's hat sitting on the bar. He'd forgotten it. She picked it up and put it in her bag. She'd drop it off to him later.

"Bye, Danish," she said, heading for the door.

"Yeah, you've got him rattled. That hat is practically welded to his head most of the time," Danish called after her.

Nina collected her laundry, then walked home through town. Just before she reached her place, a shiny red pickup truck roared past her on the narrow lane. It was going at least forty miles per hour on a stretch of road with a speed limit of twenty. It strayed slightly off the pavement, coming within two feet of Nina and spraying a shower of sand on her bare toes. She jumped as it passed and then stood blinking in its wake of dusty wind. All she could see was the back of the driver's head—a sunburned neck and short dark hair. The man was talking on his cell phone as he drove with one hand on the wheel. Nina glared at the back of his head in case he looked in the rearview mirror, but he was obviously preoccupied with his conversation.

Out of habit, Nina studied Les's bungalow as she passed. His shiny red convertible was in his carport. No Aerosmith emanated from the front deck. He must be playing his video games or doing whatever he did all day. Nina went inside to the relative coolness of her own cottage and folded her laundry and made the bed, then fell asleep on the fresh sheets. When she woke, it was already time to head over to the inn to meet Victor for a cocktail and a catch-up before getting ready for her dinner date with Ted.

She splashed some water on her face and headed out. She was looking forward to the short walk through the quiet residential streets and under the shady awnings of the shops on Water Street. She was admiring, as she always did when she passed it, the pink Victorian house with gingerbread trim and a porch swing a few doors down from her cottage when the shiny red pickup truck sped past her again, headed south toward town. The driver was still alone in the cab.

There was nothing in the direction from which he had come but the fishing lodge and The Enclave, an upscale residential development of outsize luxury villas. The island came to an abrupt end at the far side of the housing development, just a couple of miles from Nina's cottage, where the Atlantic Ocean met the Caribbean Sea at a point of land owned by a rock star and his wife. Like theirs, most of the houses in The Enclave were hidden behind fences and gates. The residents in The Enclave valued their privacy.

Nina decided that he must be a friend of Les, for no reason other than he engendered the same flavor of irritation in her as Les did. Driving fast was unusual and therefore suspicious behavior on Pineapple Cay. She sighed and focused on the profusion of flowers in the window boxes of the white clapboard house she was passing, feeling a little envious of the owner's gardening skills. She wondered where Blue lived and what his yard looked like. It must be impressive if Danish's account of Blue's dedication to gardening was accurate.

The Plantation Inn was bustling with the new arrivals, who were chatting in small groups in the lobby or checking in at the front desk. Nina didn't recognize anyone, and since Bridget was officially in charge of putting out fires until the conference formally opened the following night, Nina passed through the lobby and down the walk to the water. She slipped off her flip-flops and walked along the beach toward Victor's bungalow. It was fourth in a row of five set a discreet distance back from the perfect curve of sand. Each of the bungalows housed two private guest suites, each with its own porch separated from the other by a wall that allowed the guests on one side of the building to avoid seeing the guests on the other side. Razor Hudson occupied the other half of Victor's bungalow. Philip and Sylvia were in the bungalow next door. Definitely a less-than-ideal pairing, Nina thought, but they would be busy with the conference, and there were walls between their suites, so they shouldn't bother each other too much. Each bungalow was separated from the next by thick screens of flowering trees and shrubs and strips of mowed grass.

The powdery white strand was dotted with hotel guests enjoying the late-afternoon sun, either stretched out under blue beach umbrellas or swimming in the jewel-colored water. An attentive waiter in a crisp white shirt and navy-blue shorts delivered top-heavy fruity cocktails to the occupants of the beach chairs. It was hot, so Nina walked down to the water's edge and splashed along in the cool surf.

Victor was on his porch, leaning back in a wicker chair with his feet up on the railing. As a concession to the heat, he'd removed his jacket and rolled up his pant legs and the sleeves of his white collarless shirt. He raised his martini glass to her in greeting as she approached.

"Hello, Nina! You're just in time for the first hour of happy hour," he called to her. She rinsed her sandy feet in the basin of water that had been put there for that purpose and then walked up the steps to the porch. Victor stood and kissed her on the cheek. She sank into the chair beside his.

"Hi, Victor. Settling in all right?" she asked.

"Couldn't be better," he said. "May I fix you a martini? It's the house specialty."

"That would be just perfect, thank you," she said.

Victor strode over to the drinks tray just inside the double glass doors that had been opened wide, giving the bungalow the feel of a glamorous stone tent open to the fresh sea air.

"Do you mind if I have a peek?" asked Nina. "I've never been in these bungalows before, and I've wondered what they're like."

"Please, my casa is your casa," said Victor, shaking a silver martini pitcher. Nina strolled around the airy suite. The floors were tiled with large, creamy slabs of travertine stone, cool and slightly rough underfoot. The walls were built from chunks of light-colored coral rock. Against one wall, a richly polished mahogany desk and matching dresser sat under windows dressed up with whitewashed wooden shutters. The bed was an antique four-poster with a gauzy white mosquito net draped over it—*mostly for effect*, thought Nina. A thick oriental carpet in reds and blues had been placed next to the bed. Strings of white fairy lights crisscrossed the wooden ceiling, which was open to the rafters.

"How romantic," murmured Nina.

"Yes," said Victor. "What a waste. Have a look at the open-air shower, through that door there. I'm thinking of having one put in at my garden flat in London, just for those two days a year when one could really enjoy it."

Nina pushed open a wooden door into a small, high-walled garden. Big-leafed tropical plants surrounded a stone patio with an enormous rainfall showerhead. The high stone walls of the enclosure were draped with flowering vines. Nina noticed that along the top of the wall, jagged broken bottles had been set into the cement, presumably to deter intruders. The sharp glass poked through the leafy vegetation meant to camouflage this suggestion of possible danger in paradise. Still, it was lovely. It must be magical in the starlight. Nina rejoined Victor on the porch. There was no sound from Razor's side of the bungalow.

"Ah, well, Nina. So, here we are! You've done it! Given it all up and moved to a tropical island. Is it everything you dreamed it would be?" he asked, handing her a martini glass filled with a delicate pink liquid.

"It is," said Nina. "I have no regrets at all. There's just the small matter of earning a living to work out. But so far, so good. Philip did me a favor moving his conference here and asking me to make the arrangements."

They heard the front door of the adjacent suite open and close. A couple of seconds later, Razor Hudson came into view, trudging along the sand in billowing, black knee-length swimming trunks, his laptop computer under his arm and a straw porkpie hat perched on his head.

"I say, Razor!" called out Victor. "Care to join us onboard for a cocktail?"

Razor stopped and looked up at them. He stood without speaking for a beat, his eyes flitting rapidly back and forth between Victor and Nina. A deer in the headlights.

"No, thank you," he said. "Actually, I was just heading down to the other end of the beach to make some observations on tourist behavior. I don't usually stay at luxury resorts like this, so I thought I'd better get some work done to justify being here. I spent a month last summer hanging with the locals on the Jersey Shore, and I'm thinking I can get an article out of comparing behavior at a local working-class beach with this place. Publish or perish, eh?"

He gave them a world-weary grin and what Nina thought was a slightly judgmental look.

"Righto. Carry on, then," said Victor. Razor hesitated for a second, like he would really rather have a martini than sit on the beach taking notes on his laptop, but then he nodded slightly and continued down the beach.

"Poor Razor Hudson, the Indiana Jones of tourism studies. Its self-styled rising star," said Victor as he and Nina watched Razor go. "What a difference a generation makes, eh? There's young Razor, who'd just love to be able to claim a working-class background, to be the genuine 'voice of the people.' On the side of the angels. Unfortunately, he's just plain Raymond Hudson, burdened with an ordinary middle-class upbringing in suburbia, with all its privileges and tedium."

"I have to say, for someone who chose to make a career out of studying how people spend their leisure time, he seems pretty determined to take all the fun out of it," said Nina, watching Razor trudge through the sand with his head down.

"Mmm," agreed Victor. "Then there's Philip."

He gestured toward the shore with his chin. As if on cue, Philip had appeared, marching along the water's edge in a slim-fitting European-style swimsuit, his belly spilling out over the waistband, a towel slung over his shoulder. He did not look up toward the porch, and Victor did not call out to him.

"Philip grew up in Flint, Michigan, where his father worked in an auto plant," continued Victor. "We met at Yale. I was doing a year abroad. Philip was a little bit older than the rest of us because he'd had to work a couple of years to earn the money to attend university, and he worked part-time jobs and studied hard for scholarships to get through school. I think he felt a bit out of place when he started. He seems to be ashamed of his origins and has worked hard to become the best bourgeois striver possible."

Victor tracked Philip's progress down the beach, watching as Philip threw his towel on a vacant sun-lounger and marched into the sea with his chin up, still wearing his eyeglasses. He lay on his back in the water and kicked his legs, cutting a course through a group of other swimmers, who jumped out of his way as he churned toward them.

"Yes, rather than being proud of his hardworking forbearers, Philip seems to have a chip on his shoulder about not being to the manor born. If you're waxing lyrical about your fabulous trip to Tuscany, he's just been somewhere better and farther off the beaten track, someplace no one else knows about yet. If you're moaning about marking student papers until one o'clock in the morning, he was up until two o'clock. If you mention meeting some minor celebrity or politician somewhere, he knows them intimately, has met them many times. But perhaps I'm mistaken. Maybe it's not his humble origins for which he feels he must compensate, but simply that he's short and pudgy."

Nina knew that Victor and Philip weren't the best of pals, but she was a little surprised at the meanness of the comment. Victor was normally so good-natured. Victor took a sip of his drink, glancing over at Nina and then back out at the water, where a sailboat with billowing white sails was now tracing a path along the horizon.

"Actually, Philip's problem is that he's always taken himself far too seriously," continued Victor. "I mean, really. Our work amounts to furnishing fodder for dinner-party conversations. The amusing tidbits people feed one another so they'll have something to say other than 'Please pass the salt' or 'I've never really liked you, but I quite fancy your wife tonight.' For example, tourists on holiday in the sunny Caribbean fret about sharks in the water. But did you know that last year, only three people in the entire world died as the result of an unprovoked shark attack, and none of them were in the Caribbean. In the past fifteen years, sixty-six people have died going overboard from a holiday cruise ship. That's about four or five a year. All in all, it's very unlikely that you will die either by being eaten by a shark while on holiday or by falling off a cruise ship. You're probably—no, most definitely you are—more at risk of meeting a nasty end in your own home. It's a useful service to society we perform, generating these factoids, but it's not exactly curing cancer, is it?"

"Oh, come on, Victor. You don't really believe that," said Nina. "Why would you devote your working life to something you find so trivial? You know as well as I do that fun and relaxation are vital to human happiness and that happy people are healthier people and more productive workers. Vacations and parks save governments money on hospitals and prisons, and maybe even help prevent wars."

"Of course, you're right," replied Victor with a smile, swirling his glass. "It's the tales we tell around the dinner table years later—the family holidays, the amazing view from the top of the mountain, those crazy Australians we met in Amsterdam, or that night on Pineapple Cay. These memories bind us together and make life worth living.

What separates humankind from bird and beast." He took a sip of his martini and perused the beach in front of them.

"It's the way a pair of shy, solitary vacationers, each reading the same shockingly violent thriller at either end of a hotel beach, find a way to come together—or not." He gestured with his glass toward a woman in a raspberry swimsuit, floppy straw sun hat, and large sunglasses reclining on a chaise longue at the far end of the beach. She was seemingly engrossed in a book. Then he moved his glass toward a pale man briskly spreading his beach towel on the sand under a shade umbrella. The same paperback novel with a lurid black-and-red cover was tucked under his arm. "That is the stuff of life.

"The fact that sixty-six people have died by going overboard from a cruise ship in the past fifteen years is not the least bit trivial," he continued. "It's tragic. Many of them jumped. Either they booked a cruise with the intention of committing suicide, or, enveloped by unbearable misery among several thousand happy vacationers, they formed that intention at sea. The notes are heartrending. 'Found purse near railing.' 'Jumped following a bar-tab argument with his wife.' 'A man, age ninety, and his wife, age seventy-nine, both missing and presumed dead . . . cabin locked from the inside, two pairs of bedroom slippers neatly tucked under a balcony chair.' A female, age forty-eight, 'jumped from balcony, landed on balcony below,' then died from her injuries, perhaps believing that she had failed even at this. Most who fell were drunk at the time. These events often occurred on the very last night of a cruise. What's that tell us about human nature?"

This was a habit of Victor's that Nina recognized. He loved to play both sides of the argument. Bat it back and forth like a cat with a toy until you weren't quite sure what he really thought about something.

"How do you know those two are lonely?" she asked. "Maybe they came here to be alone. Maybe she's a frazzled mother of three who jumped at the chance to spend a few days in luxurious solitude while Daddy and the kids visit the grandparents. Or she's a teacher or a nuclear physicist looking to unwind for a few days. Maybe he's a psychiatrist or a talk-show host or a taxi driver who desperately needs a break from people jabbering at him all the time."

"Of course, you may be right, but I think not," said Victor. "For one, they've both chosen to situate themselves at the edges of the beach, where they can survey everything. This suggests that they're interested in their fellow guests. For another, her swimsuit is new and not the kind one wears to swim laps at the YMCA. It was an aspirational purchase. A sleek, chic maillot for the glamorous new life she has imagined. The one that will begin here on Pineapple Cay."

He sat up in his chair and took a deep breath of seaside air. He shot Nina a grin.

"How about we add a little zing to the week, Nina? You say those two are perfectly content alone, and not looking to change the status quo. I'll wager you that, in fact, I'm correct in my analysis of the social dynamics of this particular situation. They are primed for romance, and whether they know it or not, they're already on a trajectory that will culminate in a passionate embrace in the moonlight by the Caribbean Sea. I predict that by the end of the week, those two will have found true love, either for a night or for the modern equivalent of happily ever after—which is to say, a few months."

"Gawd, Victor!" said Nina. "How did you become so cynical? What was his name? *I'm* the one who walked in on my husband and his paralegal doing it on the red velvet sofa we bought on our honeymoon. But I still believe in the enduring power of love *and* the sweet pleasures of solitude. I know you're English, Victor, and there it's still 1965 in terms of how men view women, but here's a news flash for you: sometimes women choose their clothes simply because they like them. And they may have chosen to sit at the edges of the beach precisely *because* they want to be out of the fray."

"Yes, well. I was sorry to hear about your split from whatshis-name, Nina, darling, but I don't think you're pining away down here on your tropical island. In fact, you appear to be thriving. You're positively glowing."

"Well, thank you. All right, Victor, you're on. Although I don't know how you're going to know how long they actually stay together, even if you are correct."

"It doesn't matter," he replied. "As soon as they kiss, I win."

They clinked glasses on the bet.

4

Nina showered, smoothed sweet-smelling sesame oil into her skin until it glowed, and pulled on a new turquoise sundress she'd bought at Shelley's Beach Boutique in town. She brushed her dark hair smooth and twisted it up off her neck in a silver clip, then put on the pretty silver wire and sea-glass earrings Pansy had given her. Finally, she swiped her lips with a rose lipstick that had caught her eye in a New York department store what seemed like a lifetime ago. It was called Beach Plum.

"There." She adjusted the spaghetti straps of her dress in the miniature bathroom mirror and gave her face and hair a once-over. Acceptable. She had acquired a light tan from her time in the islands that set off the turquoise and silver nicely. She also looked better rested than she had in months. She smiled at herself in the mirror, then turned away. She was digging her one pair of dressy sandals out from under her bed when she heard a knock at the back door.

When she opened the door, Ted was leaning against the veranda post looking out at the water. The sun was just sinking into the sea, casting a pink-and-orange glow across the water and the sky. He turned around as she pushed open the screen door.

"Hi, Nina," he said with a smile. He was wearing a white shirt, open at the neck, and pressed khaki pants. His hair was still damp from the shower, and he was barefoot.

"I thought we'd take the boat down to the inn. Is that all right with you?" His skiff was pulled up onto the sand in front of the cottage. "That sounds lovely," she said. She grabbed her purse and sandals and followed him barefoot down the short sandy path to the beach and the boat. He helped her in and then pushed the boat out, hopping in as he did so. He pointed the bow in the direction of the inn, and they motored slowly southward along the shore. The lights of Coconut Cove were just coming on, golden rectangles in the windows of houses along the beach. Brighter lights emanated from The Redoubt, where reggae music drifted out across the water to them; there was a band playing tonight, and Nina could see them silhouetted in the open doorway of the bar. They passed the police station and the imposing government office building on the waterfront, the marina filled with the bristling masts of sailboats, and a string of beach houses and vacation rentals before reaching the cove where the Plantation Inn was situated.

The elegant, white colonial-style inn with its wraparound veranda was set back from the beach in the middle of a darkened lawn. Ancient mahogany and palm trees stood on either side. The windows glowed with golden light. The wooden dock was lit with pairs of tiki torches. The lights continued along a crushed-shell path across the lawn and up to the wide veranda steps.

Ted brought the boat alongside the dock and jumped out to tie it to a cleat. He held his hand out to Nina; it was warm, and his grip was firm. They slipped on their shoes and started up toward the inn. The murmur of conversation and laughter wafted down from the veranda, where elegantly dressed diners sat in clutches of twos and threes and fours around flickering candles. A pianist at the baby grand in the corner of the bar was playing mellow Cuban melodies. The inn drew a crowd of resident expats and visiting yachties most nights of the week, and tonight was no exception.

They were led to a table at the far end of the veranda, at the quieter edge of the swell of conversation and laughter.

Ted pulled out Nina's chair for her and then seated himself.

"This is very nice," said Nina.

"Yes, it is," he replied, smiling at her again across the table.

The night air was warm and fragrant. Nina breathed in deeply. "*Mmm*. Jasmine and frangipani. Michel has thought of everything," she said. They were quiet for a moment. Nina gazed down into the candle flame, listening to the roll and *shush* of the surf, the piano, and the happy murmur of their fellow diners. She looked back up at Ted.

"Well, here we are at last," he said. "I've been looking forward to this, all those nights on the road."

Butterflies took flight in her stomach and then settled again.

"I ran into Blue in town this afternoon," he said. "He was saying things have been pretty quiet around here the last few weeks. So, I guess you haven't had any more criminals to run down since I've been gone."

"Did Blue say it's been pretty quiet around here lately? That's interesting. I went to see him the other day specifically to tell him that, in my opinion, it's been the opposite of quiet around here lately."

Ted looked at her quizzically, a glint of amusement in his eyes.

"Evening, Nina." It was Victor. He was strolling up the path from the beach, his hands in his pockets. He came up the steps up and stopped at their table.

"Hi, Victor," said Nina. "Ted Matthews, Victor Ross. Victor is here for the conference. Ted owns the fishing lodge just up the shore from me."

The men shook hands.

"Fishing's good around here, is it?" Victor asked Ted.

"Some of the very best anywhere," replied Ted. "Mainly bonefish, although we fish for barracuda and tarpon on occasion."

"Out for a walk in the moonlight, Victor?" asked Nina.

"Yes," said Victor. "Strolling along, thinking big thoughts. Now I think I'll toddle off to the bar for a nightcap, then an early bed. I'm meeting Bob Mumford for breakfast to hear about his research on the economic potential of plastic-surgery package tours as a niche market.

That will furnish me with a few rounds of cocktail-party anecdotes. Wouldn't miss it. Pleasure to meet you, Ted. A lovely evening to you both. Cheerio."

Victor started to move off.

"Victor. Nina. Good evening. What a charming inn. Brava, Nina. May I join you all? Thank you."

It was Sylvia, looking glamorous in a black silk sheath and bloodred lipstick. Ted stood as she approached the table, and she smiled at him as she slipped into the empty chair beside him, rising slightly in her seat to allow him to push it in for her. Ted helped Sylvia with her chair, looking at Nina with half a smile before sitting back down.

"Victor, won't you sit down? It's straining my neck to look up at you, and I want to ask you something," said Sylvia.

Victor hesitated, glancing from Nina to Ted.

"Please," said Ted, gesturing to the other vacant chair at their table.

"Well, just for a moment, then I'll be off. Thank you," said Victor as he sat down.

"Now, who might you be?" asked Sylvia, holding one hand out to Ted and raising the other to signal a waiter.

"Sylvia, this is Ted Matthews. He runs a fishing lodge here on the island. We're neighbors," said Nina.

"Pleasure," said Sylvia with a sly smile, shaking Ted's hand and holding it for a couple of seconds longer than strictly necessary.

"Neighbors, eh?" she said, and cast a mischievous look at Nina. "I knew a Ted from Atlanta who was a big fly fisherman. Invited me to his fishing lodge in Montana one weekend. I had a hot-stone massage and a dinner of stuffed pheasant followed by a peg of forty-two-year-old single-malt scotch by a roaring fire. Then I won a hundred dollars off Clint Eastwood at poker. If that's fishing, sign me up."

"Not exactly," said Ted.

"Yes, dear. There you are," said Sylvia, turning her attention to the young waitress dressed in crisp black and white who was now hovering at the edge of the table. Sylvia put her hand lightly on the young woman's forearm and left it there while she spoke. "I must try your house specialty. What do you recommend?"

"The special tonight is snapper in a nut-and-seed crust," said the waitress.

"Excellent. Now bring me a dry martini to tide me over until the fish arrives, will you? Thank you so much." She swiveled back to Victor, who was preoccupied with catching the girl's eye before she disappeared, holding up two wiggling fingers, signaling her to bring two martinis.

"Victor, I want to ask your advice," Sylvia continued. "I've been invited to London to speak to the Royal Geographical Society about my book on nineteenth-century women explorers. Now, would you recommend I stay at Hotel 41 or my usual, The Dorchester? I've heard such wonderful things about Hotel 41 and am keen to give it a try, but if I stay at The Dorchester, I can just walk across the park to my speaking engagement. It's such a lovely walk, and there's an exhibit at the Serpentine Gallery I would like to take in while I'm there. What do you think?"

"Sylvia, my dear, I think we move in different circles. I live in a garden flat in Kentish Town. I teach at a former polytechnic, not at a well-endowed private university where money grows on trees in the leafy quad, like you and Philip. The last time I had occasion to darken the door of The Dorchester was my college roommate's wedding to a minor titled heiress twenty years ago," said Victor.

"Ah, yes. Well, I think I'm going to try something new. That's what it's all about, isn't it?" said Sylvia.

"I'm not sure I agree, Sylvia," said Victor. "I find I take great pleasure in the familiar. I almost couldn't be bothered to get off the sofa and drag myself across the Atlantic Ocean to this beautiful island. Every year about this time I reread *Cooking with Fernet Branca* by James Hamilton-Paterson. It's become a tradition. I'm transported to Italy, while I sit with a cozy cuppa in my own armchair by the electric fire in my own lounge. And who's to say *that* kind of trip is any less memorable than schlepping to the airport and boarding a crowded airplane full of yobs on stag-party weekends to Rome? I find I can't remember half the things I've done as it is, so why bother doing them? I imagine that by the time I'm truly decrepit, I'll have read *Cooking with Fernet Branca* so many times that I'll think *I* lived on a cliff top in Italy next door to a crazy Eastern European musician. It will have been a life well lived. Of course, now that I'm here on Pineapple Cay, I don't want to leave. It's a paradise of sunshine and starry skies, and packing is always so tedious and a bit sad."

"Are you doing all right, Victor?" asked Nina gently.

"Oh, I'm tip-top, Nina, darling. Never fear. Just getting set in my ways."

"Well, you can get old if you want to, Victor," said Sylvia, "but I've got a few more wild oats to sow, myself. Thank God you're back. Just in the nick of time," she said to the waitress, who had returned with their drinks. Ted refilled Nina's wineglass and then his own. Nina caught his eye and tried to communicate her apology. This wasn't the dinner he'd planned. He shrugged almost imperceptibly and gave her a resigned smile.

"Thank you ever so much, dear," said Sylvia to the waitress. She glanced at Ted's and Nina's wine. "That looks divine. Could you be a love and bring another wineglass and another bottle? Put it on my tab, will you? You, Victor?" Victor shook his head shortly, and the waitress hurried away.

"May I propose a toast?" said Sylvia, holding up her martini. The others held up their glasses as well. "It's a trite one but no less true for that—to the first day of the rest of our lives. Tomorrow we start afresh, and the world is our oyster. You too, Victor."

"You had dinner last night with Oprah, didn't you?" he said. "That's right, you mentioned it earlier. Did you two trade inspirational slogans all night?"

"Just drink up, Victor," said Sylvia.

"That I can do," he said, and downed half of his martini in one gulp.

Their food arrived.

"Victor. You're not eating. Come, you must eat. Why don't you have the mahi-mahi?" said Sylvia, picking up her knife and fork.

"I'm fine, thank you, Sylvia. I'm a bit jet-lagged, and it's the middle of the night for me. Vodka-soaked olives are more in my line for the moment. Very nourishing."

"Well, suit yourself. This snapper is divine," she said, closing her lips around a forkful and shutting her eyes in faux ecstasy. "And what are you having?" she asked Ted when she opened her eyes again, surveying his plate.

"Grilled shrimp and mango something," he said.

"Oh yes. That looks tasty. Mind if I . . . ," said Sylvia as she reached across the table and stabbed a forkful of shrimp and seared mango from his plate. He leaned back as she extended her fork toward him.

"Delicious," she said, and glanced at Nina's plate. "What a pretty salad—and french fries!" she said before focusing her attention once again on her snapper.

Fresh-cut sweet-potato fries tossed in olive oil and savory herbs, Nina thought to herself. *Lots of vitamins.*

"Now, tell me," said Sylvia after a bite and a sip of the wine Ted had poured for her. "If I were to book a fishing expedition with you, what would that entail?"

"Well, we cater to sport fishermen. Fly-fishing. Catch and release. I have several guides working with me. The best around, I'd say. If the fish are biting, they'll find them. They've taught some novice fishermen to cast like old-timers," he said politely.

"Fisher*men*. Fisher*men*," said Sylvia. "Do you ever get any women anglers?"

"Yes," said Ted. "More all the time. Some of the best fisher—anglers—I've seen are women."

When the plates had been cleared, Sylvia looked down at her watch and asked for her check.

"I hate to eat and run, folks, but I have to put a few finishing touches on my presentation slides before I put my head on the pillow. Will you please excuse me?" She pushed back her chair. Ted and Victor stood.

"I'll be off, too," said Victor. "I do apologize for crashing your dinner. I hope you will forgive us. It was very nice to meet you, Ted. Have a nice evening, both of you." He kissed Nina on the cheek, and he and Sylvia left.

Ted had just sat back down and reached for Nina's hand when they heard a voice approaching.

"Yes, Nina. There you are!" It was Philip. "I need you to go over the plan for tomorrow with me. I want to make sure everything goes smoothly." He sat down at the table and looked at Ted expectantly.

"Hello, Philip. This is Ted Matthews. We were just having a quiet dinner together before the conference starts tomorrow," she said pointedly. "Ted, this is Philip Putzel. Philip is hosting the conference."

"Yes, hello," said Philip distractedly, pulling a sheaf of papers out of the briefcase he'd placed on his lap. Ted nodded, raising his eyebrows slightly.

"Nina. We need to go over the seating arrangement for the head table at the banquet tomorrow night. I see you've got me next to Charlotte Critchlow, and that is just not acceptable."

Philip plunked his papers on the table and spread them out.

"Nina, if you'll excuse me, I think I'll go say hello to Michel," said Ted, rising.

Nina looked up at Ted helplessly. "Oh, OK. I'll see you in—"

"Also, Nina"—Philip spoke right over Nina's attempted good-bye—"I don't think you really thought through how to promote my presentation on the market potential of pet tourism. We'll need a display table of my books up front, and I'll do a signing afterward. It's a hot topic these days, and I expect it to be a popular session."

As Philip rambled on, Nina watched Ted stroll to the bar and pay their bill, then stand talking to Michel long enough for them to drink a beer together. A pair of attractive women in strappy high heels and short dresses approached the bar and stood there, repeatedly glancing over at Ted as they sipped their cocktails. He nodded at them, but he focused his attention on Michel.

Eventually, he drained his glass and looked in Nina's direction. He caught her eye. She made an apologetic face and waved goodbye, knowing it would be a while before Philip ran out of steam. Ted raised his hand in parting and then left by the side door. Over Philip's shoulder, Nina watched him walk slowly toward the dock, his hands in his pockets. Philip was still going strong.

5

After almost a month of wearing flip-flops, cutoffs, and T-shirts every day, for the second evening in a row Nina put on lipstick. She even painted her fingers and toes a sparkly shade of deep pink called Hibiscus. She donned her black silk dress, grabbed her handbag, and set off to the inn for the banquet on foot, carrying her strappy high-heeled sandals and wearing her flip-flops.

Earlier in the day she'd called Ted to apologize for the abrupt end to their date, and they'd arranged to meet in the bar at the inn after the banquet for another attempt at a quiet drink together. When she was almost at the inn, she realized she'd forgotten to bring his hat, but it was too late to turn back. The sun was low on the horizon when she entered the lobby. She made a quick detour to the banquet room and then headed to the front desk to make sure everything was going smoothly. Satisfied that all was proceeding as planned, Nina stepped out onto the veranda. She looked around to see if she could pick out any of the delegates in the predinner cocktail crowd lounging around the candlelit tables or sitting in the soft-cushioned wicker chairs facing the water, but she didn't recognize anyone. Dinner for the regular crowd of yachties and snowbirds was being served on the veranda this evening as the dining room had been turned over to the conference-goers.

On the dock, a hotel employee was lighting the tiki torches. A couple of tenders were tied up. Farther out in the cove, a large yacht lay at anchor, light from its windows glittering on the water.

"Hello, Nina. You look lovely this evening." It was Victor, making his way toward her along the veranda. "Come. Won't you join me for a cocktail before the main event?"

"Sure, that's just what I was hoping for," said Nina. She gestured toward the large, gleaming-white yacht. "I wonder who owns that boat," she said.

"That's the *Take-a-Chancy*, owned by Bubba Delancy, the patron of our conference and proprietor of Delancy's Distillery. I think I paid for at least a couple of those portholes myself in purchases of his quite-palatable dark Caribbean rum. I gather he and his wife will be joining us for dinner tonight," said Victor.

"Right," said Nina. "They certainly travel in style. That yacht's bigger than the inn."

On the way to Victor's table, they passed the woman they'd seen on the beach wearing the raspberry swimsuit and reading the lurid paperback. A few tables down was the man Nina and Victor had watched spread his towel on the sand, and he was carrying the same paperback. They were each seated at a cozy candlelit table for one with a glass of red wine in front of them.

Although they were facing each other with only a few empty tables between them, they each seemed oblivious of the other, both reading their paperbacks as they sipped their wine. Nina read over the man's shoulder as she went by: *He snatched up the phone and called his buddy at the police station. He owed him one.* His neck was red from the sun. Fresh meat tended to scorch on the first day in paradise. The woman glanced up at Nina and Victor as they passed, then quickly returned her attention to her book. Nina noted the woman's earrings: green sea glass and silver wire. They looked like Pansy's handiwork.

"Do you see what I see?" said Victor as he took his seat. He flicked his eyes in the direction of the two solo diners and then raised his eyebrows at Nina. "I think their respective evenings might take a turn toward the unexpected—but not unanticipated—very soon," he said mischievously.

Nina looked at the pair again. The man had finished his salad and was sitting back in his chair sipping his ice water. He surveyed his fellow diners with some interest now, although his eyes were focused on the far end of the veranda and not on the attractive woman sitting directly in front of him—not that she was easy to see from his vantage point. She had her back to the wall and was facing the water next to a large potted palm. She was reading her novel by candlelight. As before, she struck Nina as more interested in solitude than in meeting someone.

"What evidence would lead you to think that?" Nina asked. "I don't think they're fated even to meet on this trip, let alone fall in love."

"Oh, I don't think it's wise to leave destiny in the hands of fate, do you?" said Victor, raising his hand to signal a waiter.

"What?" said Nina.

"Well, as they say, God helps those who help themselves, and all that," said Victor as the waiter arrived.

"Yes, sir?"

"Yes, good evening . . . Samson," said Victor, reading the young waiter's name tag. "Samson, would you be so kind as to send a bottle of"—Victor snatched the wine list off the table and quickly scanned it—"Châteauneuf-du-Pape to the lady and gentleman sitting just over there, with my compliments? Thank you so much."

The waiter looked in the direction of the hapless subjects of Victor's experiment. He turned back with confusion on his face.

"Excuse me, sir, do you mean the lady and gentleman who are seated at separate tables?" he asked.

"Yes, I mean just that, Samson," said Victor, enjoying himself. "And Samson, please pour them each a glass, then leave the bottle on the gentleman's table. Oh—and please bring a bottle of the same magical elixir for us as well, would you? That's a good man."

71

The waiter moved off, and Victor grinned at Nina. He then settled in to watch the tableau he had orchestrated unfold.

"That's not fair play, Victor," said Nina. "You have tainted the sample and biased the results. Now we'll never know what might have happened."

"Oh, poppycock," said Victor. "Now the fun begins! You see, if he's any kind of gentleman, he will be obliged to go over and refill her glass. Then nature will take its course."

The waiter returned with the bottle of wine for Nina and Victor, then went to fetch the other.

"Here, let me charge your glass, Nina, darling," said Victor, pouring wine for the two of them. He raised his glass. "To love, by which I mean predictable, instinctual human behavior."

"To . . . serendipity," Nina countered, and they drank.

"Oh, look sharp now, Nina. The game is afoot!" said Victor, rubbing his hands together.

The waiter had reappeared and was standing beside the woman's table, gesturing to the bottle of wine in his hand, then to Victor, then to the man sitting on his own near her, and finally to her glass. The woman looked at Victor and Nina for a moment, then at the man, who was now looking at her, his attention no doubt attracted by the waiter's arm gestures. She looked alarmed and did not return his smile. Hesitantly, she finally nodded at the waiter; he filled her glass, bowed slightly, and moved on to the man's table. With the air of someone who was doing something out of duty rather than pleasure, the woman raised her glass in Victor's direction and gave him a brief smile and a nod before returning her attention intently to her book.

The waiter filled the man's glass and left the bottle, and the man turned around in his chair to look at Victor and Nina. He nodded his thanks and raised his glass in Victor's direction before taking a sip. He nodded and smiled at Victor and Nina again. Then he turned toward the woman with his glass raised and seemed to be trying to make eye contact with her, but she was staring intently at the open book in front of her on the table, her glass of expensive French wine untouched beside her. Having failed to make eye contact with her, the man glanced back at Victor and made to get up from his seat.

"Retreat! Retreat!" Victor whispered to Nina, snatching up the bottle of wine and both of their half-filled glasses and ducking through the nearest set of French doors into the lobby. Nina hurried after him as best she could in her high-heeled shoes, catching up with him as he hurried down the steps and into the bar.

"Victor, what on earth?" she said, leaning against a stool, a bit out of breath. Victor deposited the bottle on the polished mahogany bar and handed her glass of wine to her, cool and unruffled.

"He was about to come over and talk to us, and that would ruin it. I don't want to know him or look at pictures of his kids from his failed marriage or hear about how he won this trip for being top salesman of the year. Or worse yet, have him say that he's here for the conference and why don't we all have dinner together tomorrow night? I just want to observe from a distance," said Victor.

"Hmm," said Nina.

Victor took a sip of his wine and then moved swiftly across the room to the door that led out onto the veranda. He stuck his head out, peering down the veranda to where the man and woman were sitting. Nina sighed and followed him.

"Where did she go?" said Victor. Nina stuck her head out. The woman's table was empty. The glass of wine Victor had sent her still sat untouched. A waiter cleared the table as they watched. The man was still seated at his table, but he had been joined by the two young women Nina had seen in the bar the previous night making eyes at Ted. They were all drinking Victor's wine and chatting amiably.

"That's nice," said Nina. "He seems like a nice man. He made an effort to thank you, and he found someone to share the wine with. I like him."

"Nina. He could be a psychopathic murderer, for all you know," said Victor.

"And I'm feeling a bit sorry for her and a bit guilty," said Nina. "She seemed to be having a good time until we came along. I think we—well, you—made her feel uncomfortable, and she left. Looks like your scheme backfired, Victor. She's run away, and those three are getting along like a house on fire."

"Those young ladies are not looking for romance, Nina. They're both wearing wedding rings—they're strictly in the adventure market. Which is not to say that is always the end of it, but I'd say, judging by the extra attention paid to their hair, freshly manicured nails, and just slightly risqué dresses, they're friends on holiday. A week stolen out of busy lives in different cities, perhaps. A chance to wear those party frocks that are just a bit too shiny for dinner alfresco on a tropical island but must be worn now or maybe never."

Nina looked over at the two women, who were laughing and clapping as a waiter flambéed some exotic dessert at their table with a blowtorch. Yes, maybe Victor was right. They weren't on the prowl; they were just having fun where they found it. Of course Ted had caught their eye. He was very eye-catching.

"Oh, it's early days yet, Nina, darling," said Victor, patting her on the shoulder. "Progress has been made. Our subjects are now aware of each other. That's how it starts. All it takes is proximity and opportunity," said Victor. "The foundation of all great romances."

"Gawd, Victor. I still don't believe you're really that cynical. Haven't you ever been in love?"

He shrugged, drained his glass, and set it on the bar. Then he grabbed the still half-full bottle and gestured for Nina to go ahead of him out the door.

"Shall we? I guess there's no respectable way to avoid Philip's grand oration this evening. We might as well join the others," he said.

Michel's staff had done a wonderful job arranging the dining room for the banquet. Nina had kept the bride's choice of beach-themed table decor. Eight round tables were topped with taupe linens and sparkling crystal and silver. Candles in little glass globes filled with beach sand and seashells flickered on each table, and their light reflected on the glass of the mullioned floor-to-ceiling windows that faced the water and the sunset-streaked sky. The windows were open, and the sound of the waves and the soft sea air drifted into the room. Cuban piano music wafted in from the bar. Nina began to think she might actually have a good time at dinner.

"Nina. There you are. Where have you been? We start in fifteen minutes." It was Philip, stalking toward her across the dining room.

"Everything is fine, Philip," said Nina. "It's all ready. The microphone at the podium is working and ready to go when you are. They'll start serving dinner as soon as everyone finds their seats. I just heard the gong sound for dinner."

Delegates began to drift in, searching through the tables until they found their names on the place cards. A number of delegates were already sitting and chatting among themselves. The servers in white shirts and black ties began to circulate with bottles of wine.

"Ah yes. Well, then. Let's sit down," said Philip.

Nina had taken one for the team and seated herself next to Philip, with Bridget on his other side. She'd put Victor and Sylvia at the same table for the perhaps selfish reason that she liked to talk to them; plus, she figured they'd temper Philip's bluster. She put Razor there because he seemed to know Victor. And Philip had requested that Bubba and Nancy Delancy be seated at his table. Nina glanced around. She didn't see any sign of a rum magnate among the gathering group of diners, but then again, she wasn't quite sure what a rum magnate looked like.

There was a commotion by the door, and there was her answer. A sleek, silvered-haired man with a statuesque, raven-haired woman in a red dress on his arm entered from the veranda. They paused in the doorway and looked around.

"There's Mr. Delancy now. I must go greet him," said Philip breathlessly. He hustled across the room toward the pair. Nina could see the tall woman's eyes widen slightly as Philip bore down on them, but she smiled broadly and laughed good-naturedly as Philip awkwardly grasped and kissed her outstretched hand. She was a good head taller than her husband, all strong curves and bold colors beside him in his understated rich man's uniform of a well-cut navy-blue blazer and light-gray slacks. The top of his balding head, face, and neck were all deeply tanned with mottled brown patches, indicating a life spent in the sun. Mr. Delancy shook Philip's hand and nodded curtly, then put his hand on the small of his wife's back to guide her across the room toward their table.

"Please, please have a seat," Philip said to Mrs. Delancy, ostentatiously pulling out her chair for her.

"Well, hello you all," she said, plunking her evening bag down beside her plate and looking around the table with a white-toothed smile. She looked to be in her early sixties and well preserved. Not the ingenue one expected to see on a rich playboy's arm.

"I'm Nancy," the woman said, holding her hand out to Razor, who had slipped into his place beside her. He froze. A deer in the headlights again.

"Dr. Razor Hudson, Carmichael Institute of Leisure Studies. Hello," he said, pumping her hand rapidly.

"Very nice to meet you, Razor," said Nancy, gently freeing her hand. "What an unusual name. How did you come by it? I'm guessing your mama didn't name her little bitty baby Razor."

"He earned that nickname the hard way," said Victor, jumping in quickly as Razor squirmed in his seat, going a bit red in the face. "A razor-sharp mind that cuts through the fluff and dross that lies thick on the field we work." Victor raised his glass in Razor's direction.

"I see. *Very* interesting. I'll be on my toes, then," said Nancy. "And who are you?" she said, turning to Bridget.

Victor leaned over and whispered in Nina's ear, "Old Razor gave himself that name a year or two back. Product of an unhappy youth, I'd guess. I'm all in favor of reinventing oneself. More power to him."

"Lots of fluff on the field you work. What's your specialty?" Bubba asked Victor gruffly.

"My area of expertise is workingmen's clubs in London—from 1890 to 1945, to be precise," said Victor. "I also teach history to young people who text one another about their evening plans while I stand in front of them describing how their great-great-grandparents died in the hundreds of thousands to rid the world of the Nazi scourge."

"What? You run a club? Who's your liquor supplier?"

"I study working men's recreational clubs in England around the turn of the century. Pool, bingo, dances on a Saturday night. That kind of thing."

"That's a job, then, is it?" asked Bubba.

"I'm afraid so," replied Victor.

"Victor, you are far too dismissive of your own work. I read your last book. It was wonderful," said Sylvia from across the table. "It captured a piece of history we don't want to forget. Our finest hour, some might say. When we tire of it, we'll need some kind of blueprint to find our way back from this video-game imitation of life we've created for ourselves."

"You are too kind, Sylvia," replied Victor. "I think this island is the perfect antidote to all the excesses of modern life. I haven't been able to establish e-mail contact with my office since I arrived, and more importantly, they haven't been able to reach me. Well done, Nina," he said, smiling and raising his glass in Nina's direction.

Nina smiled and sipped her wine along with the others.

"I'm in rum," said Bubba brusquely. "We make and sell six million cases of the stuff annually. It was my grandfather's business. Then my father's. I thought I'd be my own man. I'd show them. I liked fast cars, so I invested heavily in a car factory up in Canada. The Bricklin. Ever heard of it? Neither has anyone else. I lost a bundle there. So, I went to work for my father. Doubled the business in the last decade. Turns out I have a knack for it. But now everyone's becoming a whiskey connoisseur. Obsessed with being the only one in their gang with a bottle in their cupboard that was made in small batches ten years ago in some dank old castle on a Scottish island. The rum's still flowing, but it's flatlining." He shrugged. "Still keeps us in groceries, though, eh, Nance?"

He wife glanced over at him and smiled vaguely, then turned back to her animated conversation with Sylvia. Bridget was listening eagerly, her hands folded on the table in front of her, chiming in with an occasional comment or peal of laughter.

"Well, I'm doing my part to keep your enterprise afloat," Victor said to Bubba. Bubba nodded and chuckled appreciatively.

Nancy turned to her other side and engaged Philip in conversation, and Philip looked pleased. Nina sat back in her chair and sighed contentedly. The planning and organizing were over, and things seemed to be unfolding nicely. Now she could just relax and enjoy herself. Maybe she'd take in Sylvia's talk on women explorers and the lecture on Caribbean history by a professor from Barbados tomorrow. She turned her head and listened to Victor tell amusing war stories from the classroom while the meal was served.

"I'll have the jerk chicken, please," she heard Philip tell the waiter. "I am allergic to shellfish. I'm surprised my conference organizer put lobster on the menu tonight, knowing that."

Did Nina know Philip was allergic to shellfish when she and Josie discussed the menu? No, this was the first time she'd heard that, she thought. Anyway, she was sure the inn had sent messages to all the guests asking them their food preferences and any allergies before they arrived. Nina pretended not to hear Philip.

Once the waitstaff had cleared their dinner plates and served dessert, Philip began to stir in his seat, straightening his bow tie and looking around the room at the gathered delegates. It was time for his keynote speech to kick off the conference. He had arranged for a good-natured Canadian specialist in culinary tourism to introduce him. As she finished telling the audience how much she was looking forward to his remarks, he pushed back his chair and scooped up the sheaf of notes from beside his plate. He marched to the front of the room, then stood at the podium surveying the gathering before him.

"Well," he began, "here we are, ladies and gentlemen. The world's leading lights in the field of leisure studies. Many of us now distinguished scholars with years of experience and numerous accolades to our credit. But once upon a time, we were all keen and hungry. Bright new stars on the hunt for the truth."

"Bit of a mixed-metaphor salad to start. Vintage Philip so far," muttered Sylvia, reaching for her glass and taking a generous mouthful of wine.

"I'm still hungry," said Bridget. "If he gave me a raise, I could afford to eat once in a while." She snorted at her own wit.

"Yes, here we are," continued Philip. "Once upon a time, relentless in our quest to understand ourselves and our fellow human beings. Now—now, we are content to tuck in to a fine dinner at a luxury hotel and call it work!"

Nina turned to Victor. "This whole thing was his idea," she said.

"My message to all of you this evening is simple," Philip said, strafing the guests with an intense glare. "We, as a profession and as members of the human race, need to get back to what matters. Let me tell you why."

"Wait. He skipped right over the *what matters* part. I need to know what matters before I decide whether or not I want to get back to it," said Victor.

Philip paused for dramatic effect, taking a sip of water to allow the suspense to build. Nina glanced around the room. Some delegates had pushed back their chairs and were listening politely with their hands folded on their laps and faintly bored expressions on their faces. Others were focused on their coconut cupcakes. After a moment of silence, Philip began again in a booming voice that made Nina and everyone else in the audience jump. He had everyone's attention now.

"As I sat in my study in New York pondering what I should say this evening, a cut-glass tumbler of Delancy's fine rum at my elbow, I recalled something Rudyard Kipling once said. 'The first condition of understanding a foreign country is to *smell* it.'"

He took an exaggerated deep breath with his eyes closed, fanning the imaginary scents of exotic lands into his nostrils with his hand. He was too close to the microphone, so it sounded like Darth Vader. Undeterred, he continued.

"When I was a young man, just starting out in this field, I once walked four days through the mountains to sit at the feet of a wise man. A shepherd. We dined together on boiled chicken feet, sitting by his modest campfire under a starlit sky, and although I could not speak his language, nor he mine, we shared that moment in time, fellow travelers on this blue planet hurtling through space. It was an *authentic* moment. I can still recall the smell of the sweet mountain grass, the tang of the wood smoke, and the intoxicating aroma of the simple but delicious meal we shared."

"Why were there chickens roaming around in the mountains?" said Victor, leaning across the table to help himself to another glass of wine. "If the man was a shepherd, wouldn't his diet be sheep or goat every day of the week? I smell a rat."

Philip scanned the audience again and then shook his head slowly.

"I cannot help but be struck by the contrast with the gathering here this evening. We've become soft, my friends. If you can believe it, I actually saw an article on the surfing culture in Wisconsin in one of our learned journals the other day." He chuckled, shaking his head. "I guess they will print anything these days. Pandering to the illiterate nineteen-year-olds who come into our classrooms to nap every afternoon."

Beside her, Nina felt Razor sit up in his seat and exhale angrily.

"Did you hear that?" Razor said indignantly. "That was a shot at me! I've had just about enough of that washed-up old has-been. Where does he get off?" He looked around the table for support. Sylvia met his gaze and pursed her lips, then turned her attention back to the podium without comment. Bubba and Nancy Delancy looked at each other. Bridget was wide-eyed.

"Don't let it rattle you, old boy," said Victor. "Water off a duck's back. Philip revels in being provocative. It's his idea of being cutting-edge."

"Your paper sounds very interesting. I'm looking forward to reading it," said Nina, touching Razor lightly on the arm. He startled at her touch, and she quickly withdrew her hand. His face was red with embarrassment and anger. He nodded curtly and stared down at his plate for a moment. Then he abruptly pushed back his chair, mumbled, "Excuse me," and rose and walked briskly to the bar adjoining the dining room. Through the door, Nina saw him climb onto a bar stool and signal the bartender with two fingers.

"What a shame," said Nancy Delancy sympathetically.

Up at the podium, Philip was just getting warmed up.

"I guess we should not be surprised that such rubbish is being produced these days," he continued. "I have not had a single graduate student of decent intellect in the last ten years, let alone one with real promise."

Bridget let out a startled whimper. Her face flushed crimson.

"Oh, Philip. For heaven's *sake*! Put a sock in it," yelled Sylvia. "For once in your life, try to be the man your dog thinks you are!"

Philip was undeterred.

"John Steinbeck, one of America's foremost writers, wrote in his novel *Travels with Charley*, 'We don't take a trip; a trip takes us.' He was talking about the transformative power of travel. When asked why he wanted to climb Mount Everest, mountaineer George Mallory famously replied, 'Because it is there.' Today, if you ask the average person how they chose their travel destination, they're likely to say, 'I got a really good seat sale, and the hotel has free Wi-Fi.' The young men of Mallory's generation forged their characters paddling the uncharted rivers of Amazonia or trekking across the ice floes of Antarctica on a quest to reach the pole. Today's generation is made up of drunken louts on spring break whose idea of adventure is a wet T-shirt contest at an all-inclusive resort! I fear, my friends, that it signals no less than the end of our civilization."

Sylvia rolled her eyes and took another large gulp of wine.

Bubba turned to Nina with a baffled look on his face. "What is he *talking* about? The end of civilization? Drunken louts on spring break? We sell rum. Does he know that? We sell good times. I sponsored this event because I wanted to polish the brand a bit, grab some market share in the snob segment. He just insulted my core customers! I sell a lot of booze to the beach resorts when the temperature starts to drop up north. It's a solid revenue stream."

Philip wasn't finished.

"It is our duty as sociologists in the field of leisure studies to document this alarming societal transformation and to seek out authentic cultural experiences to share with our less learned fellow human beings. However, our profession is now filled with mediocrities and lushes who dole out infotainment just to please the masses."

"Oh, how flattering. He didn't forget me," said Victor. He stood and raised his glass in Philip's direction. "Cheers, old man! Here's a quote for you: 'We are *all* in the gutter, but some of us are looking at the stars!' Oscar Wilde. Emphasis added."

Victor bowed and sat down. He smiled and looked around to acknowledge the smattering of applause.

Philip jutted out his chin and clutched the edges of the podium with both hands.

Nancy Delancy clapped and whistled. "All right, Victor! Good one. This is getting interesting! Usually I want to stick a fork in my leg at this stage in the evening."

Philip pounded the podium with his fist.

"I will not be silenced! It is my duty to speak truth to power!" he shouted.

"Just what power is he speaking truth to, I wonder?" mused Victor. "I can't imagine Philip considered himself inferior in authority to any of us."

At the other tables, people were beginning to look at one another, confused. Some were laughing. A few had thrown down their napkins in apparent disgust, pushed back their chairs, and made their way to the bar. Philip had lost his audience.

The Canadian culinary-tourism expert Philip had lassoed into serving as mistress of ceremonies for the evening quickly made her way to the podium and squeezed in front of Philip to reach the microphone.

"Yes, I'd like to thank Professor Putzel for opening the conference with his thought-provoking remarks. You have given us much to think about as we meet over the next few days. As a token of our appreciation, please accept this coffee mug and a gift certificate for Shelley's Beach Boutique. Thank you, Dr. Putzel." She demonstrated to the audience that they should clap, and there was a half-hearted smattering of applause as Philip took the gift bag from her hands with an abrupt nod.

"We'll get under way at nine o'clock sharp tomorrow morning with a panel discussion on Leg Room: The Airline Industry's Dirty Little Secret. That should be a lively discussion. See you all then," she concluded.

The gathering began to disperse.

"Well, it's never easy to be the truth-teller, but I think that went well," Philip said as he approached his table.

"Put that in the next newsletter, will you, Bridget?" he continued as he sat down. "Something like this: 'At this year's very successful Delancy Symposium organized by Philip Putzel on Pineapple Cay, Dr. Putzel delivered a keynote address on the importance of academic rigor in the field of leisure studies. The address was well received, with one delegate remarking that Dr. Putzel had given her much to think about.' Have you got that?"

Bridget didn't answer, just rose and stalked to the door. Philip gazed after her with a puzzled expression for a short moment, then turned to Bubba.

"Did you notice how I slipped in a reference to Delancy's right up front? In the same sentence with Rudyard Kipling, to elevate the tone a bit. I thought you'd appreciate that."

"All I noticed was your fatwa against my core business from the podium I paid for," said Bubba. "Let's go, Nancy. I need a drink."

The Delancys got up and left, and Victor laughed quietly. Philip looked around the table. His eyes alighted on his first ex-wife.

"So, Sylvia—"

"No, Philip, sorry," said Sylvia firmly, tucking her bag under her arm and rising to leave. "Massaging your ego is no longer something I do. Nina, Victor, I'll be having a nightcap in the bar later if you care to join me. Right now, I need some air."

They watched her make her way to the door.

"Fascinating oratory, Philip," said Victor across the now nearly empty table. "And interesting that you've already concluded that the conference has been *very successful*, when in fact it has not yet begun. The night is young, so to speak, Philip. Anything could happen. There could be a renewal of hostilities between the water-park crowd and the wilderness-canoe faction, for example. The first rule of rigorous academic research: never assume anything."

Philip looked at Victor for a moment with pursed lips, but he did not reply. He turned to Nina and announced, "I want to get an early start tomorrow. Meet me here at eight o'clock, please, to go over the last-minute details."

"Yes, Philip. Of course," said Nina, thinking she would be very glad when he boarded the plane back to the frozen north.

"Dr. Putzel?" A young woman stood by Philip's chair, holding a copy of his latest tome. "I just finished your book on pet tourism, and I wanted to tell you how much I enjoyed it."

He rose quickly to his feet.

"Thank you, yes. It is a terribly understudied area of research, given the central importance of pets in modern society. Let me buy you a drink, and I'll answer any questions you may have." He put his hand on her back and propelled her ahead of him in the direction of the bar.

"There is always one, and that is always enough," said Victor.

"I told Ted I'd meet him for a drink after we finished. He's probably waiting for me in the bar," Nina said, standing up and stretching her arms.

"Don't worry. I don't intend to be a third wheel again tonight," said Victor. "I could use some peace and quiet after all that. I think I'll take a walk on the beach. See you in the morning, Nina."

He smiled and strolled leisurely to the door and down the veranda steps with his hands in his pockets. Nina watched him cross the lawn to the beach and disappear from sight before she made her own way to the bar.

Ted was standing at the bar talking to Michel, who was mixing drinks behind the long, polished wooden counter. Philip was ensconced in the corner with his young admirer.

"Hi," Ted said, greeting her with a smile. "How did it go?"

"Oh, well, no one threw anything," said Nina. They chatted with Michel for a few minutes, then took their glasses out onto the veranda, looking for a quiet corner. They sat and talked for an hour, undisturbed. Ted told her about his visit home to Florida to see his family, including his three sisters. Nina told him about growing up with her two brothers in Maine. He asked about her old life in New York, and she answered as best she could without dwelling on the gory details of her expired marriage. She asked him about life at the fishing lodge, and he made her laugh. Nina glanced at her watch. It was ten o'clock. They stood and walked down the steps onto the beach.

Sylvia was walking toward them from the direction of her bungalow, her four-inch heels dangling from one finger.

"I'm just headed to the bar for a nightcap. Care to join me?" she asked as she approached.

"Thanks, Sylvia, but I think we're going to head out," said Nina.

"All right, then. I could use a drink." She exhaled sharply. "I just saw Razor Hudson, and he's still in a state. Pacing the beach in front of his bungalow. I wonder if Philip has any idea of the upset he's caused. No, of course he doesn't. Well, I'll see you tomorrow, Nina. Good night, Ted."

She trotted up the stairs to the veranda and into the bar. Through the lit doorway, Nina could see Philip at the bar, talking in an animated fashion to someone just out of sight and having a grand old time. Nina watched Sylvia give him a wide berth and disappear from sight. Nina looked at Ted and was just about to say they should head home when she heard someone call her name.

"Hiya, Nina!" It was Bridget careening toward them arm in arm with Nina's neighbor Les, the professional gambler.

Where had she picked him up? They both looked like they'd had a few too many piña coladas. The expression of shock and dismay Bridget had worn while Philip was making his speech was gone. In fact, she was beaming. Bridget and Les stumbled to a halt in front of Nina and Ted, holding each other up. Les looked at Nina warily through half-closed eyes and wagged his finger at her before focusing on Bridget. She was laughing in snorts.

"Can you believe that arrogant son-of-a-beach-ball?" she said, her speech slurred. "*I* did that research! That was *my* work he was talking about as if he'd done it all himself. Bwana Putzel and the mountain shepherd. Ha!" She stumbled, and Les pulled her up. They swayed in unison on the sand.

"I've worked for him for five years. Philip, I mean," said Bridget. "I have worked for him for *five years*." She imitated Philip Putzel's patronizing nasal drone: "Bridget, please go read every book in the library and have a concise summary on my desk by Monday morning." Then she imitated herself, the ever-eager, perky assistant: "'Of course, sir. Yes, Professor Putzel, I'll get right on that.' *Five years*! And then he spelled my name wrong on the letter of reference I asked him to write for a new job I really, really wanted. The letter was a paragraph long. Talk about damning with faint praise! I didn't get the job. Well, to hell with him. I quit! I'm going to work at A Cuppa Joe instead. Gladly. And right now, we"—she looked at Les—"what's your name again? Anyway, we're going to celebrate by going skinny-dipping in the ocean followed by a soak in the hot tub on the roof of my villa. Yahoo! Freedom! Want to come?" She looked expectantly at Nina and Ted.

"Well, maybe not tonight, but thanks, anyway," said Nina.

"Nina's a bit uptight. *Repressed*," Les said in a confidential tone near Bridget's ear—but loud enough for everyone to hear.

Nina bit her lip hard to prevent herself from replying.

"Too bad, but the night is young. See you tomorrow, then. Bye!" said Bridget, waving goodbye as she and Les lurched away toward Bridget's rental villa, which was on the far side of Sylvia's bungalow.

Nina and Ted motored slowly back to her cottage in Ted's boat. He sat in the stern with one hand on the tiller. Nina sat on the bench facing him, the warm wind whipping loose strands of hair across her face. They passed Bubba's enormous, brightly lit yacht and headed up the shore. The Redoubt was a glowing beacon in the middle of the darkened, sleeping village. They could hear the band from across the water. There was a bonfire on the beach in front. It looked like a good time, but they didn't stop. Ted beached the skiff on the sand in front of Nina's cottage, hopped out, and extended his hand to Nina, helping her out of the boat while she clutched the hem of her silk dress and shoes in her other hand. The water felt warm lapping over her feet, ankles, and shins. They paused for a moment and faced each other. The moon was high in the sky, lighting a glittering path across the water to the beach where they stood. He smiled at her. She smiled back. She marveled again at his long blond eyelashes and warm brown eyes.

"I've got your hat. You left it at The Redoubt the other day. Would you like to come up for a cup of tea?" she asked, her heart pounding.

"Yes, I would," he said with a slow smile. She turned to make her way up the sand, but Ted caught her hand and drew her back beside him. He kissed her lips tenderly, and she felt her knees buckle slightly.

"You smell wonderful," he said softly in her ear.

"So do you," she whispered.

Hand in hand, they walked slowly up the sandy path from the beach and through the small grove of tall coconut palm trees that stood in front of her veranda. The cottage was dark. Ted kissed the back of her neck as she pushed open the unlocked door and dropped her shoes on the floor inside. He shut the screen door behind them softly, then put his arms around her and kissed her again. She kissed him back, feeling his heart pounding against her chest.

"We should tell them we're here," said Andrew Gallagher's voice in the darkness.

The lamp by the sofa snapped on, and Pansy, Andrew, and Danish rose slowly up from behind the sofa.

"Surprise!" said Pansy weakly.

"Awkward," said Danish.

Nina and Ted let their arms fall to their sides.

"Um, happy birthday, Nina," said Pansy. "Sorry. We'll get out of your hair. Um, hi, Ted."

"Hi," said Ted. "Is it your birthday?" he asked Nina.

"Um, yes. How did you know?" she asked the three still standing behind the sofa.

"I work at the post office," said Danish. Danish's day job was delivering the mail in Coconut Cove. "Three card-size envelopes delivered to your address in the past week. All postmarked Maine. One was a little thicker than the others. Maybe one of those talking cards from Grandma. One small package from a Louise Ely in New York. Probably earrings, something like that. I cross-referenced this information with the photocopy of your passport obtained by Pansy when you bought your house—"

"Sorry, Nina," Pansy broke in. "I didn't think you'd mind if I told him your birthday."

"—and bingo. Nina Spark, thirty-seven years old today. I'm a professional investigator, don't forget," said Danish, obviously pleased with himself.

Nina was touched, but she thought it best to put the kibosh on Danish's idea of investigating. "*Professional* usually means somebody is paying for your services, Danish. No one has ever paid us to do anything investigation-wise," she reminded him.

"You can be a professional artist without getting paid," replied Danish. "Ever hear of Vincent van Gogh? He painted more than nine hundred paintings in his lifetime and only sold a couple to friends and relatives who felt sorry for him. I rest my case. Anyway, happy birthday."

"Thank you. You're very thoughtful," said Nina as she walked over to the little group by the sofa and gave them each a hug. Her eyes fell on the birthday cake and a pitcher of piña coladas on the table. "Oh, that's so nice. Come on. Let's have a drink and a piece of cake. I can't think of a better way to celebrate!"

"Bet you can," said Danish.

"Well, all right, if you're sure," said Pansy. She gestured for Andrew to press the "Play" button on the portable stereo they'd brought. Bob Marley started singing "Stir It Up."

Nina walked briskly over to the kitchen and got some glasses and plates out of the cupboard. Ted followed her to help.

"Happy birthday," he said, taking the dishes and cutlery from her and kissing her on the cheek.

They sat around the table eating cake and drinking piña coladas. Danish drained his glass and jumped to his feet.

"That hit the spot," he said, patting his belly. "Speaking of covert or otherwise-awkward nighttime entries and exits—"

"Which we weren't," said Pansy.

"—did I ever tell you about my roommate Bram?" Danish rose from his seat and began dancing around the room to Toots and the Maytals. "Ibrahim West. We were both bodywork majors at the Boulder College of the Healing Arts. Tall, skinny guy. Well, one night Bram was working late in the homeopathy lab. He had a weapons-grade cleansing tea he thought he could patent, sell a ton of, and retire at age twenty-five. Anyway, lights went out, and he got locked in the lab with nothing to eat or drink but his glow-in-the-dark tea. The campus was deserted. Meanwhile, he *had* to be on a five thirty flight to Austin the next morning to keep a date he'd made with a girl he'd met there the year before. Just like in a movie," he said.

"How romantic," said Pansy, looking at Andrew.

"Yeah, so, anyway, Bram decides the only way to go is out the window and rappel down the side of the building. He ties the curtains together, anchors them to the radiator, and swings over the window ledge. So far so good. Only thing is, these drapes are one hundred percent organic cotton grown and loosely woven by flower children. So, *rrrip*! Bram said he swung like a pendulum across the facade of the building and ended up in the butterfly garden. Still made it to Austin, though. Oh, sorry, Nina."

The story involved a lot of wide arm gestures, and Danish had managed to knock a whole shelf of books onto the floor.

"Just leave it," said Nina. "I'll get it in the morning. Let's go outside and look at the stars."

"So, what happened to Bram and the girl from Austin?" asked Pansy as they gathered their things and headed outside.

"Actually, she didn't show," said Danish. "Bram was bummed for about five minutes. Funny thing, he never patented his tea. He's a TV weatherman in Phoenix now."

Pansy made another pitcher of piña coladas, and Ted lit a drift-wood fire on the beach in front of the cottage. They sat around it talking while they finished off the pitcher, and then another. After a while, Pansy and Andrew went home, and at some point, Danish disappeared. Ted kicked the remains of the fire apart and sprinkled sand on the ashes, then he and Nina walked slowly back up to the cottage. Nina was beat. She curled up on the sofa while Ted put the dirty glasses and plates in the sink. The next thing she knew, the sun was streaming in through the big windows, and Blue Roker was banging on her front door.

6

Now Nina was in the passenger seat of a police Jeep beside Deputy Superintendent Blue Roker, and Philip had been discovered unconscious on the beach at the Plantation Inn. She was still struggling to sort out the chain of events, and her head ached. She wondered if it would be appropriate to ask for a glass of water and a Tylenol at the police station.

They cruised through town at just the right speed for the residents of Coconut Cove to get a good look at her en route to the police station. Blue rolled to a stop, and they got out.

"After you," he said, gesturing her to go ahead of him up the walkway into the station. She did as she was told. Her flip-flops slapped the polished concrete floor. Behind her, the heels of his boots struck the floor with a heavy thud. She waited while he opened the metal door into the squad room, then followed him in. He led her not to his office at the back but into a small, windowless interrogation room with a tiny table and two chairs in it—nothing else.

"Please have a seat," he said, pulling out the cheap plastic stacking chair for her. He sat down across from her and pulled a digital tape recorder out of his pocket. He turned it on and set it on the table between them.

"OK, Nina. Please tell me what happened last night. When did you last see Professor Putzel?"

Nina looked at the tape recorder. "Shouldn't you take notes, too? What if that thing malfunctions? Then you'd be in a pickle."

He looked at her for a moment. A trademark Blue Roker inscrutable blue stare.

"Can you please just answer the question?" he said.

Nina sighed. "OK, of course. Well, Philip gave his speech. Nobody knew quite what to say after that, so everyone just sort of drifted away. That must have been about nine o'clock. Some people went into the bar. Some went out to have a nightcap on the veranda. The others just went to their rooms, I guess. Philip went off toward the veranda with a young woman. A fan. I didn't see him for a while. Then I saw him in the bar, talking to someone."

"What time was that?"

"Ten o'clock, or just after. I know because I looked at my watch to see if it was too early to go home."

"Pardon me?"

"I wanted to leave, at least to get away from the crowd at the inn, but things had kind of unraveled during Philip's speech. I thought maybe I should stick around for a while to make sure everything was all right because Philip had hired me to organize the conference—or at least to look after the local logistics."

Blue looked at her intently for a second, then took a deep breath and asked, "Who was he talking to?"

"I couldn't see the other person. I just saw Philip through the open door."

Blue took a small notebook and pencil out of his shirt pocket and made a note. She couldn't see it; his hand was in the way.

"What was his demeanor?"

"Sorry?"

"You said he was speaking with someone you couldn't see. Did it look like an argument, or like he was telling a joke, or like he was giving directions?

"No, it didn't look like an argument. It just looked like he was holding forth like he usually does."

"What do you mean *holding forth?*"

"To put it bluntly, Philip likes the sound of his own voice. He tends to monopolize conversation. He gives the impression that whatever he has to say is more important than whatever anyone else has to say."

Blue made another, longer note in his book.

"Does Dr. Putzel have any enemies?"

"Like I said, Blue, he's not very nice to a lot of people. He's downright cruel to Bri—some of them." She didn't want to point the finger at Bridget.

"Bridget Neary," said Blue.

Damn.

"Dr. Putzel's assistant. You saw him treat her badly?"

"Yes, he belittles her in front of her peers and treats her like an intern—which she's not. But he treats everyone badly. He insulted both Razor and Victor last night, probably not for the first time. I don't imagine Sylvia has any great affection for him. Or his other ex-wife. And who knows how his current wife feels about him these days. If being the target of Philip's offensive behavior is your criteria for drawing up a list of suspects, you might as well put my name down there, too. For that matter, Bubba Delancy wasn't too thrilled with Philip's speech last night, given the money he put up to sponsor the conference. But being offended is a pretty weak motive for murder, isn't it?"

"*Mmm,*" said Blue noncommittally. "What about something more concrete? Money. Professional jealousy. Scorned lovers. Anything like that you are aware of?"

"I'm mercifully ignorant of Philip's love life. I do know he remarried a year or so ago and that he and his wife just had a baby. I wasn't invited to the wedding, and I've never met her. Nor his second wife. That was before I knew him. Sylvia, his first wife, is in the same field, so I see her once in a while at conferences. She always seems very content and to be enjoying her life post-Philip—they split up a long time ago.

She's here at the conference. I can't imagine money would be a motive, at least not for anyone attending the conference. They're all in the same boat, financially speaking. As university lecturers and professors, none of them has the kind of money you'd kill for, but I don't think any would be in dire need of money, either. They all make a good living."

Except for Bridget, perhaps, thought Nina. *Philip probably didn't pay her much, and certainly not what she was worth. Maybe she was bitter about it.* But Nina wasn't going to tell Blue that. It wouldn't be fair.

"Professional jealousy. I suppose there could be something there," she continued. "You know what they say: academic politics are so vicious because the stakes are so low."

"Are you aware of anyone attending the conference who may have had a grudge of that nature against Dr. Putzel?" Blue asked.

Nina felt uncomfortable. She didn't know Razor at all. He hated Philip, that was obvious, but he didn't seem like the kind of person who could commit murder. Victor was a friend, and she'd known Sylvia for years.

"Look, as I mentioned earlier, Philip probably only had direct interaction with about a dozen of the delegates before this week. And their interaction was probably limited to e-mail—correspondence about research papers and things like that. I'm sure his e-mail records could tell you. Among the conference delegates, the group who knew him best or worked with him on a regular basis were those sitting at our table last night—Sylvia, Bridget, Victor, Razor, and me. And he's burned all of us at one time or another."

She felt a pang of guilt, remembering everything that Philip had done for her despite himself since her abrupt move to Pineapple Cay.

Blue shifted in his seat.

"Where were you between ten o'clock last night and seven o'clock this morning?" he asked, looking directly into her eyes.

So, she *was* a suspect.

"Ted picked me up at the inn after the banquet broke up. We had a drink on the veranda, then went by boat back to my place. Pansy,

Andrew, and Danish were there. It was a surprise. It was my birthday yesterday. I'm thirty-seven. Still not an *old lady*, in my opinion," she said, trying to inject a bit of levity into this increasingly tense situation. Blue did not react. Nina took a breath and continued.

"We sat on the beach and talked. It was nice. I had rather a lot to drink, I'm afraid. Coconut rum goes down very easily. Like liquid ice cream. Then I guess I went to sleep, until you knocked on my door this morning."

Blue looked at her without speaking for a moment.

"What time did Ted leave?" he asked.

"I don't know," Nina answered, her cheeks burning. "I must have fallen asleep on the sofa." Blue didn't ask about Pansy, Andrew, or Danish, and she didn't volunteer anything. She still wasn't quite clear how Danish had ended up in her bed.

Blue reached out and turned off the recorder.

"OK. That's all for now, Nina. I may have more questions for you later. I can get one of the officers to give you a ride home, if you like."

"No, thank you. That's OK. I'll walk."

They stood, and he walked her to the door.

"If you think of anything that might be relevant to the investigation, please give me a call," he said as he opened the heavy metal door. "Otherwise, I'll be in touch."

"I will," said Nina.

Blue nodded briskly and disappeared again behind the metal door. Nina walked out into the brilliant sunlight. She'd forgotten to bring her sunglasses and hat, so she put her head down and walked to the waterfront. She'd decided to walk home along the beach rather than through town, where she'd likely be quizzed on Philip's assault by random passersby. The Pineapple Cay bush telegraph must be humming by now.

Her bedroom door was wide open when she arrived home, and Danish was gone. The only sign that he'd been there was a huge hunk newly missing from the collapsed birthday cake on the kitchen table. Nina wrapped up the remaining quarter and put it in the fridge. She made

96

coffee and sat down on the veranda with her bare feet in the cool sand to think things through. She looked over at Les's bungalow. No signs of life and no loud music. Apparently, he and Bridget had hit it off last night. *Thank you, Bridget, for your questionable taste in men,* Nina said to herself. Another run-in with Les was more than she was up to today.

Nina took a sip of her coffee and looked out at the water. Shades of turquoise and jade deepened to sapphire blue out past the reef. The sky was bleached white in the building heat. A breeze rustled the palm fronds. Another perfect morning in paradise. Not for Philip, of course. Could Razor possibly have been angry enough to try to kill him? It suddenly occurred to Nina that she needed to make a decision about the conference. There were fifty—well, forty-nine—conference delegates milling around the breakfast buffet over at the Plantation Inn likely in shock and wondering what would happen now. Philip was supposed to make a presentation this morning, but that obviously wouldn't be happening. She'd better head over there to check on him and sort things out.

She heard her front screen door slam, five heavy footsteps through her house, then the screen door onto the veranda burst open. It was Danish, of course. Despite knowing each other less than two months, he'd given up knocking when he came over.

"Hey, Nina. Wow. I just went home to the inn, and the police were all over the joint."

Danish taught yoga classes at the inn in exchange for room and board.

He said with excitement, "Sophia, one of the chambermaids, told me that the guy you were working for, the professor, washed up on the beach this morning, about seven o'clock! He was lying in the surf with a huge syringe sticking out of his leg. Red as a lobster, patchy all over. Unconscious. Nothing on but boxer shorts, Sophia said. She heard it directly from the old lady who found him. She's totally out of it now, the old lady. They had to sedate her."

"Blue's been here already. Danish, what were you doing in my bed last night, dare I ask?"

"I had a tad too many celebratory beverages at your birthday bash, so I crashed here. I figured you'd end up at Ted's," he said.

"I fell asleep on the sofa here. What's with all the towels?" She gestured inside to where there was still a trail of wet towels from the bathroom to the bedroom.

"Sorry—I went for a swim at some point last night, and I had to shower to get the salt off before I went to bed," he said. He went inside with Nina following him and began gathering up the towels, then looked around for somewhere to put them. He stashed them behind the bathroom door.

"OK, whatever. I've got to get over to the inn now. Are you driving your mail cart?" Nina asked.

"Yeah, sure. I'll give you a lift," he said. Nina grabbed her bag, hat, sunglasses, and sunscreen, and they headed out the door. They climbed into the red Pineapple Cay Postal Service golf cart.

He looked over at her as they drove through the back streets of Coconut Cove. "I guess we're back in business," he said.

"What do you mean?" asked Nina. Her head hurt. She still needed to find some Tylenol.

"I mean, we're a crime-solving unit with a stellar track record. I wonder if Pansy can get someone to babysit her kids this afternoon so we can get cracking," said Danish.

"Hold on. Danish, our one and only adventure in crime fighting was a fluke. We're lucky we didn't end up in jail—or dead. This doesn't involve us. Please. Well, it doesn't involve you, anyway, unless you killed Philip Putzel. It seems I'm a suspect."

"What?"

"Danish! Watch the road!" They narrowly missed sideswiping a recycling bin on the sidewalk. After yanking the steering wheel to swerve back onto the road, Danish turned his head to stare at Nina again.

To avoid a crash, she spoke rapidly. "Blue is drawing up a list of everyone who might have had both a motive and the opportunity to murder Philip. It looks like I'm on it, at least until he talks to you, Pansy, and Ted about where I was last night."

Ted. A wave of nausea washed over Nina. Blue was going to question Ted sometime today about her alibi for last night. That was embarrassing.

Danish turned off the main road into the shade of the long, tree-lined lane to the inn.

"Well?" asked Danish, turning to stare at her.

"Well, what?" said Nina.

"Well, did you do it?" he said.

"Yes, I did, Danish. I tried to kill my former boss, then went home and had piña coladas and birthday cake with you. *No*, of course I didn't do it."

"Well, that's good. I had to ask, you know. To eliminate you from our inquiries."

Nina snorted with exasperation.

"So, does Blue have any leads yet?" Danish asked as they came to a stop in the inn's parking area. There were a couple of police Jeeps by the curb. "Did you see anything suspicious last night at your wingding? A few of those characters looked a little shifty, if you ask me. A couple of ladies attended my afternoon yoga class yesterday, and I did my usual 'Where are you from/What are you doing here/How are you enjoying Pineapple Cay so far' thing—and they wouldn't look me in the eye. It was like they couldn't get out of there fast enough. They ignored each other, too. Not to brag or anything, but I'm usually quite popular with the ladies on vacation."

"Well, they're academics, Danish. That's pretty standard behavior in that crowd."

"Uh-huh," said Danish, leading the way across the lawn. "The action is this way."

Nina followed him. There was a small crowd clustered at the far end of the hotel beach, just past the last guest bungalow—the one housing Philip's and Sylvia's rooms. Yellow police tape surrounded the bungalow and blocked access to the beach in front of it.

Oh dear, thought Nina. *Michel is not going to be so delighted this morning that I brought the conference to his inn.*

She could see Blue Roker on the other side of the tape, standing with his hands on his hips talking to another officer. A police photographer was moving methodically around the building. A couple of other officers were wading through the crowd of onlookers, asking questions and taking notes. Philip was nowhere to be seen.

This is just surreal, thought Nina. She slowed her pace unconsciously as Danish charged ahead to join the group standing along the tape.

"Nina!"

It was Victor. He was standing on the porch of his bungalow watching the scene unfolding next door. Nina changed course and walked over to join him. They stood side by side for a moment, watching the activity.

"Blimey," said Victor. He had a martini in his hand. It was shortly after eleven o'clock.

"Yes," said Nina. "Poor Philip." She said it, but did she really feel it? Philip was arrogant, insensitive, and self-centered. She didn't like him much. But no one deserves to be violently attacked. So, yes, she did feel sorry for poor almost-dead Philip.

"Have you heard any news of what happened?" asked Victor.

"No," said Nina, "except that the police seem to think it was attempted murder."

"Blimey," Victor said again, and sat down. He took a long sip of his drink. Nina sat down in the wicker chair beside him.

"Where are my manners?" said Victor, slightly flustered. "Can I get you something?"

"No, thank you. I'm fine, Victor," said Nina. The smell of the gin was making her feel sick again. "Did you see or hear anything last night or this morning?" she asked.

Victor looked like she felt. Like he'd had a bit too much to drink last night and was paying the price this morning: tired eyes, and his normally immaculate attire somewhat wrinkled, like he had dressed in a hurry. Understandable under the circumstances.

"I must have crawled into bed about midnight last night," he said. "I walked into town and stopped in at the bar on the waterfront, then I wandered home, had a nightcap in the hotel bar, and slept like a log until I was awakened by a woman shrieking on the beach out front this morning. She kept it up, so I stumbled out onto the veranda to see what the fuss was about, and there was Philip, lying faceup on the sand. He was sloshing back and forth in the surf like a dead fish brought in on the tide." Victor went silent.

"Did you see Razor or Sylvia? Did the woman's scream wake them, too?" asked Nina.

"Well, Nina, darling, between you and me, I don't think dear Sylvia made it home last night. I think perhaps she put another notch in her belt last evening and bedded down aboard a sailboat at the marina. She and a well-preserved old salt were getting pretty chummy in the bar by last orders. A fellow from South Carolina who lives on his boat, if I recall the tale he told me."

"And Razor?"

"Razor was already down on the beach when I stumbled out onto the veranda. He rose to the occasion, old Razor. Had his arm around the elderly lady, and he shouted to me to fetch the police, which I did. They've been here for hours now. I've been told to make myself available for questioning."

Nothing seemed to be happening behind the police tape. Blue had gone inside Philip's bungalow.

"I'm not sure what we should do about the symposium today. Has anyone seen Bridget this morning?" Nina said to Victor. "A lot of people have traveled a long way to be here. But it doesn't seem right to just carry on as if nothing has happened. People are bound to be a bit rattled."

"Yes," said Victor. "All of us must quietly hope that our passing— or near passing—might cause at least a ripple in the daily activities of the people we know, even if life in the rest of the world goes on, oblivious."

"*Mmm.* Maybe we should cancel the program for this morning and move it to later in the week. We'd planned to give people some time to explore the island and enjoy the hotel amenities, anyway, so there's a bit of breathing room in the schedule. I should see if I can find Bridget and then go down to the office to make the arrangements and get the word out."

Nina pushed herself up and out of the chair. She looked over at Philip's bungalow. Danish was working the crowd, talking to hotel staff and conference delegates.

"Have you seen Philip?" she asked Victor.

"No," replied Victor. "There was an ambulance here earlier. The paramedics went inside for a while, but they came out again empty-handed and drove away. My guess is Philip wouldn't agree to go to the hospital. I think he must still be in his room. A couple of hotel workers took him in on a stretcher when he was found."

Nina sighed.

"I guess the right thing to do would be to go over and check on him," she said.

"I'd volunteer to go with you, but I don't think Philip would find my presence very comforting," said Victor.

Is that another allusion to some conflict between Victor and Philip? Nina wondered.

She sighed again. "OK. Bye, Victor. Why don't you come down to the inn for a coffee later, when you're ready. I'll be in the lobby."

"Yes, all right," he said, running his fingers through his hair. "I'll freshen up and join you presently." He went inside, and Nina started up the beach toward Philip's bungalow. Danish came loping toward her.

"Got some good intel from the bystanders. Where were you?" he said.

"I stopped to see Victor," Nina said.

"Victor Ross, I presume? According to my sources, Philip's arch nemesis. Rivals from way back. Hate each other's guts. Maybe there's a woman to blame, somewhere in the olden days?" mused Danish, a finger on his chin.

"No, I don't think so. I don't think they're in competition that way. Victor's my friend, Danish. And professors of leisure studies do not have arch nemeses," replied Nina.

"Well, anyway. Get this—there was something written on the guy's chest in black marker: 'I win.' Permanent marker. Sounds like something an arch nemesis would write, doesn't it? The giant syringe was an EpiPen. The kind allergic people use when they get stung by a bee or something like that."

"A shot of Adrenalin. Who told you that?"

"Mike, the security guard. Ross burst into the lobby, yelling, 'Get the police, there's a dead man on the beach,' which freaked everybody out. Mike ran over to preserve the crime scene until Roker got there. Turned out the guy—Putzel—wasn't dead, but Mike saw the message written on his chest."

"Oh my. Well, I guess that would explain why the police have ruled out an accident."

"Yeah. Well, I've got a yoga class in five. Michel wants to keep things as normal as possible. Catch you later. I'll come by your place later, and we can go over what we've got so far."

"No, Danish!" she yelled after him, but he didn't seem to hear.

Nina walked across the sand to Philip's bungalow. Blue was back outside, and his officers were taking down the crime-scene tape. Nina walked over to Blue.

"Hi again, Blue," said Nina. "May I go in and see Philip?"

He hesitated for a moment. "Yes," said Blue. "Follow me."

Philip was sitting up in bed when they entered the bungalow, a bank of thick pillows propping him up. A nurse in a starched white uniform and cap was gently dabbing a sponge on his face. His face and hands—all that was visible above and below the hotel-issue terry robe he wore tightly wrapped up to his neck—were covered in angry red welts and patches of scaly skin.

"Nina!" he shouted when he saw her. There was certainly nothing wrong with his voice. Nina took a deep breath and moved to his bedside. Blue took up a position opposite her, behind the nurse's chair.

"How are you feeling, Philip? Can I get you anything?" Nina asked.

"You can get me the hell off this island!" he shouted. Nina flinched. Blue looked at Nina, but kept silent.

"I have never had such a horrific night in my life!" said Philip forcefully. "First the kitchen mixes up my room-service order and nearly kills me with a shellfish appetizer, then the nonexistent security at this hotel fails to detect a thief breaking into my bungalow and *dragging* me down the beach in the middle of the night!"

He shouted at Blue, "I will be pressing charges!" Blue's expression did not change.

Would it be possible to avoid Michel for the rest of my life here on Pineapple Cay? Nina wondered. *Maybe if I do my grocery shopping at*

seven o'clock in the morning, right when the store opens, and limit myself
to my cottage and environs, and never go to another village function . . .

"I'm really sorry about what happened to you, Philip," she said.
"Of course, I'll help you make arrangements to leave, if that's what you
want." Philip was quiet for a moment, glaring at Nina. He looked out
the window and then back to Nina.

"No. I have my reputation to uphold. Fifty people have traveled
around the world to hear me give my paper on pet tourism. I am a
professional. I've done fieldwork on Daytona Beach at spring break. I
can take it. We will stick to the program."

"Yes, Philip," said Nina. "So, was anything taken from your bungalow?" she asked. Out of the corner of her eye, she saw Blue stand
up straighter.

"No. He must not have expected me to be here. I fell asleep on the
floor next to the bed after injecting myself with the EpiPen. I didn't
wake up until bloody Razor Hudson started slapping my face and
splashing sea water on me this morning. I was lying on the beach in my
underwear! What if Charlotte Critchlow from Westbury College had
looked out her window and seen that? That woman *thrives* on being
the bearer of other people's bad news."

Nina was thinking that pretty much everyone already knew exactly
what he was wearing when he was found and what was written on his
chest. And, unfortunately, after his speech last night, most seemed
to find it funny, rather than tragic. He didn't actually die, after all.
Anyone who didn't know the details would find out at the scheduled
midmorning break.

"So, the person who broke into your bungalow didn't take anything but hauled you down the stairs onto the beach while you were
sleeping and wrote something on your chest? Odd kind of thief," said
Nina.

"Already the gossip has started!" shouted Philip. "Who told you
about the message?"

"All right," said Blue. "I need to question Dr. Putzel further, Nina. You'll have to go now."

"Of course," said Nina. "Philip, if you need anything, just give me a call. I'll talk to Bridget and move things around a bit to give you some time to recover."

Philip just said, "Humph."

Blue's eyes followed Nina as she left the room.

Back out on the beach, Nina glanced around. To her right, a police officer was sitting on a beach lounger talking to two women in maid uniforms sitting opposite him. To her left was the white stucco two-story villa where Bridget was staying. Nina hiked her bag up on her shoulder and plodded down the sand to the villa. She rang the bell several times without any luck and was just about to leave when the door opened, and there stood Les. Mercifully, he had a towel wrapped around his waist.

"Well, good morning, Nina," he said. "What a—surprise. What can I do for you? We were in the middle of an epic session in the hot tub." He stood in front of the door to bar her entry—and her view—into the house.

"Oh, it's you. Why are you everywhere I am all of a sudden? I'm here to see Bridget, if you don't mind," Nina said, peering over his shoulder. The door swung wide open.

"Hi, Nina!" said Bridget with a big, gummy smile. She was wearing a flowered bathing suit that accentuated her matronly figure. "Come on in! You've got to see this place! It's amazing! We're having breakfast up on the rooftop terrace. Come on up!"

Bridget was off and up the stairs before Nina had the chance to get the news about Philip out. She followed Bridget up to the roof. Les trailed behind.

Nina had seen the rooftop terrace before, when Pansy had shown it to her. The view was spectacular. A row of teak sunbeds with thick mattresses and linen shade canopies was positioned to take in the long sweep of beach and the turquoise sea. At one side of the terrace, the hot tub was boiling away. Out of the corner of her eye, Nina saw Les shed his towel and climb into the hot tub with a loud, obnoxious sigh. He popped the top off a beer. Nina pointedly looked at her watch. He closed his eyes and lay back against the built-in headrest.

"Isn't it amazing?" said Bridget, spreading her arms wide and grinning contentedly. "Who needs Philip Putzel when you have this? He was so mean last night. I decided to skip his stupid presentation on dog vacations this morning and just hang out here with Les."

Does she really not know what happened? Nina wondered. Philip's bungalow was right next door. Nina looked over at the hot tub. It was on the side of the terrace away from Philip's bungalow. If Bridget and Les had been over there all morning, she supposed it was conceivable they hadn't noticed the activity down below.

"Can I tell you something a little bit naughty, Nina?" said Bridget conspiratorially, snorting a giggle through her nose as she walked toward the edge of the terrace facing Philip's bungalow.

"OK," said Nina warily, following her.

"Last night, I saw Philip in his outdoor shower, just before the banquet." She put her hand over her mouth, widened her eyes, and laughed her big, inelegant—but joyous—laugh. "Yeah," she continued in a whisper. "He stood in front of his shaving mirror and practiced his speech—totally in the buff. It was like watching a train wreck. I couldn't tear my eyes away."

Nina wondered how much she knew about Les's nudist lifestyle.

"Look," said Bridget. "You can see right into the walled garden behind his bungalow from here." She gestured toward the bungalow and then turned to look herself. "What's going on?" Bridget asked, looking at Nina questioningly. She seemed to be noticing the police officers and the crowd for the first time.

"Philip was attacked last night. Someone tried to kill him," Nina said.

Bridget's hand flew to cover her mouth.

"Oh my God!" said Bridget. "Is he all right? What happened?"

"He's OK," said Nina. "He's in bed recovering, but he'll be all right. Did you see anything last night?"

"No!" said Bridget. "Les and I came back here after we saw you on the beach after the banquet, had a few more drinks with my housemates up here on the roof, and sat in the hot tub for a while. We went out for a moonlight swim—the moon was almost full last night, you know? Spectacular. That was maybe about one o'clock. I got excited because I saw some tracks in the sand, like turtle tracks, you know? Like in a David Attenborough documentary? I thought maybe some giant turtles were coming ashore to lay their eggs. It was a big, deep groove in the sand. I thought maybe we could watch. That would be so cool, but Les pointed out that they were running parallel to the water, not away from the water. Duh, Bridget."

Nina glanced over at Les, who raised his beer bottle in acknowledgment.

Nina was thinking about what Philip had said about being dragged out of his bungalow and down the beach by his assailant. So, if those were the tracks Bridget saw, it happened sometime between ten o'clock and one o'clock. Philip ordered room service, too, she remembered. If she could find out when that was, she could narrow down the time frame of the attack.

"Where did you see the tracks, Bridget?" she asked. Bridget walked to the front of the terrace and gestured to the left, up the beach away from the inn.

"Going that way," she said. "We went for a swim, had another soak in the hot tub, then went to bed," she said. "I didn't hear anything."

Nina looked over at Les again. He was lying back in the hot tub with his eyes closed.

"What about you, Les?" Nina asked. "Did you see or hear anything strange last night?"

He opened his eyes slowly and focused on her. "Well, here's a clue, Nancy Drew. I was otherwise occupied all evening. I saw and heard lots of strange and wonderful things, but not from your professor friend."

Bridget giggled.

"All right, Bridget, thanks," Nina said, turning back to her. "We need to reorganize the conference schedule for today. I can go get started with Josie, but can you come over when you're ready?"

"OK," said Bridget.

Nina walked down to the water in front of Bridget's rental villa, then up the beach a short way. She didn't see any sign that a body had been dragged through the sand. Of course, any tracks below the high-water line would have been washed away by now. She sighed and headed back down the beach to the inn. *What started out as a simple assignment has turned into a sticky mess,* she thought. *Open revolt and wounded egos at the opening banquet. Attempted murder. What next?*

Nina spent about an hour in Josie's office rejigging the conference schedule and contacting as many of the delegates as she could to inform them of what had happened. Groups of them sat talking in hushed tones on the veranda as the day wore on. Eventually, Bridget appeared and took over on the front line. Nina sent a message to Philip's wife, informing her that there'd been a mishap, but that he was fine. When she was finished, she went out into the airy lobby to wait for Victor. She'd just sat down on a sofa in the corner when Michel came in from the side veranda where lunch was now being served. She could hear the parrot who lived in a cage on the veranda shriek after him in a Parisian accent, "Yes, I hate you, too. Don't worry."

"Stupid bird," he muttered. He saw Nina and sat down beside her in a deep club chair. He leaned back, crossed one knee over the other, draped his hands over the armrests, and surveyed her for a moment before he spoke.

"Well, Mademoiselle Spark. Quite a morning. How are you managing?" he said. His concern was unexpected. She'd thought he would be at least annoyed at the police tape festooning the shrubbery at one end of the hotel beach.

"Michel, I'm so sorry for the disruption. I hope your other guests are not too upset by what's happened," Nina said.

"My dear mademoiselle, unless you poisoned Monsieur Putzel, you have nothing for which to apologize. In the past, I've paid for a troupe of actors to stage something called a murder-mystery weekend, primarily to entertain our resident expatriate clientele. The natives get restless after several months of golf and cocktails. They begin to act out—scandalous wagers on the weekly crab races, a surge in clandestine rendezvous in our upstairs guest rooms, entrées sent back to the kitchen for no reason other than our patrons are craving a little drama. Some distraction. Now that the professor is making a good recovery, I'll admit that I much prefer the real thing. In fact, I should thank you again for the honor of hosting your conference. The phone is ringing off the hook for dinner reservations this evening." Michel smiled mildly.

"Well, thank you for your understanding," said Nina uncertainly. She paused and then asked, "Michel, can you tell me what time Philip ordered room service?"

Michel smiled. "Ah, Mademoiselle Spark, has your previous success encouraged you to change careers and become an investigator? *Bien.* Deputy Superintendent Roker has also asked me these questions, but I will play along. Monsieur Putzel called for room service at ten thirty. The kitchen tells me that a plate of seafood and spinach tartlets, two slices of guava cheesecake, and a bottle of rosé were delivered to his bungalow at ten fifty. The professor was in the shower, so the waiter left the tray on the table and departed."

"Is there any chance the food was accidentally contaminated with shellfish? By a knife used to prepare two different orders, perhaps?" Nina asked.

"I would not let Chef Dionne hear such suggestions. He prides himself on running a hygienic, well-regimented kitchen. As I told the police, no chance at all. Monsieur Putzel took great pains to emphasize his allergy to shellfish when he placed his order."

So, someone entered Philip's room and tampered with the food sometime after it was delivered, hid and watched or came back later, and dragged the unexpectedly alive but unconscious Philip into the water, hoping to drown him—although he'd only ended up with an awful sunburn. It must have all happened before one o'clock, when Bridget said she saw tracks in the sand. But who would have done this?

"Is that all, Ms. Spark?" asked Michel, preparing to stand.

"Yes, I guess so. Thank you, Michel," said Nina.

"Not at all," he said. "My pleasure. I shall be interested to see if it is the deputy superintendent or yourself who captures the villain this time. Even innkeepers need their amusements. *Bonne journée*, mademoiselle. Do take care." Michel nodded to her, then strolled leisurely across the lobby and into the dining room.

Victor breezed through the side door shortly after Michel left, looking much better than he had when Nina first arrived—freshly shaven and dressed in a cool white-linen shirt and gray trousers.

"Let's have our coffee out on the front veranda, Victor. I find the view of the ocean and the sound of the waves soothing, and I, for one, could use a bit of that right now," said Nina.

They went through the open French doors onto the veranda. The sea at the foot of the lawn was sparkling in the sunlight. Some guests were playing croquet on the grass, chatting normally as they whacked the wooden balls through the hoops. A few other guests were ensconced in the comfortable wicker rocking chairs facing the water, reading or chatting over post-lunch frosty drinks in highball glasses. Things seemed to be returning to normal, at least on the surface, after the morning's shocking discovery. Perhaps unsurprisingly, the conference attendees who knew Philip only slightly, if at all, were finding things to do on their unexpectedly free day at a lovely inn on a beautiful tropical island. Nina felt a pang of sympathy for Philip. Life was strange.

"There's Sylvia, back from her adventures," said Victor. "Shall we join her?"

Sylvia was at the far end of the veranda reading a newspaper, with a cup of coffee on the railing beside her. She was dressed in tennis whites. She looked up as Nina and Victor approached.

"Well, hello, Nina. Victor. What a spectacular day. I think I'm going to take a tennis lesson this afternoon, perhaps get a massage, and then lie on the beach with a good book before the four o'clock session. Won't you join me for coffee?" She smiled broadly and gestured for them to sit in the chairs facing her. She raised her hand to attract the attention of a waiter.

Sylvia doesn't seem too shaken by the recent attempted murder of her ex-husband, thought Nina. Then again, Sylvia was always a cool customer, not given to flagrant displays of emotion. Nina sank down into the thickly cushioned seat, breathing in the fresh sea air and the setting.

"Well, Sylvia. What do you make of it?" said Victor as he settled into his chair. "Was it you who tried to off Philip, by any chance?"

Sylvia glanced at him and tsk-tsked. She lit a cigarette and took a long draw, exhaling slowly through her nose before replying.

"Victor. Always so refreshingly direct. Generally a quality I admire in a man. Deputy Superintendent Roker asked me more or less the same thing in a similarly direct manner. A very impressive man. Such extraordinary eyes. If anyone has reason to wish Philip dead, it's me," she said. She drew on her cigarette again, blowing a delicate puff of smoke toward the croquet players.

"I had two small children at home. I put my career on hold when they were born, taking piecemeal work here and there to make ends meet while Philip finished school and then got a job at the university, whining all the time about how busy he was, how stressful his work was. He was advancing in his career, making a name for himself while I changed diapers and drove carpool. Then the bastard left me with two kids for one of his doe-eyed adoring students. Not the one he's with now. What a pathetic cliché." Sylvia shook her head slowly.

"That poor deluded girl. Of course, she ended up the same way. He left her for the next adoring student. Now he has a baby with that one. I bet she doesn't think it's so glamorous now, being the wife of the great Philip Putzel, stuck at home with a crying baby while he swans off to the Caribbean. That man cares about nothing but himself. His great contribution to humankind is in finding more things for doting doggie parents to spend their money on. Guest rooms for dogs in five-star hotels. Room service for animals on holiday. He wrote an article last year on the growing market for swimming pools for dogs. I mean, really. When we met, at least he was doing real research." Sylvia sniffed derisively.

"I guess you're more of a cat person, am I right, Sylvia? I guess I should have known that. You have some very feline qualities," said Victor.

Sylvia ignored his comment.

"Of course, I'm sorry about what's happened," she said in a more measured tone. "However, as I told the dashing deputy superintendent, I didn't try to kill Philip. If I were going to do it, I would have done it years ago while he snored next to me in bed having rolled in from some faculty party with booze on his breath, hours after the children had gone to bed. No, I picked myself up, finished school, and got on with it. The children are now thriving, no thanks to him. Maria's a pediatrician, and Sally is a white-water rafting guide in Colorado, of all things. I'm very proud of them."

Nina admired Sylvia, but she couldn't help thinking that Sylvia's expensive education and help from family had given her a boost that others in her situation might not have had.

Sylvia stubbed her cigarette out in a saucer.

"I hear it was shellfish," she said. "That'd be the way to do it. Philip's highly allergic to shellfish. He also finds it hard to resist both a tasty morsel and a compliment. Slip some lobster or crab into a plate of delicacies, deliver it to him on a silver tray, and perhaps tell him that it comes with the compliments of the chef because the hotel is so honored to have him as a guest. He would scoff it right down and be dead in minutes. He had a lucky escape, I'd say."

So, Philip's attacker must have been someone who knew about his allergy, thought Nina. Sylvia knew, because she had been married to him. Victor might have known because he and Philip were at college together, maybe living in the same student residence all those years ago. Bridget probably knew because she'd have made arrangements for Philip many times by now. It was unlikely, though not impossible, that Razor knew. But maybe the shellfish was just an accident. Philip ate something he shouldn't have, then a burglar discovered him behind the bed and dragged him outside for some reason. None of it made much sense. Lots of people found Philip extremely obnoxious, but why bother killing him?

Nina stood, and Victor got to his feet as well.

"I've got to get going and help Bridget reorganize a few things," she said. "Tomorrow morning we had planned for excursions, anyway, so Philip has some time to rest up. See you later."

"All right, Nina, darling. Have a great day. You are doing a fantastic job. Top-notch. This place is gorgeous. I might just sell my apartment in Old Town and move here myself," said Sylvia. She laughed at the absurdity of the idea and waved her fingers in parting.

"Righto, Nina. Adieu," said Victor. He sat back down to finish his coffee as Nina made her way down the steps and around the side of the inn to the driveway. As she walked, she passed a constable interviewing a couple on the lawn, notebook at the ready. *He'll be talking to every single guest today,* Nina thought. She looked around for Blue, but he was nowhere to be seen. Feeling the effects of her late night and early morning, Nina decided to go home and take a nap before the afternoon session. She'd catch up with Bridget a bit later.

~

The afternoon's presentations, if a bit dull, at least went off without a hitch after the tech guy came in and fixed the overhead projector, which had been working only minutes before the room filled with delegates. Nina had supper with Victor, then made her excuses and headed home as he wandered into the bar where a few people were gathered.

Nina glanced over at Les's house as she pushed open the gate in her waist-high white picket fence. His house was dark.

Where is he? she wondered. He hadn't gone out at all in the past two weeks since they'd met. His bungalow was usually ablaze with light until midnight. She shrugged and went inside. One mystery at a time. She shucked off her clothes, had a nice warm shower, and went to bed early. Her last conscious thought was to wonder what Ted was up to that night.

7

It was a beautiful morning on Pineapple Cay. A rooster crowed in the distance as Nina stood on the gravel drive in front of the Plantation Inn. She and Josie had organized a choice of excursions for the conference delegates for the day, and she watched as several white vans pulled away. Some guests were headed for the dive shop and a day of snorkeling, while others were going to the museum and on a historical walking tour of Coconut Cove. A final group was on an island sightseeing tour with stops at the brewery, the rum distillery, and a beach bar for lunch. When they had all gone, she turned to head back into the inn—and saw that Razor was sitting on the steps with his backpack beside him, scribbling in the Moleskine notebook he carried everywhere.

"Razor. You didn't feel like getting out for the day?" she asked.

"I'm totally not into that tourist crap," he said. "I want to see the authentic Pineapple Cay. Experience the real culture. The yoga instructor here said he'd line up a couple of local guys to show me around."

"Danish?" asked Nina.

"Yeah. He's super cool. He's been here awhile. Knows what's going on," said Razor.

"Uh-huh," said Nina.

Danish came striding across the lawn from the staff quarters near the tennis courts.

"Yo, Razor, man. Are you up for it? The guys are set. They'll be here pronto. Howdy, Nina. Are you coming with us?" he said.

"I wasn't planning on it. Didn't actually know you had arranged this bespoke tour. Where are you taking Razor, dare I ask?"

"A couple of my buddies, Warren and Fuzz, give nature tours in the bush down past Smooth Harbour. They know all about traditional medicine, local plants and animals, stuff like that. Then I thought we'd sample some local cuisine down in Sandy Point before I take my man Razor here to cool down at a hidden beach only the locals know about."

"Sounds great," said Razor. "I want to try some real local food. We can skip the beach, though. Is there a factory of some kind here? I want to see the real Pineapple Cay."

"The real Pineapple Cay is rimmed by white-sand beaches, Razor. The locals swim, too, and fish for a living," said Nina.

Razor didn't reply.

Nina considered Danish's invitation. She could go home, but why not see more of the island? She had only planned to do some housework, and that could wait.

"All right. I'll tag along, if you don't mind," she said. Razor looked like he did mind, but she sat down on the step to wait, anyway. Danish lay down on the grass and put his hat over his face. About a half hour later, a beat-up van with tinted windows rolled up. The doors opened, and two guys with long dreadlocks spilled out, the sweet tang of ganja billowing out with them. They were both wearing soccer jerseys and baggy shorts. A woozy reggae beat seeped out of the van.

"Warren, man. You're late," said Danish to the taller of the two.

"Sorry, brother. They were doing pumpkin ravioli and brazed kale with poached pears for dessert on the telly. Must-see TV," said Warren. He came slowly around the van and heaved open the sliding door, then gestured casually for them to get in.

"All right, y'all. Load 'er up," said the other guy—Fuzz, apparently. He bounced on the balls of his feet, his eyes bright. He seemed to have energy to burn.

"Guys, this is my man Razor. He wants to see the real Pineapple Cay," said Danish.

"Respect, brother. Sister," said Warren, slapping Razor's hand with his own and letting it fall slowly. "We gonna do that. I'm going to teach you about bush medicine—like what my granny showed me from a baby."

Razor looked delighted for the first time since he'd arrived on Pineapple Cay. Genuine sort-of Rastafarians.

They all got in the van. Fuzz got in back with Nina and Danish, and Razor rode shotgun beside Warren. They turned right on the main road heading south. They rolled past the row of beach houses lining the shore south of the village, only their roofs and the tops of cabbage palms in their gardens visible from the road. The van wound through the sun-dappled green tunnel of trees.

"Fuzz, man. Roll me a marley," said Warren from the front seat. Nina's eyes were already burning from the joint they must have smoked on their way to the inn. She pushed open the window.

"No, no, lady from NYC. Keep the windows tight. It's too hot out there. We got the AC," said Fuzz.

Fuzz rummaged around in the back seat of the van and came up with a cookie tin, which he opened carefully on his lap. Inside were the makings of a marley. He proceeded to roll a big fat spliff, lit it, then offered it to Nina.

"No, thank you," she said. Fuzz held it out to Razor. Razor seemed to hesitate. She could see the wheels turning. The When in Rome principle and building credibility with the local guys versus *Midnight Express* and ten years in a local jail. He shook his head no.

"No, thanks, man. Never on an empty stomach," said Danish. Fuzz shrugged, took a drag, and passed it up to Warren.

They turned off the main road onto a narrow rutted track that led into the nature preserve. The van bounced over the potholes. A forest of extremely tall, straight pine trees with an understory of spiky palmetto palms soon surrounded them. Warren stopped the van, and Nina wrestled the door open as quickly as she could, gulping in the hot, fresh air outside the vehicle. She was beginning to feel a bit buzzed from the secondhand smoke.

"Let's walk a bit, stretch the legs," said Warren, heading off down a faint path through the trees. They followed him in single file.

"This here is a pine forest," said Warren. "Yellow pine. Latin name, *Pinus caribaea*. Once used as ship masts for the English. The littler ones are palmetto palms; they are dried and used for weaving baskets and mats."

"Yeah, my granny sells them in the market. I can get you a good deal if you want, man," Fuzz said to Razor. "You can take one home to your woman. And your mother and your granny and all your sisters."

"She isn't your granny, and those baskets you sell are made in China, man," said Danish. "It says so right on the bottom." He turned to Razor. "If you want a souvenir to take home, I'll help you pick one out. Some are genuine, some aren't."

Razor stiffened. "I'm a traveler, not a tourist. I'm very accustomed to haggling in the market, but I'm not interested in souvenirs. I'm here for work. But, thank you," he added, as if remembering that that's what a polite human would say in that situation.

"OK, whatever you say. Just offering," said Danish.

Boy, Razor has a lot of sharp edges. Maybe his nickname does suit him, after all, thought Nina.

They kept walking. Gradually, the tall pines thinned out and gave way to scrubby, leafed trees and sand. The trees got shorter and the light got brighter. They emerged onto an empty beach and halted in the shade of a tall palm tree.

"We will start with a refreshing beverage," said Warren. "Coconut water. Cleans your insides. The yummy mommies and investment bankers stateside all gaga now about coconut water. We been drinking it every day, our whole lives. You sit here, watch the sea, chill, be cool. Good for you."

Danish flopped down onto the sand, and Nina sat beside him. Razor tentatively joined them.

Fuzz shimmied up a nearby coconut tree, his biceps and quads straining, machete in one hand. He hacked half a dozen green nuts loose, and they fell to the sand with soft thumps. Warren picked one up and bounced it in his hand a few times, shook it, then took the machete from Fuzz and sliced the top off. Fuzz reached into his knapsack and came out with a box of plastic straws. He took the green coconut from Warren, stuck a straw in it, and handed it to Nina. Warren hacked open another one for Razor.

"When you done drinking, you can eat the jelly," said Warren to Razor. "Here, I show you." He took the machete and chopped the top off another green nut. He lifted it to his lips and threw his head back, drinking the water inside in several long gulps. When it was empty, he split the coconut in two with one powerful swing of the machete and held half of it out to Razor. Fuzz reached into his knapsack again and fished out a couple of spoons. He gave one to Razor and one to Warren.

"See here," Warren said, scooping the soft, white flesh out of the green husk with a spoon. "You eat it just like this. *Mmm-mmm.* Coconut is a miracle food. It got everything, man. Electrolytes, vitamins, antioxidants. That's why I look so good."

Razor scooped out some jelly and took a small spoonful, chewing it tentatively.

"Yes, yes. It's good. I like it," he said.

"That's right, man. Nature's Viagra. It keep you at twelve o'clock all day. Not nine o'clock. Twelve o'clock all day," said Fuzz, demonstrating the hour hand of the clock using his bent forearm as a visual aid.

Razor stopped chewing and swallowed quickly. He set the coconut gently on the rock next to him. "That's fascinating. I didn't know that piece of local lore," Razor said, scribbling in his notebook.

"I said no tourist crap, Fuzz," said Danish.

"That's not tourist crap, man," said Fuzz. "A genuine coconut demonstration like that cost you ten dollar easy at some fancy hotel on the big island."

"Let's go for a walk," said Warren, heading down the beach. Nina slipped off her sandals and followed the group. It was midmorning, and the sand was hot underfoot, so she veered down to the water's edge and splashed along in the surf.

Warren stopped beside a tall, leafy tree on the edge of the forest. The others gathered around. Nina joined them, her feet now coated in wet sand. That was always the issue at the beach. Whether to trudge through the sand in street shoes, wear sandals and get sand inside them, or go barefoot and wade in the refreshingly cool water, knowing that eventually you'll have to stuff your sandy feet back into your shoes. *Someone should have invented a fix to that by now,* Nina thought, brushing sand from the soles of her feet.

"This is what we call a Tourist Tree," Warren was saying. "See how its bark is peeling, leaving red patches on the trunk and branches, just like a tourist who stay in the sun all day drinking margaritas." He snickered. "Gum Elemi, Latin name, *Bursera simaruba*."

"And what did your ancestors use this tree for?" asked Razor earnestly.

"Yes, this tree is very valuable in our culture. If you get stung by a bee or a wasp, you make a poultice from the leaves and put it on the sting to get the poison out and relieve the pain. Also good for cuts, burns, rashes, and measles. The old people boil the leaves and add the liquid to their bathwater. It relieves rheumatism," said Warren. "If you got another kind of problem, you can drink the tea instead. The men use it to make a bush tea called Twenty-One Gun Salute. Nature's Viagra."

"Fascinating," said Razor, nodding his head vigorously.

"Yeah, we're going to follow this bush trail now. I want to show you something," said Warren, starting along a narrow sandy path back into the forest behind the beach. Nina sighed and slid her feet back into her sandals, feeling grains of sand push under her toenails and rub uncomfortably between her toes. She heard her grandmother's voice in her head, could see her in her flowing red tie-dyed dress and chunky necklace of wooden beads, gesturing with a highball glass in her hand. *"That's what we call* champagne problems, *darling. Don't sweat the small stuff. And it's all small stuff."*

"Listen. You hear that?" said Fuzz. "We call it Woman's Tongue, because it never stops chattering." He laughed loudly at his joke.

"Poinciana," said Warren. Nina listened. She could hear the faint rattle of the long seed pods in the treetops around them, and she realized she'd seen the same trees along the road in town. They walked on, following the path as it wound around dense stands of trees and coral rock outcroppings.

"This here, this is Love Vine, also known as Dodder," said Warren, gently lifting the tender green leaves on a wiry orange vine wound round and round a tree so many times that it seemed to be smothering it.

"Let me guess," said Nina.

"It is a traditional cure for backache. You have backache, you cut the vine and tie it around your waist. Your backache will go. That's what my grandmother says," said Warren.

"Cool," said Razor.

"Also an aphrodisiac," said Fuzz. "You boil it and drink the tea, it get you in the mood."

"Oh, brother," said Nina. "And what if I've just got a headache? Is there any plant on this island that can cure that?"

"Sure, mama," said Fuzz, holding out a coconut. "You get your man to eat the jelly of a coconut, and your headache be gone, no problem," he said. "Best cure there is, know what I'm sayin'?"

"Good one, Fuzz," said Danish, high-fiving him.

Nina rolled her eyes. They walked on.

The path reemerged on the beach. They turned and walked back in the direction they had come from in the shade of the fringe of trees bent over the dazzlingly white sand. A short distance along, Warren stopped abruptly in front of a tall, leafy tree with a broad, dense canopy.

"All right, look here, man," he said forcefully, pointing at the tree and looking at Razor. "Stay away from this tree, right? This here is manchineel. If you stand under it, it drip poison sap on you. If rain drips off a leaf into your eye, you can go blind. If you brush against it, it will burn your skin raw and red. No joke. Hurts like nothing you have ever experienced, man. Also, don't eat the fruit. The death apple. They taste sweet at first, like a woman, but they will blister the inside of your mouth, close up your throat so you can't breathe. Then you die."

Nina looked at the tree. It looked harmless. Small, bright-green fruits littered the sand beneath the tree. They did look fresh, juicy, and tempting in the heat.

"Definitely not an aphrodisiac," said Danish.

"Wait. What?" said Nina. She thought of the red blotches all over Philip's body. Blotches and blisters. *Maybe it wasn't a sunburn, which didn't make any sense. He went missing after dark, and was discovered unconscious on the beach shortly after sunrise. Maybe it was a rash, maybe from a manchineel tree. Maybe he ate the fruit for some reason.*

"This one no good for starting a fire, if you follow," said Fuzz.

"Are there many of these trees on the island?" Nina asked, turning to Warren.

"Here and there. They grow along the beach, and close by the mangrove," he said.

"If they're so poisonous, why aren't they cut down?" she asked.

"Well, they were here first. Also, the large root system keeps the beach from eroding," said Warren.

"Are there any manchineel trees near the inn?" she asked.

"Yeah, there's a big one, a ways down from the inn, away from town," he said.

"Huh," said Nina. They started walking back to the van. Fuzz was lecturing Razor on Pineapple Cay culture. Danish fell in beside Nina.

"What are you thinking?" he asked her. "You got something? Do you think someone fed Philip Putzel a death apple?"

"No. Maybe, I guess. But I was thinking about the red rash all over his face and chest. He said he was dragged down the beach. What if his attacker left him under the manchineel tree down the beach from the inn? That could be how he got the rash. After his attacker left, Philip could have revived, staggered up the beach toward his bungalow, and collapsed again on the sand in front of the guest bungalows. Then the tide came in, washing away the footprints of both Philip and his attacker."

"Yeah, I can see that," said Danish. "So, we're looking for a sadist. Or at least someone who really, really hates Putzel. Other than Victor Ross, does anyone spring to mind?"

Nina looked ahead at Razor Hudson's hunched shoulders, braced under the weight of his knapsack containing a computer, a notebook, and who knew what else. He was nodding his head eagerly as he listened to Fuzz.

Surely not, thought Nina.

"I really don't know," she said aloud to Danish. "Let's just hope it was a one-off random act of craziness and that whoever did it has gotten whatever they have against Philip out of their system."

They had reached the van.

"Everyone in," said Fuzz. "We're going to Rosie's for lunch. It's a local place, down in Sandy Point. You're going to try her conch salad," he said to Razor. "It's the best in the islands."

124

A short while later, they were sitting on the outdoor patio at Rosie's Restaurant in Sandy Point, at the very southern tip of the island. Nina had been there once before with Ted. The setting was spectacular: turquoise water all around and a view of the Diamond Cays trailing off over the horizon. A couple of sailboats were anchored in the sheltered cove below the restaurant, and a table of jovial yachties had already built up a collection of empty beer bottles and cracked lobster shells.

After eating, Danish, Fuzz, and Warren wandered off on some mission of their own. Nina was sitting with Razor at a table by the railing, listening to him rant about the cutthroat world of academia. Razor was peeling the label from his beer bottle in tiny pieces, making a little pile of them on the table in front of him. Nina was fighting the urge to reach into her bag, pull out her sunscreen, and squirt some on the top of his head, which was starting to glow red.

"The sun is pretty intense here," she said. "Do you have a hat? Would you like some sunscreen for your . . ." She gestured to the top of her own head and face. She didn't know how to reference his shaved head. Some men were so sensitive about baldness. Razor just batted her question away with his hand as if it was a mosquito buzzing around his face.

"I mean, you wouldn't believe some of the lame-o project proposals they accepted this year. Another study of how backpackers rejoin the workforce after bumming around the world for a year. I mean, that's already been done to death!" he said. For the past half hour, he had complained bitterly about not winning a grant for his latest project—research into how business travelers behaved on airplanes.

"I mean, I was going to spend a total of *one thousand hours* in the air, observing business travelers on both international and domestic flights. It was going to be groundbreaking."

He grabbed a french fry off his plate and chomped it angrily. He picked up another and jabbed it at Nina as he spoke.

"And then! And then! Guess what I hear through my contacts? It was *Philip* who recommended that the committee reject my request for project funding! According to my sources, he called my project *amateurish*. But I know what's going on. He feels threatened by the cutting-edge research I've been doing on hot-tub etiquette at ski resorts, the participant observation stuff that he's too old and lazy to do, and so he used his position to kill my project!"

Razor munched his fry as he looked out at the water and the small islands trailing off over the horizon.

"He *knew* that I need that funding to do the project so that I can get tenure in my department. Without it, my career will screech to a halt, and if I am lucky, I'll grind out my remaining days on earth teaching Sociology for Engineers for what amounts to minimum wage as a contract instructor. So, if he should have an unfortunate accident, good riddance, I say, and I don't care who knows it!"

Razor grabbed the sweating bottle of beer in front of him by the neck and chugged it in what Nina could only describe as an aggressive manner. When he was done, he slammed it down on the table, rattling the salt and pepper shakers. Danish, Fuzz, and Warren had settled at a nearby table for a game of dominoes, and they looked over in unison at the bang. Seeing nothing but a very intense, thin-lipped small man with a shaved head picking at the label on his beer bottle, they turned their attention back to their game.

"Excuse me," said Razor, rising quickly and stalking away toward the restaurant, presumably to find the restroom.

Wow, thought Nina, watching him go. *He really hates Philip. Forget about not speaking ill of the almost-dead.*

But in the world of academics, it's all about tenure. You get it, and you've got it made. A well-paid job for life, prestige, autonomy, a sabbatical every few years so you can rent a villa in the South of France to "write a book" or live in a yurt in Mongolia to study local handicrafts—whatever. If you don't publish, or you don't publish in the right journals, you don't win research grants, and you don't get tenure. Game over. No doubt people have killed for less. *Could Razor really have done it?* she wondered.

When Razor returned, they settled up with Rosie and piled back in the van. Fuzz flared up a postprandial hooter, and the vehicle filled with weedy smoke. Nina cracked the window, but that let the hot, sunbaked air of midday inside, so she closed it again and rested her head against the back of the seat, her eyes closed. Fuzz, Warren, Razor, and Danish were talking about the strategy behind dominoes. Razor was peppering the others with questions about the significance of dominoes in local culture. His questions were urgent, their answers unhurried and amused. Nina tuned them out.

By the time they passed the **WELCOME TO COCONUT COVE, POP. 3,000** sign on their way into town, she was feeling very drowsy and more than a little buzzed. She pictured her hammock swaying in a gentle breeze and a cold glass of iced tea in her hand. With any luck, she'd be in it very soon. Still, she couldn't shake the feeling that she should tell Blue Roker what Razor had said about Philip ruining his chances at a prestigious grant. She felt sorry for Razor. He seemed like a fish out of water, uncomfortable even in his own skin. But despite any personal feelings about Philip or Razor, it was her duty to pass on any possibly useful information to the police.

They dropped Razor off at the inn.

"Warren, man, just drop me at Nina's," said Danish drowsily from the back seat. "We've got some work to do before my shift at The Redoubt."

Nina swiveled her head around to look at him. He was leaning back against the headrest with his eyes closed. She let it pass.

Without asking directions to her house, Warren drove through town and slowed to a stop in front of Nina's yellow cottage. She didn't bother asking him how he knew where she lived. She assumed now that everyone on Pineapple Cay knew not only where she lived but also that she had bought the cottage off the Internet in the middle of the night not long after walking in on her husband and his paralegal in flagrante delicto on the living room sofa. That was several months ago now. Old news.

Nina heaved herself out of the van at her front gate.

"Thanks, guys. That was very educational," she said to Warren and Fuzz.

"Respect, sister. Anytime you need a sachet of my special Twenty-One Gun Salute bush tea, give me a call. I'll fix you up. That fisherman's getting old and rusty," said Fuzz, snorting laughter at his own joke. She could hear Warren join in as they drove off.

Does he mean Ted? Nina wondered. Did everyone except her know everything about everyone else around here? She pushed open her unlocked front door and went inside. Danish followed her into the cottage, opened the fridge door, and started rooting around inside for something to eat or drink. Even though she was still feeling woozy from the ganja smoke, she went to the phone. Better call Blue and say what she had to say before she lost her nerve.

The phone rang twice before he picked up.

"This is Roker."

Nina told him what Razor had said. There was silence on the other end of the line.

"I wasn't interrogating him, Blue. We were eating lunch together, and he brought it up," Nina said. Another second of silence.

"All right, Nina. I'll look into it. Thanks for the call," said Blue. Nina hung up the phone and sighed. Distasteful duty done.

"Was that Blue you were talking to?" asked Danish from the kitchen.

"Yup," she said. She stepped out onto the veranda and stretched her arms above her head and breathed in deeply. The steady rhythm of the surf was making her even sleepier. She'd get rid of Danish and curl up in the hammock for a nap this afternoon. But just then, a screechy metal guitar riff assaulted her eardrums.

"Oh, come *on*! Not again!" she exclaimed.

Les was on his back deck barbecuing in the altogether. His stereo was blasting Guns N' Roses. He set a platter of raw meat by the grill and disappeared back inside his house. With her hands on her hips, Nina stood glaring at his deck, waiting for him to reappear. Danish burst through the door onto the veranda and flopped into a deck chair. He was carrying the last bottle of beer from her fridge.

"What is it they use to house-train puppies? A squirt gun. I need a squirt gun with a very long range," Nina said, still staring at the deck, where Les had reappeared with his condiments.

"I've got a paintball gun," said Danish from his reclined position.

"Really?" she said, turning to look at him with interest.

"Yeah. Two, actually. The Supershot IV and the Rainbow Dynamo 500. Both rated to a hundred and fifty yards."

"I knew you were the man for the job. Listen, I'm trying to train Les to keep his clothes on in my line of sight. As soon as his bare bum strays off his deck, I want to land a fluorescent green blob on each cheek. Punishment must be delivered as soon as the offense is committed, or the puppy never learns. Are you in?"

"Are you kidding? Right on! I'll be back in a flash with the guns and ammo." He chugged the beer, then took off at a trot around the side of the house and down the street.

Nina sat on the veranda and made her way through a bag of tortilla chips while she waited for Danish. She trained her eyes on Les, enjoying being irritated by him. She watched Les eat his burger. Then she watched as Les painted a birdhouse in what Nina would have thought were bird-repelling black-and-yellow stripes. *He must think it looks homey,* she thought. It was almost sweet. Almost enough to make her stand down from her mission. But not quite.

Danish came back a short while later, dressed in neon paint-splattered army-surplus fatigues, a plastic toy gun in each hand.

"I could only find pink paint pellets. They're not that easy to come by around here," he said.

"That'll do," said Nina. "OK. How do I work this thing?" Although she grew up in Maine—big deer, moose, and bear country—she had never learned to shoot a gun.

"Well, you look through the sight at your target, and when you've got him in the crosshairs, let 'er rip. Press the trigger," said Danish.

"Does it hurt?" asked Nina.

"No," said Danish. "It's like being pinged with a rubber band. I've adjusted the velocity so we can lob the paint pellets at him like Nerf balls."

"OK. Let's do it," said Nina, shaking her head to clear it. She squinted up at the crowns of the palm trees towering over her cottage. The rustling of the fronds was almost deafening. She and Danish sat cross-legged on the edge of the veranda facing Les's deck, following his movements through their gun sights. Les finished painting his bird feeder and set it on the deck's railing to dry. He stood at the top of the steps down onto the beach, stretching his arms above his head, then doing a few lunges, oblivious to the crosshairs on his butt.

"Why does he bother you so much?" asked Danish while they waited for Les to stray off his deck into the forbidden zone. "Is it his scrawny little butt? Why don't you just look the other way? Up the beach toward Fortress Matthews, maybe. In fact, I think you should take a good hard look in the mirror, Nina, and ask yourself this: If that was Ted frolicking on his deck in his birthday suit, would you be so offended? Are you just targeting Les just because he doesn't have the posterior of a male swimsuit model?"

She turned to look at him sternly. "The point is, Danish, that a normal person like Ted would not do that. Why should I have to suffer for Les's lifestyle choices? Look! There he goes!"

She retrained her sights on Les and watched him trot down the three stairs onto the beach and stroll toward the water, doing arm circles as he went. Nina began to have second thoughts about the wisdom of her plan. Perhaps shooting Les wasn't the best tack after all. She started to lower her weapon.

"Oh, I don't know, Danish. Maybe this is wrong," she said. As the words left her mouth, Danish pressed the trigger on his paintball gun, and a fraction of a second later, a splat of fluorescent pink appeared on Les's backside. He yelped and spun, looking around wildly for his assailant. He looked first down the beach toward town, then up the beach toward the fishing lodge. Nina and Danish flattened themselves on the deck of her veranda.

"I didn't give the word!" hissed Nina.

"I didn't know that was the plan!" whispered Danish. "I thought this was what you wanted!"

"I know, I know!" said Nina. "We've got to get inside before he sees us. If I open the door, he'll notice." She crawled on her hands and knees to the edge of the veranda on the side away from Les's house and rolled off it onto the patchy grass. Crouching, she edged along the side of the house to the front door, Danish right behind her. They straightened up as they rounded the corner. The screen door was unlocked, and they slipped inside, hurrying to peer out the window at the beach in front of Les's house. He had disappeared.

"I think I may have to reevaluate the Les situation," said Nina, collapsing onto the chintz sofa. "My strategy might be veering a bit off course. I'm going to have a nap first, then think about it." She lay down and closed her eyes. A few minutes later, she heard a car drive up and stop in front of Les's house, then two car doors slamming shut.

"It's the police!" Danish hissed. "Les called them! If Roker catches me, I'm done. He already has it in for me. He's never thought I was good enough for Alice."

"This is my fault," said Nina. "Go out the beach door and leave through the vacant lot. I'll take the heat."

After Danish took off, Nina casually situated herself on the sofa with an iced tea, the paintball guns stuffed under the seat cushion. She felt strangely calm as she waited for the police to knock.

A couple of minutes later, two young officers were at the door, their uniforms too big for their barely postadolescent frames. The one with glasses cleared his throat.

"Ah, Ms. Spark? We've had a report of a paintball shot in the area. Have you heard or seen anything unusual?" he asked.

Nina was never very good at lying, and she caved immediately. She held out her hands for the cuffs.

"OK, it was me. Take me away. Let's go."

The officers looked at each other, then the same officer motioned for Nina to follow him to the police Jeep. At the station, they put Nina in a holding cell in the basement, and then she was alone. She sat on the hard bench and stared at the wall, trying to clear her still-fuzzy head. She watched a gecko scurry along the wall and up into the rafters. The room didn't offer much else to look at—the two holding cells along the back wall, a small metal desk and chair, and a poster above a chipped white porcelain sink in the wall opposite reminding everyone to wash their hands.

After several minutes, Nina heard footsteps coming down the corridor toward her. The slow, measured gait of Blue Roker. He entered the room with a couple of file folders in his hand, pausing at the door to look at Nina for a moment before walking over to stand in front of her cell.

His mouth was a straight line, and his eyes radiated annoyance. "So, Nina. You decided to disregard my advice to live and let live and have gone vigilante."

She looked up at him from the bench. "I know, I know. He's just so *annoying*."

She clutched the edge of the bench with both hands to keep from sliding off. She was feeling a bit dizzy. Blue stared at her for a long moment, his eyes trained on hers. His nostrils flared briefly.

"Yeah," he said, and turned away from her, crossing the small room to sit at the metal desk. He took a pen out of his shirt pocket, opened a file folder, and proceeded to ignore her. Nina sat on the bench with her head in her hands, watching him read.

"Are you going to charge me, Blue, or what? I don't think you are allowed to just throw people in jail and leave them there to rot."

He turned toward her, leaned back in his chair, stretched his long legs out in front of him, and sighed.

"It's been five minutes. Nina, you are *high*. Way up in the clouds on your own magic-carpet ride. Your clothes reek of marijuana. I'm keeping you here for your own good. What are you doing? Shooting your neighbor with a paintball gun. Smoking ganja. I'm baffled and, to be honest, disappointed. I thought you were a woman with more sense."

"It's a contact high!" Nina protested. "I was trapped in a van all morning with Danish, Razor Hudson, and a couple of local businessmen—Warren and Fuzz? Perhaps you know them? With the windows up and the AC going full blast!"

Something occurred to her. "And may I refresh your memory and remind you that that's how we know Razor has a major-league grudge against Philip. A *motive*, you might say. I took a reefer for the team!" She giggled at her own joke.

Blue stared at her, tight-lipped, for a couple of seconds more, then turned back to his papers and started writing again. Nina rested her head against the bars of the cell and watched him. What could he possibly be writing in that big, thick file? She read the Pineapple Cay weekly newspaper. The crime reporter usually had so little to report that he had also been assigned the "Dear Auntie" advice column for the lovelorn. And he wrote the recipe section. Blue was left-handed. Very interesting.

He closed the file and pushed it to the edge of the table, then pulled another one closer. He opened it, scanned the first page, then quickly signed the bottom. He did the same with the next page and the next. Requisition orders or other administrative papers of some kind, Nina deduced. How very exciting. This was getting old. She shifted her attention from the files to the man himself.

He was tall and muscular, his hair shaved close to his skull. He had a coiled intensity as he sat folded in the battered metal chair. It was hot in the room with the small, high windows shut and the ceiling fans turning slowly overhead. Nina could feel a trickle of sweat running down her neck and her thin coral-pink T-shirt sticking to her back, but Blue's khaki uniform was still crisply pressed, his trouser legs tucked into polished black leather boots. He glanced up at the clock on the wall, his ice-blue eyes startling her as they always did. He lowered them again to his paperwork, and it was like a light had blazed briefly and been extinguished.

It occurred to Nina that every time she'd seen him since she arrived on Pineapple Cay, he'd been in uniform. Did he own a pair of jeans? He must do his gardening in civilian clothes. She tried to imagine him in a T-shirt, shorts, and flip-flops. Sneakers with grass stains on the toes. In a bathing suit, emerging from the surf like Daniel Craig in *Casino Royale* . . .

"Nina, really!" she whispered aloud to herself. Blue looked up at her for a moment, then back at his paperwork.

Nina scrutinized the chipped pink polish on her nails, thinking—not for the first time—that she really shouldn't bother with the nail polish. She couldn't keep up on it. She wanted to be a glamorous woman with polished nails, but maybe that just wasn't who she was. She looked over at Blue again. She wondered if he was the type of man who liked ladies who wore nail polish, or if he went for the no-frills, outdoorsy type, being a no-nonsense man himself. She wondered if he had a type at all. In her two-plus months on Pineapple Cay, she'd never seen him

134

with a woman or heard about any hot romance involving the chief of police, something she'd think the Pineapple Cay bush telegraph would be all over. Strange. He had the tall, dark, and handsome thing down cold, but if any of the numerous females drawn into his orbit had stuck, Nina hadn't heard about them. Maybe she'd just ask him.

"So, Blue, did anyone ever tell you that you have the most beautiful eyes in the world?" she said. His pen paused for a millisecond, then he resumed writing, without looking up.

"Of course they have," she said. "It must get *so* boring, people always telling you how handsome you are. How smart. How *scary*."

He glanced up at her briefly and sighed audibly, then looked back down at the file in front of him. She watched him in silence for a moment, then ran her eyes again over the stained concrete wall, looking for the gecko. It was now watching her with its beady little eyes from the crumbling concrete sill of the small barred window up high in the corner of the cell. Watching her judgmentally, it seemed to Nina. OK, so that was a bit tacky. Flirting with the chief of police while she was in a holding cell. Especially when kind, handsome, upstanding Ted was out somewhere on his boat with his fishing rod, hatless. She giggled. What was wrong with her? She *must* be high. She rolled her head back toward Blue, who was still reading his file.

"You know, Blue, this place could use a coat of paint. It's sort of depressing. I saw a documentary once on television where they found that painting prison walls pink made the inmates calmer. Ever heard that?" she asked. No answer. "And upstairs. That's a really nice, bright office. That dirty blue paint doesn't suit it. You should paint it a nice fresh green or yellow, and maybe hang a few pictures."

Still no answer. Blue turned a page in his document and kept reading.

"So, what were you like as a little boy, Blue? Little boy blue." She giggled. "Did you always want to be a police officer? What did you study at the University of the West Indies?"

Blue looked up at her and sighed. Again.

"Marine biology," he said shortly. "This is a police station, not a day care center. Although, lately, it is hard to tell the difference. I don't want people to get too comfortable here. Being locked up is meant to be a deterrent to antisocial behavior." He looked at her meaningfully.

"Oh, how very *interesting*," said Nina, turning her whole body toward him and resting her chin on her palm, and her elbow on her crossed knee.

A man in a faded red T-shirt, shorts, and flip-flops shuffled into the room carrying a battered black leather briefcase. He looked to be in his late fifties, with longish gray-blond hair swept back off his face, a lush handlebar mustache, and a small beer belly.

"OK, Roker. My client will not be making a statement, so unless you have the evidence to hold her, I suggest you let her go," he boomed, ambling toward Nina's cell.

"Who are you?" asked Nina.

"Frank Carson, attorney-at-law. Duty counsel."

"I didn't call a lawyer," said Nina.

"You think I don't know everything that goes on around here, sunshine? I know," he said. "Let me do the talking, okeydokey?" He turned to face Blue.

"What we have here, Deputy Superintendent, is a classic case of he said, she said. Now, I happened to have just run into the complainant on the sidewalk in front of his house, and he is baked like a cake. Can't clearly say whether the alleged assault came from the right or the left or from on high. Maybe it didn't happen at all. My client here"—he glanced at the paper in his hand—"Ms. Spark. She does not admit to any wrongdoing. Anything she may have said to you or to your officers to this point, I will argue, has been drawn from her under pressure. So, what have you got, Blue?"

Blue rubbed his temples and stood, his hands on his hips and his weight on one leg. He glared at the lawyer for a couple of seconds, then shifted his gaze to Nina.

"Nina, I know you shot a paintball at Les. You know you did it. *He* knows you did it," he said, gesturing at the lawyer. "It's assault. A very serious charge. Not funny. However, as it happens, Mr. Carson is right. We do not have the evidence to press charges. Please find another hobby."

"So . . . shall we?" The lawyer looked at Blue and gestured to the big lock on the cell door.

Danish strode into the room just then, brandishing an official piece of paper, which he slapped down on Blue's desk. "Sharon told me to come on down and give you this," he said to Blue confidentially, like it was the two of them against Nina and the other miscreants of the world.

"Well, well, Nina. You have been a naughty girl," Danish said, shaking his head. He had changed his clothes and was now wearing his official Pineapple Cay Postal Service uniform.

Nina glared at him.

"Fortunately, Deputy Superintendent Roker here has shown you some mercy and is releasing you into my custody with a warning. I came as soon as I got the phone call," Danish said. Nina turned her head to stare at Blue.

"Seriously?"

"What I *actually* said was that if Mr. Jensen went to the town office and paid your fine, he could come by and give you a lift home. I'll inform Mr. Jones that justice has been served to its meager limits so he'll get off my back, and we can all just get on with our day. I've got bigger issues to deal with, including fifty conference delegates and assorted members of hotel staff to interview this afternoon."

Blue pulled a bulky ring of keys from his belt and unlocked the door, giving Nina a stern look as she rose and floated out of the cell.

"Aw, so you were going to let me go, anyway. That's so sweet." Nina smiled up at him. He stood aside in stony silence to let her pass.

Danish sidled over to Blue and said to him in a low voice that Nina could still hear, "Just for future reference, Blue, mano a mano, you didn't do yourself any favors locking her up. It's a rare woman who can overlook being thrown in jail by a prospective suitor."

Blue glared at him with his arms crossed until Danish exited the room, Frank Carson trailing behind. Nina started to follow them with her head down, not wanting to see Blue's displeased expression, but the police chief caught her by the arm, and she looked up.

"Nina. Do me a favor and go directly home and sleep this off. Please leave Les alone. There's more to life. All right?"

She smiled up at him. "All right, Blue. Sorry. I'm going to be a model citizen from now on, you'll see. By the way, thanks for the gardening tip. My hibiscus is perking up."

Nina could feel Blue's steely glare on the back of her head as she hurried out of the room.

Mystery lawyer Frank Carson was waiting with Danish on the sidewalk in front of the police station when Nina emerged into the intense sunlight and heat of midafternoon. Frank dug around in his shorts pocket and brought out a bent business card, which he held out to her.

"If anything else comes up, here's my card," he said.

"Thanks," said Nina. She stuffed it in the back pocket off her cutoffs.

"Now, it's illegal for me to counsel you to destroy evidence," said Frank, "but it's possible that Roker will get a search warrant to look around your house for proof that you painted a pink flower on Les's backside. If the evidence is not there"—he gave Nina a meaningful look—"well, then, that's that. Now, if you'll excuse me, there's a cooler full of beer and a few bonefish down near Sandy Point calling my name."

"Wait," said Nina as Frank started to walk away. "How did you know I was here?"

Frank fixed her with a pair of sharp hazel eyes from under his bushy eyebrows.

"I've been keeping tabs on you since you arrived on-island, sunshine. You've got issues with the neighbors, a history of getting mixed up in police matters, and maybe a litigious streak. I'm thinking you could be my retirement plan."

Retirement from what, exactly? Nina wondered, looking at his flip-flops and T-shirt.

"I'm practically broke, but thanks for your help today," said Nina. Frank chuckled, raised his hand in parting, and shuffled off down the sidewalk toward a giant boat of a car. It was a vintage 1950s Oldsmobile convertible, baby blue. Nina had seen it around town a few times and had wondered whom it belonged to. Now she knew.

8

Nina was fast asleep in her bed when the phone rang. What time was it? Moonlight spilled in through the open window, and the curtains gently lifted and fell in the soft night air. She leaned over and felt on the floor for the old-fashioned rotary-dial telephone she'd inherited from Miss Rose.

"Hello?" she said, glancing at the clock on the bedside table. It was after midnight.

"Nina, it's me," said Pansy breathlessly. "There's been another incident at the inn. This time it looks like Sylvia Putzel-Cross was the target. Andrew just got home. He was in the bar with his golf buddies when Blue and a couple of his officers showed up looking very official."

"Oh! Was Sylvia hurt?" asked Nina, already wriggling out of her nightie and into the jeans and T-shirt she'd left on the floor by the bed last night.

"No, I don't think so. Andrew said he saw her in front of her bungalow talking to Blue."

"Well, thank goodness," said Nina, stepping into her flip-flops. She ran her fingers through her hair. "What is going on? Why would anyone want to hurt Sylvia? This conference is going downhill fast. I'd better get over there and see what I can do."

"Hold on. I'll give you a ride. Be there in ten minutes," Pansy said quickly, and hung up. Nina splashed some water on her face, brushed her teeth, grabbed her bag, and was pacing the sidewalk out front when Pansy rolled up in her turquoise golf cart a few minutes later.

The inn was quiet when they arrived. The dining room and bar had been shuttered for the night, and most of the guests had retired to their rooms. A few lingered on the veranda, chatting quietly in the dark. A light was burning in the lobby, and in its yellow glow through the open door, Nina could see Michel's silhouette as he stood talking to Josie, his hands in his pockets. Nina sighed. She couldn't imagine he'd be thrilled with this latest turn of events.

"Let's go to Sylvia's bungalow first," she said to Pansy. "I'll talk to Michel later."

They cut across the lawn in the moonlight to the bungalow where Sylvia and Philip were quartered. Several people were sitting and standing on the porch of Sylvia's side of the bungalow, which was closest to the inn. Philip's half was in darkness. Nina picked out the tall frame of Blue Roker, a uniformed officer at his side. Blue was talking to Sylvia, who was barefoot in a red-silk kimono tied at the waist. She was perched on the porch railing with a martini glass in her hand.

"I wonder what Danish is doing here," said Pansy. Nina followed Pansy's puzzled gaze. Danish was standing under the porch light talking in an animated fashion to Mike, the inn's security chief. He was bare-chested and barefoot. He appeared to be wearing only blue boxer shorts.

Philip was nowhere to be seen. Strange that he hadn't been drawn out by the commotion next door. They reached the foot of the stairs.

"Evening, Blue," sang out Pansy. The chief of police looked in their direction. Blue's eyes narrowed when he saw Nina and Pansy. He looked tired.

"We heard Sylvia was attacked and have come to see if she needs anything," said Pansy.

"Evening, ladies," he said, nodding to them politely. "I appreciate your concern, but this is a crime scene. We haven't finished our investigation."

"I'm absolutely fine, thank you, girls," said Sylvia. "Just a little excitement. It's all over now. We seem to have some sad prankster in our midst, but I have every confidence that the deputy superintendent here will soon root him out."

She took a sip of her martini and looked at Blue over the rim of her glass. He remained stone-faced.

Danish trotted down the steps and joined Nina and Pansy on the sand.

"Hey, ladies. This stuff is getting out of control. Some psycho climbed over the wall into Sylvia's outdoor garden shower. Scared the crap out of us," he said.

"Us?" said Nina. "How is it you happen to be here in the middle of the night wearing only your boxer shorts, Danish? Did you hear Sylvia scream from all the way over in the staff quarters?"

"Not exactly," said Danish, running his fingers through his thick mop of dark hair and glancing up at Sylvia. She blew him a kiss through bloodred lips and a hand tipped with long crimson fingernails. Danish grinned and lazily slid his gaze back to Nina's face, the smile still on his lips. She glared back at him, her hands on her hips.

"You're kidding me. You and Sylvia? What about Alice? Boy, you thought Uncle Blue had it in for you before. He must *really* be loving this," said Nina, slowly shaking her head.

"Actually, Alice and I broke up," said Danish, looking out at the sea, which was a black void in front of them.

"Oh, Danish. I'm sorry. You seemed like such a cute couple," said Pansy, reaching out to squeeze his arm.

He shrugged and looked away. "It was fun while it lasted, but you know. You only live once."

"Unbelievable," said Nina.

Danish turned to face them head-on.

"OK," he said. "So, there's a limit to how many documentaries about rusty cannonballs found in a field that a man can watch before he goes mental. Especially with old Aunt Agatha sitting over there in the corner in her vintage recliner talking to the television like the people on the screen can hear her. And the doilies. I've never seen so many doilies. On the coffee table where you're not supposed to set your glass of lemonade unless you put one of the Will-and-Kate commemorative coasters under it. But you'd better not get that wet, because then it would be *ruined*. Doilies on the arms of the sofa where I was allowed to sit next to Alice—but not too close, unless I wanted a hole drilled in my head by Aunt Agatha's evil glare. Doilies on the backs of the chairs. Like cobwebs, everywhere! I felt like I was trapped in a web!"

"Um, given that Agatha's brother is just a few feet away," Nina said, gesturing at Blue, "maybe you should keep your voice down." Alice was Blue's niece, and she lived with his extremely devout sister, Agatha.

"Excuse me if I'm confused," said Nina. "A couple of weeks ago, you were so lovesick for Alice that you almost got us both thrown in jail. And now it's over and you don't care?"

"People change," said Danish.

"In two weeks?" asked Nina, incredulous at this turn of events.

"I realized that I'm not ready to be tied down with a wife and mortgage and two kids," he said.

"Last I heard, Alice was *the one*. It can't all be Aunt Agatha's fault. You and Alice must have spent some time together without her aunt around."

"Yeah, sure," said Danish with another shrug. "We hung out at The Redoubt, went to the beach. And I must say for the record that Alice looked fine in a two-piece. But let me put it this way. There was way too much homework involved in getting to the main event, if you catch my drift."

"You mean that you're a shallow, pleasure-seeking cad," said Nina.

"Oh, come on. Like your interest in Ted is purely intellectual," he said with an eye roll. "I know it can't be his sparkling conversation that you doll up in a fancy dress and lipstick for. The guy never says more than ten words in a row."

Nina sniffed and looked away. "You might try that sometime," she said. "Sometimes not talking is just the right thing to do."

Pansy giggled.

"Just remember, Nina, if you point your finger at someone, there are four pointing back at you." Danish looked down at his hand for a moment, his eyebrows knitted, his fingers going through the motions of pointing and counting.

"Well, three, actually, because thumbs don't bend that way, and I'm not sure if technically they are called fingers, but *anyway*, there was a lot of talk about feelings that just seemed to go around in circles with no obvious point."

Alice again, apparently.

"She liked to talk about *the future*—her career, stuff she was going to do, what color she was going to paint her living room in the house that didn't even exist yet, *what she wanted to name her kids!*" exclaimed Danish. "Her other favorite topic was stuff that happened three hundred years ago. King this-or-that did this-or-that in 1672. I, on the other hand, am a man of action. I live in the here and now."

Given that Alice was the curator of the Pineapple Cay historical museum, Nina had wondered what the two possibly talked about.

Danish continued, "We discussed the situation in a very mature manner, and we decided to treasure the sweet memories but to move on down our separate paths in life."

"Really?" said Nina in a gentler tone, fixing him with what she meant to be an I'm-not-buying-it look.

Danish sighed heavily, and his shoulders drooped. "OK, so her hotshot ex-boyfriend, Dr. Brainy McBrainiac from the main island, chased her down over here a couple of days ago, and they've reunited. Apparently, they're *soulmates*. They're getting married. I was her rebound, if you can believe it," he said.

Pansy cooed sympathetically.

"Oh, Danish. I'm sorry," said Nina. She was pretty sure he was more upset than he was letting on.

"No biggie," he said, looking down at his feet then over at Sylvia, wrapped in her red-silk kimono. She blew him another bloodred kiss.

"So, Sylvia is *your* rebound," said Nina.

"Well, I guess *technically* that honor would go to Stephanie. She's a dog groomer from New Jersey. She left yesterday . . . Sylvia and I ran into each other in the hot tub today after my yoga sesh. She's dynamite. We're on the same wavelength."

"Really," said Nina.

"Nina, I know what you're thinking, and that's sexist. If I was a hot young chick who enjoyed fine wine and talking about real things, and Sylvia was a mature gentleman with a zest for life, no one would have anything to say," said Danish.

"OK, OK. I don't want to know anymore," said Nina, shaking her head to get rid of the image that was just beginning to form. "Just give us the facts about the break-in."

"Listen to you, Nina Spark, PI! 'Just give me the facts. I'm on the case.'" He imitated her in a gruff, hard-boiled Hollywood-detective voice.

"OK. We were relaxing in the bedroom area. Sylvia asked me to get her a glass of wine, so I went out to the veranda to get the bottle we'd left there. I was trying to find it in the dark when I heard her shouting. 'Hey! What're you doing! Get back here!' Like that. I hotfooted it back into the bungalow, and she was in the outdoor shower whacking the back fence with a broom."

"A broom?" asked Pansy.

"Yeah. The chambermaid must have left it," said Danish. "Anyway, I was, like, 'Hey, Sylvia, what're you doing?' And she said somebody had come into the bedroom. She'd drifted off, and when she opened her eyes, someone was standing next to the bed. She yelled, and he took off through the shower. She took off after him and was trying to whack him down with the broom, but he escaped over the fence. I ran around the side of the bungalow, but I didn't see anything. Then I called Mike, who called Roker. And that's it. Now you're up to speed."

"So, did Sylvia recognize the intruder?" asked Pansy.

"No, she said she didn't get a good look at him. It was dark, and he was wearing a hoodie and something over his face, like a bandana," said Danish. "She did say that he was on the short side. Not as short as her, but not tall like your friend Victor."

"Victor is just about the last person who would climb over a garden wall to murder someone," said Nina. "It really would not be his style. Strychnine served to the victim in a crystal tumbler of aged scotch whiskey would be more his speed."

Razor is on the short side. So is Philip, she thought. *Bridget is almost as tall as Victor.*

"I'd like to have a look in the bungalow and at the garden wall," said Nina. "I just can't make sense of any of this."

"First Philip, and now Sylvia. Maybe it's someone who doesn't like professors for some reason," said Pansy. "Maybe it's someone who has a grudge against Philip and Sylvia, in particular. Someone they knew while they were married."

There was movement on the veranda. Blue Roker went into the bungalow. The officer moved into position on the top step, standing guard over access to the crime scene. Sylvia squeezed past him and sashayed down onto the sand to where Nina, Danish, and Pansy stood.

"Well, kids. This is one for the books," Sylvia said.

"Are you all right, Sylvia? Danish was just telling us what happened," said Nina.

"Absolutely fine. The villain escaped over the back wall, but not before I got a piece of him." She smiled wickedly, slipped her hand in the pocket of her robe, and pulled out a ragged piece of dark-blue jersey cloth.

"A piece of his hoodie," she said triumphantly.

"You should give that to Blue so he can get it tested for DNA or something," said Pansy.

"Oh, I will. I just wanted to show you gals first. I had him by the foot as he was trying to get over the wall. He kicked me off, but not before snagging his sweatshirt on the broken glass on the top of the wall. I bet he cut himself. We had quite a tussle. I told the deputy superintendent that much, and he's got someone looking for blood on the wall as we speak."

"You're surprisingly calm, considering all this, Sylvia," said Nina.

"I assure you, I've had worse scares than this in my lifetime, Nina, darling. I once went to a dinner party at the embassy in London and found I was to be seated with a lawyer on my left, another on my right, and a third across the table from me. It still frightens me to think of the evening I might have had to endure if I hadn't had the presence of mind to switch the place cards and put myself next to the fellow who walked across Ireland with a refrigerator on his back.

As it turned out, I had a fantastic time that evening." She threw back her head and laughed.

Nina, Pansy, and Danish looked at one another.

Is it normal to be so unaffected by an attempt on your life? Nina wondered.

"Well, I think I've had enough fun and games for one day. I'm going to call it a night," Sylvia finally said. "The dashing deputy superintendent promises he'll be finished here shortly, and then I'll toddle off to bed. Thanks for checking in on me, girls. You're very sweet. Good night, Danish. I'll see you later, I'm sure." She gave him a girlish grin.

"Sylvia. What on earth is going on?" It was an irate Philip, strutting up the beach from the direction of the inn.

"Such a shame, Philip. You missed all the excitement. Well, I must toddle. Nighty night, everyone," said Sylvia, turning and jogging back up the stairs and into the bungalow before Philip could say anything else.

Nina, Pansy, and Danish exchanged glances again. Where was Philip coming from? Did he have an alibi, or was he just circling back after going over Sylvia's garden wall? Nina looked to see if he was bleeding anywhere. Philip looked at Nina expectantly, his chin jutting upward, and she gave him a bare-bones account of the event.

"I don't know what to say," he huffed. "Crime appears to be rampant on this island. This inn has appalling security. The police are incompetent. No one has been brought to account for what happened to me two days ago. And now this. I am extremely disappointed, Nina."

That made two people who had expressed their disappointment in her that day, Nina noted.

"Nothing like this has ever happened in all the twenty-five years this conference has been held," stormed Philip. "It will be a black mark on my record, and for that I hold you personally responsible."

He jabbed the air with a finger pointed at Nina's face. Her hands went to her hips.

"Hey, man," said Danish. "Chillax. I'd like to point out that nothing like this ever happened here on this island or at this hotel before you rolled into town. Chicken and egg. Kettle and black. Or pot, kettle, and black. You know what I mean."

Philip huffed angrily and glared at Danish. He opened his mouth to reply, but Nina jumped in.

"I'm sorry, Philip. I'm sure the police are working as hard as they can to find out who attacked you," she said.

"*Anyway*, how was your evening, Philip?" asked Pansy, gracing him with one of her brilliant smiles. "Were you out on the sunset dinner cruise with some of the others? I hear it's fabulous."

Philip perked up. Good old Pansy.

"Actually, I found a charming local rum shop," Philip said. "An authentic island watering hole called The Pirate's Wake. I spent the evening with some genuine Pineapple Cay residents observing island culture. Quite invigorating. Razor Hudson thinks he's got a monopoly on participant observation research methods. I was doing it before he was born. I sat and had a few bottles of beer with some locals, and as a result, I think I've uncovered a novel island custom that I've never seen written up in the literature. It is the public display of undergarments in social clubs. I don't know what it means yet, but I'm going to research it further and write an article. I'm aiming for the *Annals of Tourism Research*. That's a top-ranked journal."

Nina, Danish, and Pansy exchanged another silent look. The Pirate's Wake was a sleazy bar a few miles south of town frequented primarily by afternoon drinkers and college spring breakers looking for a walk on the wild side. The walls and ceiling were adorned with hundreds of pairs of women's underwear and brassieres.

"I'll tell you what it means," said Danish. "People blow in here on vacation for a few days, get drunk with people they'll never see again, and either convince themselves or their girlfriends that nailing their leopard-print undies to the wall means they are *not boring*, unlike the schmucks they left behind in cubicle land."

"Well, young man, I think there may be a bit more to it than that, as will be revealed by a rigorous ethnographic study," said Philip, chuckling condescendingly.

"Doubt it," said Danish.

"It's almost two o'clock in the morning," said Nina. "Let's go, Pansy. I've got to be back here in a few hours. Philip, I've arranged for you to go bonefishing tomorrow morning, as you requested. We'll meet by the fountain right after the breakfast keynote, all right? We'll be back in time for the afternoon session on the impact of hotel-room decor on vacation spending."

"Fine," said Philip.

Really, he was infuriating. Couldn't he just say thank you? Nina could see why someone would want to off him. But Sylvia? Sylvia seemed to get along with everyone and stayed clear of the petty turf wars that were Philip's favorite pastime. Nina watched him march up the steps into his half of the bungalow and shut the door firmly.

"Night, Danish," said Nina. His love life was his business. She had nothing more to say on the subject.

She and Pansy strolled back to the parking lot.

"I wonder what Blue is making of all this," said Pansy.

"Mmm," said Nina. "It'll be days before he gets the results of any lab tests on blood, if they find any. Or the results from tests to know for sure if Philip ate shellfish, I suppose. He looked tired."

"Yes, I noticed," said Pansy. They were quiet for a moment.

"So, is Ted taking Philip out fishing tomorrow?" Pansy asked.

Nina nodded.

"Sorry about the other night," said Pansy.

"That was very nice of you all," said Nina. They walked on in silence a few steps.

"So, you and Ted seem to be getting along pretty well," said Pansy with a giggle.

"Yes, I guess so," said Nina. "He's a nice guy."

"*Mmm,*" said Pansy.

~

Ted's Jeep circled the splashing dolphins fountain in front of the inn at precisely nine o'clock the next morning, coming to a stop beside Nina, Philip, and Sylvia. He had a seventeen-foot Boston Whaler with a folded Bimini top trailered to his Jeep. Sylvia had gotten wind of the planned fishing trip and was enthusiastic about giving it a try.

"Morning, all," Ted said as he came around the front of his Jeep. "Hope you're looking forward to a day of fishing. The boys have been radioing in to say they are biting hard. Should be good."

"Yes, about that, Ted," said Philip confidentially. "I'm wondering if it might be possible to be in a separate boat from Sylvia. You see, she is my bitter ex-wife. One of them, anyway, and I find it rather puts a damper on things to have her within eyesight. In fact, I'm not entirely sure she isn't trying to kill me."

"Philip," said Sylvia in a bored monotone, looking at her nails. "If it sets your mind at ease, while you were getting your just deserts—or almost getting them, in any case—I was drinking champagne aboard a sailboat captained by a dashing gentleman from South Carolina, who reminded me, yet again, why my life is so much better now that you are just a risible footnote to it. If we're keeping score, I might also add that some unknown person tried to smother me in my sleep last night. I know it wasn't you, because you don't have the . . . *nerve* for it, shall we say. Nevertheless, I think we're neck and neck in the attempted-murder category."

Philip crossed his arms and turned his back on Sylvia.

"Sorry, Phil," said Ted. "It's two rods to a boat, and Nina has agreed to crew for me today"—he smiled at her—"so that makes the four of us. Is that going to be a problem?"

"Not in the least," said Sylvia, flashing a smile at Ted. "Philip," she said in a colder tone, "grow up. You can rest assured, I will not be observing your technique on the water. I'm sure there will be more interesting things to occupy one's attention out there. Get over yourself, please." She rolled her eyes at Nina.

"Oh," said Philip to Ted, "are you our guide? I thought we were going to have a local guide. I'm not a tourist, you see." He laughed his fake self-deprecating laugh. "I have a professional interest in authentic island culture and lore. I'm sure Nina's told you about my work."

Nina winced, embarrassed. She knew Ted had given up a rare morning off to take them out as a special favor to her.

"Well, all the guys are out on the water today. We've got a full house at the lodge, so I guess you are stuck with me," said Ted as he put their bags into the back of the Jeep. "Hop in."

"Philip," said Nina, "Ted has fished his entire life. People travel thousands of miles to come here and fish with him. We're extremely lucky that he's taking us out. He knows these islands inside and out."

"Yes, Philip," said Sylvia. "Really. Can you not just let things unfold as they will, for a change, instead of trying to orchestrate everything?" She turned to Ted and smiled. "Ready when you are, Captain."

Philip huffed a little and jutted his chin skyward but didn't say anything else.

They drove to the same boat ramp Ted and Nina had used the day he had taken her out fishing. It seemed like ages ago, but it was really only a month prior. She and Sylvia watched as Ted expertly backed the Jeep down the boat ramp and unhooked the boat from the trailer. Ted waded into the water, pulling the boat out until it floated free. Philip splashed in after him, grasping the gunwale on the opposite side in an ineffectual effort to help.

After Ted parked the Jeep in the shade, they waded out to the boat, and he helped them in. He stood with one hand on the wheel and the other on the ignition and looked around to make sure they were all seated before he started the engine and moved slowly away from the dock and through the mangroves.

It was cool and shady in the channel, but as the mangroves thinned, a vista of brilliant turquoise water and creamy-white sandbars appeared in front of them. Ted opened up the throttle and they flew along the shoreline, the wind whipping their hair. Nina realized that once again she'd forgotten to bring Ted's hat. She looked over at him. He didn't look sunburned yet.

The water grew shallow beneath the boat, and Ted slowed and then stopped. He gently dropped the anchor over the side.

"This is a promising spot. Let's give it a try," he said. He took two rods from the racks running along the gunwale and handed one to Philip and one to Sylvia. He opened a bench and took out his tackle box.

"Let's go with a Crazy Charlie," he said, tying the fly to Sylvia's line. "Phil, can I give you a hand with that?"

"I think I can take it from here," said Philip, fumbling with the fly. "I'm not one of those citified sissies who needs the guide to tie the fly on and cast for me. This place looks like a children's theme park compared to some of the wild water I fished in Montana last summer."

"Sure," said Ted. "'Though most people find it helpful if we give them a bit of an introduction to saltwater fly-fishing the first day out. It's a whole different kettle of fish from the freshwater angling you might have done up north."

"Kettle of fish. That's funny," said Nina, trying to spark a festive mood onboard.

"I'm from Michigan. Fly-fishing is in my blood. Hardwired," said Philip. He managed to tie on the fly; then, grasping the rod in his right hand, he maneuvered himself to the bow of the boat. He climbed up onto the deck and looked around, holding the rod at the ready.

"Hold on a moment, Sylvia, then we'll get you going. Let's just let Phil get a few casts in first," said Ted.

"Yes, please do," said Sylvia. "I'm perfectly content to wait my turn."

"OK, then, Phil. Let's see what's out there today," said Ted. He stood still with his hands on his hips, scanning the flats through the polarized lenses of his shades. Several quiet moments passed.

"There. Twelve o'clock. Thirty feet," said Ted quietly. "They're tailing near that mangrove. Cast your line."

"Got it," said Philip, raising his arm and cracking the long rod like a bullwhip above his head three times in rapid succession before letting the fly drop to the water's surface. The line whipped back and forth over their heads, the barbed fly pinging off the metal frame of the Bimini top and the gunwales of the boat. Nina, Sylvia, and Ted flattened themselves against the deck until the barrage ended. When they raised their heads, Philip was standing serenely on the prow of the boat, his chin up, looking rather pleased with himself.

"There. What did I tell you? First cast. On the money." He stood motionless, watching the surface of the water expectantly, waiting for the fish to bite while the line slowly sank in the water. Even Nina, who'd only been fishing once in her life, knew that wasn't how you did it.

"Good God, Philip!" said Sylvia. "You almost harpooned us!"

"Phil, I'd ask you to be careful when you false-cast," said Ted calmly.

"What do you mean, 'false-cast'? That was bang-on."

Ted paused for a second, looking at him.

"What I mean is, throw your line from shoulder height, like this," he said, taking a rod from the rack and deftly demonstrating a cast. The line zipped off the reel.

"You don't want the line circling back behind you, maybe hooking someone," Ted said. Out of habit, he pulled the line in slowly, foot by foot, stripping it in with his hand and reeling up the slack, playing the fly like a shrimp—the bonefish's preferred delicacy. Philip watched Ted's hands surreptitiously for a moment, then imitated his movements.

"Why don't you show me how to do it," said Sylvia to Ted. "You'll find I am a much more pliable pupil."

"Of course," said Ted. He showed Sylvia how to cast and threw the line out for her several times until she hooked a fish.

"I've got one!" she squealed.

"OK now, Sylvia. Take it easy. Let it run. Good. Now bring in the line like this. Good. Keep the tip of your rod up. Good. You're doing great," murmured Ted. The long, slender silverfish came to the surface near the boat. Ted slipped over the side of the boat into the thigh-deep water and cradled it gently in his hands for her to see.

"Good job, Sylvia," he said with a grin. "It's a beaut."

"It's gorgeous! Here, Nina, will you take a photo of me, my fish, and the handsome fishing guide? I want to send it to all my friends!" said Sylvia, pulling her cell phone out of one of the many pockets in her new fishing vest and handing it to Nina. She smiled for the camera.

"Fabulous!" she said.

Ted gently removed the hook from the fish's mouth and released it into the crystal-clear water. It was gone in a fraction of a second. Philip stood silently on the deck at the bow of the boat. Nina could feel his discontent, which was visible in his tightly pursed lips.

"Well, thank you so much, Ted," said Sylvia. "Now I can say I've bonefished—is that really a verb?—with the best in the business on a spectacular day in the islands. Fantastic. But it's rather a lot of work, so I think I'll just relax and enjoy the scenery from here on in." She fished two bottles of orange juice out of the cooler, offered one to Nina, and with a contented sigh, settled down beside her on the bench in the shade of the Bimini top.

Philip continued to cast authoritatively but fruitlessly up at the front of the boat. His movements telegraphed his growing frustration.

"Have a seat," said Ted. "We'll try another spot."

He started the engine and the boat gathered speed, skimming over the surface of the turquoise water and leaving a wake of pure-white froth.

The speed of the boat and the wind in her face were exhilarating, and Nina smiled, despite Philip.

Ted steered the boat in a wide arc around a sandy point of land and into a shallow circular cove rimmed with white sand and low cabbage palms. The sunlight reflected off the tops of the palms' shiny emerald-green fronds. He cut the engine.

"Throw out the anchor, please, Nina?" he said.

She scrambled to her feet and chucked the anchor overboard. She looked over the side. The water was only about two feet deep over a sandy bottom. A stubble of sparse turtle grass covered the bottom. Among the gently waving sea blades, Nina could see little circles in the sand. A sign that bonefish had been feeding here.

From its cradle along the gunwale, Ted picked up a long aluminum pole and kicked off his boots. He sprang up on the raised deck of the boat and scanned the surface of the water in silence, holding the pole motionless in his hands for several long moments, the sunlight reflecting off the gold rims of his aviator shades. Then he stuck the end of the pole in the sand and leaned on it, pushing the boat around until they were facing the direction they had come from. Nina could see the muscles in his forearms and calves straining beneath his deeply tanned skin.

"OK, Phil. They're over there. Nine o'clock. Forty feet," he said, gesturing with his chin. "Cast off the port side."

Philip didn't move.

"Cast off the port side. The left-hand side of the boat. At nine o'clock."

Philip made several frantic casts, each one landing only a short distance from the boat.

"Hold on," said Ted. "I'll get us a little closer." He motioned to Nina to haul up the anchor, then poled the boat forward, toward the school of fish he'd spotted. He stopped, and Nina dropped the anchor gently over the side. Ted climbed softly down from the raised platform and gestured for Philip to come stand beside him.

"OK now. They are really close. Short-cast them," he said in a hushed voice. Nina didn't dare move.

Philip wound up and threw his line out hard. It squealed off the reel and landed a good distance out. He pulled it in foot by foot as he had seen Ted do. The soggy bit of pink fluff on the end of his line came out of the water without a fish on the end of it, again. He turned to Ted.

"This water is fished too hard. There are no fish left," he said petulantly.

"You lined the fish," said Ted. "If you throw the line over the fish, it spooks them. That's why I told you to short-cast."

"You brought us too close. You spooked them. I can't make a decent cast when we are sitting right on top of them like that," said Philip testily.

"Well, you can't long-cast either, it seems," Ted replied calmly. "Don't worry. It takes a bit of time to get the hang of it. Just enjoy the ride, and you'll get there eventually."

He poled them around again, scanning the horizon. He maneuvered the boat into position, straining against the pole.

"All right. Off the starboard side. The right side. Three o'clock. About a hundred feet out."

Philip scrambled up to the bow. He threw his line out. The breeze caught it and blew the fly back toward him. It caught on his multi-pocketed fishing vest. Ted stepped forward to help Philip untangle his line and detach the hook.

"OK, Phil. May I give you a little tip? You're right-handed, correct?" Ted asked. Philip nodded. "So, I have positioned the boat so that you can cast directly out from the starboard side, not across your body, like you have just done. Try it. You'll find it much easier."

"Ted, I took an advanced fly-fishing workshop in Pennsylvania a few years ago with Hook Dobson, the fly-fishing legend. Have you heard of him?"

"Sure," said Ted.

"Yes, well. Hook Dobson told us to do it this way," said Philip.

"Is that so?" said Ted. "When he was down here a couple of months ago, he spent a whole night on my front porch arguing the exact opposite, and when I saw him at the sportsman's show in Maryland last week, he was all excited about some new technique he'd picked up in Patagonia. But that's Hook for you, eh? A contrarian by nature and inclination. He'd argue the moon was made of Swiss cheese until the sun came up, just for the exercise. Don't get discouraged, Phil. Like I said, saltwater fly-fishing is another game altogether. Keep at it. It rewards the dedicated."

They slogged away in the sunshine for another half hour or so, then Ted pointed the boat toward home and they flew back to the dock. Philip didn't say anything on the ride home, and after saying a curt "Thank you" to Ted in front of the inn, he strode away with his head down.

"I'm afraid you had to work awfully hard this morning, Ted," said Sylvia. "But thank you so much. I enjoyed the lesson immensely."

She waved goodbye and went up the front steps of the inn and into the bar. Nina watched her go, then turned to Ted.

"I'm so sorry, Ted," said Nina. "I should've known it would be like that."

He chuckled.

"Don't worry about it. He's just a garden-variety know-it-all. We deal with several of those each season. Comes with the territory." He glanced at his watch. "I've got to get back to the lodge."

He leaned down and kissed her lightly on the mouth. His lips were silky soft. "I'll see you soon," he said, and walked around the front of his Jeep to climb in the driver's seat. She waved goodbye as he steered the boat trailer around the fountain and down the long driveway to the main road.

When? she wondered, and sighed.

She went slowly up the front steps of the inn to sit through a presentation entitled "Who Needs Paris? Hallucinogenic Holidays and Zero-Carbon Mind Trips" to be given by a professor from Danish's alma mater, the Boulder College of the Healing Arts. She ran into Bridget in the lobby, and a thought occurred to her.

"Bridget, did you see anything from the rooftop of your villa last night? Any activity around Sylvia's bungalow?" she asked.

"No, the police asked me that, too, but I went out to supper at The Redoubt with some of my housemates. I ran into Les there and, well, you know. . ." She giggled. "I didn't get back here until this morning. Don't tell my grandmother."

That's an alibi for Bridget for last night, and a dead end on Sylvia's attacker, thought Nina as they went into the conference presentation together. Perhaps not surprisingly, Danish was sitting in the front row. He sidled up to Nina at the refreshment table during the coffee break.

"Howdy, Nina. Professor Watson's great, eh? I took Intro to Medicinal Plants from him back in the day. Got a B⁺. My brownies didn't rise. I forgot to add the baking powder."

"Uh-huh," said Nina.

Bridget hurried over breathlessly with one of her housemates in tow.

"Tell them what you told me, Dan," she urged her friend.

"OK. Like I told the police, last night Janet and I were sitting on the rooftop terrace just talking, about eleven thirty, maybe. We were sitting at the table on the side nearest the inn. I heard Sylvia shouting, so I got up to look. I saw someone climb over the back wall of her bungalow and take off running across the lawn to the driveway. I ran downstairs to try to see where the burglar went, but by the time I reached the driveway, I'd lost sight. I went to the front desk and told the guy there what I saw, and he called the police right away."

"Now we're getting somewhere!" said Danish, rubbing his hands together. "Did you get a look at the person?" he asked urgently.

"No," said Dan. "It was dark under the trees. I just saw a silhouette."

"Short hair, long hair? Male, female? Help us out here, Dan," said Danish.

Dan thought for a moment.

"It was a woman," he said.

"How do you know?" asked Nina.

"She ran like a girl," he replied. Dan lifted his arms and banged them against his sides.

Nina rolled her eyes but held her tongue. No use antagonizing a possibly useful witness.

"That could be any of them. Philip, Razor, Victor. Maybe not Victor. He's too tall," Danish said. "The only one it *couldn't* be is Bridget, because she was at The Redoubt when it happened. I made a call—your alibi checks out." He looked at Bridget.

"My *alibi*? Why would I want to kill Sylvia?" Bridget asked. She sounded genuinely curious. Danish ignored her question.

"Victor was also at The Redoubt last night, and on the night Philip was attacked. It took a while, but I got Veronica to confirm that much," said Danish. "If Philip's claim that he was hanging out at The Pirate's Wake all night checks out, the only suspect who doesn't have an alibi for either night is Razor. He says he was in his room, alone, at the time of both attacks."

They all looked down to the far end of the long table, where Razor was going through the fruit basket. He selected a banana and wandered back to his seat. Bridget gasped and covered her mouth with her hand.

"OK, everyone! We're going to get started again. Please find your seats!" said the nice Canadian culinary-tourism expert.

9

The next morning, Nina had a craving to see the sun rise, so she pulled on a sweater and took her coffee out on the veranda before even the birds were awake. The island's beauty was more apparent in the quiet of the morning. A gentle breeze rustled the fronds of the coconut trees, and the waves gently lapped against the beach. Les's bungalow was dark. *Maybe I have Bridget to thank for that,* Nina thought. She wandered down to the shore in the half-light before dawn with her coffee cup in her hand and strolled along in the surf toward the fishing lodge, her eyes searching the sand for pretty shells washed in on the tide. She picked up two perfect, pure-white scallop shells and a glossy white-and-yellow butterfly shell, as delicate as a piece of fine china.

In the shallows, several large orange sea stars were scattered across the sandy bottom. Nina reached down and touched the rough, textured back of one, then stood in the water up to her knees and watched the sky turn a delicate shade of pink. The pink changed to china blue, which became more and more saturated until the sky was an intense cobalt and lit with brilliant sunshine.

Pineapple Cay started to come alive for the day. Nina saw a couple of cars passing on the road behind her house, and somewhere down the beach toward town, someone started hammering and sawing wood. As she walked back toward home, Nina looked beyond the grove of palm trees beside her cottage and noticed a couple of joggers go by on the sidewalk. She recognized Veronica's upright posture, and—*Victor?* She'd never have guessed he was a runner, but that was certainly his tall, thin frame trotting along beside Veronica. He was heading back into town from the direction of The Enclave.

Well, good for him, thought Nina. As she rinsed her feet in the basin of water on the veranda steps, Nina decided she'd give the morning session of the Delancy Symposium a pass. She'd done her part in organizing the venue and the on-site activities, and Bridget was handling the rest of it. She needed a break from Philip and PowerPoint presentations.

It occurred to Nina that she hadn't really done much exploring of Pineapple Cay on her own since she'd arrived. She'd always had Ted or Pansy or Danish in tow. She got out the guidebook she'd bought at the gift shop in town and decided to hike up the highest peak on the island, where there were some ruins of an old loyalist plantation house. But first she'd stroll into the village center, pick up a few postcards to send home, and have breakfast at the sidewalk tables in front of the bakery. She grabbed her bag and headed down the sidewalk toward town.

A short while later, Nina was sitting at a café table in front of the bakery with a cup of coffee and a warm banana muffin, a copy of the Pineapple Cay weekly newspaper, and a view of the sea. The smell of baking pineapple turnovers wafted out the screen door of the shop. A slow but steady stream of shoppers strolled up and down the main drag of Coconut Cove, bringing life into the little town. Nina was reading an article on preparations for the upcoming homecoming parade when the noise of a loud V-8 engine made her look up. A shiny red truck zoomed past.

That guy again, she thought, wondering again what his story was. She drained her coffee cup, gathered her things, and wandered down to Joe's Boat and Golf Cart Rentals. The trail to the top of Lime Tree Hill was a couple of miles south of the village, so she thought it'd be best to cruise down there in a golf cart. She picked out a nice banana-yellow cart and hit the road. There were no other vehicles in the small parking area at the side of the road that marked the trailhead. A small wooden sign with LIME TREE HILL and an arrow carved into it had been pounded into the ground at knee level; the arrow pointed up a sandy path into the bush. Nina shouldered her backpack containing a bottle of water, sunscreen, and her guidebook and headed up the path through a grove of stalky palmetto palms and shiny-leafed cocoplum bushes.

The heat was intense, and as the path started to climb, the footing changed from sand to uneven coral bedrock. Nina was glad she'd worn her sun hat—a purchase from the straw market—and her hiking boots. She stopped to apply a fresh layer of sunscreen to her nose and shoulders. Cicadas sang loudly in the bush. The path ran alongside the remnants of a thick wall, about three feet high and at least two feet thick, made of coral stone. According to her guidebook, it had been built by loyalist plantation owners who'd fled the American Revolution to make a new life on Pineapple Cay more than two hundred years before. They'd built the wall to pen in the sheep and cows they'd brought with them. The animals didn't thrive in the tropical island climate, and those few settlers who hung on eventually switched to growing pineapples, oranges, and mangoes. They sent tons of exotic fruit to England, first as ballast on the ships that brought stores to the islands, and then, when the aristocracy developed a taste for it, as coveted delicacies for the banquet table. But farming was hard on this coral island, and many settlers gave up after a few years. The stone shell of the manor house, visible through a stand of hardwood trees at the base of Lime Tree Hill, as well as the thick stone wall that surrounded it, was now grown over by scrubby hardwoods and vines.

The hike to the peak of Lime Tree Hill took Nina less than an hour. Pineapple Cay had a few low, rolling hills, but no mountains. Standing on the top of Lime Tree Hill at just 250 feet above sea level (according to her guidebook), Nina had a panoramic view down the length of Pineapple Cay in both directions. She took a drink from her water bottle and looked north. Just south of town she could see the roof of the Plantation Inn, the beach in front of it dotted with sunbathers. Bubba and Nancy's big white yacht was anchored out in the cove, and several dozen sailboats with tall masts were tied up at the marina. And there was Coconut Cove, with its neat grid of streets lined with prettily painted cottages, built alongside the cove. The peppermint-pink government building stood next to the blue police station on the waterfront, and the lemon-yellow primary school was next to the gleaming white church on the edge of the village. North of the village, past her own little yellow cottage, she could make out some of the large, gated villas in The Enclave. She could see the dark, heaving ocean and the white froth of the waves crashing against the rocky cliffs on the Atlantic side, while a few hundred yards away on the Caribbean side of the island, the water was calm, and a cheerful shade of turquoise.

Nina swiveled her head to look south down the island. There were just a few small, scattered fishing settlements south of Coconut Cove. A creek wound its way to the sea through a vast tract of bush and mangrove. Farther south, Nina could see a patchwork of white-rimmed salt ponds. Near the ponds were several huge, gleaming white hills. At first, her northerner brain registered them as piles of snow, but of course they were giant heaps of sea salt. Ted had told her there was a saltworks on the island. Trailing off the end of Pineapple Cay was the long chain of small, mainly uninhabited islands that were preserved as Diamond Cays National Park. It was serenely beautiful. Nina smiled and took a deep breath of sweet sea air.

As she exhaled slowly, she looked directly in front of her. Lime Tree Hill overlooked a long swath of undeveloped white-sand beach. From what she had learned about island history and the ins and outs of island real estate from Pansy, Nina figured that it was probably generational land—land collectively owned by the inhabitants of the island who had descended from the slaves of the original plantation owners. Generational land could not be easily sold. Otherwise, the beach would have been lined with vacation homes by now.

There was a boat a short distance offshore. Not the typical pleasure craft loaded with holidaymakers in bathing suits doing some snorkeling. It was an industrial vessel. A barge or a dredger. Nina could hear the drone of a large diesel engine from where she stood at the top of the hill. There were two men in blue jeans, work gloves, and ball caps moving back and forth on the deck. They seemed to be positioning some piece of heavy equipment at the stern of the boat. And there was the shiny red truck parked on the beach! A man wearing a ball cap and sunglasses leaned against the front grill of the truck with his arms crossed, watching the men at work on the barge in front of him.

Nina guessed they were building something in the water. Maybe a wharf. Nina didn't know anything about construction. Maybe it was a commercial fishing boat, but it seemed too close to shore. There was no one else on the beach and no houses visible in either direction. Just several acres of bush and the potholed dirt road Red Truck Man must have driven in on.

Something moved in the bushes directly below Nina, about a hundred feet down the hill. It was Les. Nina recognized his scrawny backside and pudding-bowl haircut. He was crouched behind a clump of palmetto palms. As she watched him, he scurried a short distance away to take cover behind a boulder. He raised a camera to his eye and took several pictures of the boat and the guy leaning against his truck on the beach.

Suddenly, Nina felt exposed. If Les was hiding from those guys, maybe she should be, too. As quietly as she could, she moved back from the edge so Les wouldn't see her if he looked up, and she crouched behind her own clump of palmetto palms. Almost as if Red Truck Man had sensed he was being watched, he turned his head and looked up at the summit of Lime Tree Hill, scanning the peak with his sunglass-shaded eyes. Nina stayed very still, suddenly glad that she'd worn her olive-green T-shirt this afternoon. It seemed like he was staring right at her for a long moment, but then he looked away, back out to the barge offshore. He walked to the edge of the water and yelled something to the men onboard. Nina couldn't hear it. She didn't know what they were doing, or why it was so interesting to Les that he was taking pictures of it, but she had a strong sense they shouldn't know she was there. When she was sure Red Truck Man and the guys on the boat were fully occupied again with whatever it was they were doing, she crept back away from the summit and walked quickly back down the path to her rented golf cart, glancing frequently over her shoulder to see if Les or Red Truck Man was following her. There was no sign of either.

So much for a relaxing afternoon hike, she thought as she motored back to the village. As she drove past the school yard full of children running and laughing in their neat navy-blue-and-white uniforms, she decided it must just be her overactive imagination that had made her think anything sinister was going on. The attacks at the inn had her seeing suspicious behavior everywhere. But it *was* strange that Les just happened to be at the inn the night Philip was attacked, and now here he was skulking around in the dunes. It seemed like all this started when he arrived back on the island. Pansy said he was from Connecticut. Philip went to Yale, which is in Connecticut. Maybe they'd met there somehow, sometime. Bridget said she'd run into Les at The Redoubt the night Sylvia was attacked. Being spotted in a crowded bar on the night in question would provide a good alibi, and also enough cover to slip out for a few minutes and commit a crime. But how did Red Truck Man fit in?

Not everyone's a criminal, Nina, she reminded herself. *Some are just jerks.*

She decided to stop in at The Redoubt to say hi to Veronica and maybe have a quiet, cool drink on the back deck before heading home. She returned the golf cart, then headed down the sidewalk to The

Redoubt. It was quiet. Just a few scattered tables of vacationers. Bob Dylan was warbling away on the jukebox. Veronica stood behind the bar, drying glasses with a white towel. Frank Carson sat at the bar talking to her. Nina made her way over.

"Come on, what do you say, Veronica?" Frank was saying. "You know we were made for each other. We're both strong, independent thinkers with a low tolerance for bull crap. How about a moonlight sail on my boat? You can sit back and relax while I cook up my famous seafood paella for you. We'll drink champagne, dance under the stars. I might surprise you."

Veronica smiled and shook her head slowly, still drying glasses.

"Frank, as I've told you at least a hundred times, thanks for the invitation, but no. My bull-crap detector starts beeping every time you walk in here. You and I both like things just the way they are, so don't pretend you don't."

Veronica smiled at Nina as she slid onto a stool beside Frank. "Hi, Nina, how is it? What can I get you?"

"Hi, Veronica," Nina said. "How are things? I'll have an iced tea, thanks."

Veronica moved down the bar to pour her iced tea and serve a couple of customers who had just sat down.

"Hi, Frank," said Nina.

"Hello, Nina Spark. Start any neighborhood wars lately?" He grinned at her as he slowly spun his bottle of beer on the bar top.

Veronica set Nina's iced tea in front of her with a smile and moved away again.

"Actually, I'm giving some serious thought to taking things to the next level and suing Les for polluting my visual environment and stressing me out with his music. Would you be interested in the case?"

He took a long pull on his beer, then turned to face her. "Although it's against my professional interests to do so—and I have no love for that Jet Ski–joyriding fish-terrorist Jones—I'm going to give you a piece of advice on the house: Live and let live. Life is short, sunshine. Be happy."

"That's really deep, Frank," said Nina. "The problem is, I can't hear myself think when I'm sitting on my back porch." She took a sip of her iced tea. "Ah, I get it. You're a genuine hippie. 'Everybody get together, try to love one another' and all that. I thought that didn't work out."

"Ain't nothing wrong with that sentiment, sunshine, but that was just a little before my time. I made my poke as a tax attorney up north. More libertarian than liberal, politically speaking. All I'm saying is you'll get more out of life if when Les plays his music, you just take off your clothes and dance on the sand, instead of wasting your time arguing in court or shooting spitballs at him over the hedge."

"Well, thank you for your advice, I guess. I'll think about it," Nina said.

"Hello, Ted. I was hoping I'd run into you today," said Frank, looking over Nina's shoulder. Ted slid into the vacant seat beside Nina. Her stomach did a little flip.

"Hi, Frank. How're you doing?" he said. He removed the ball cap he was wearing in place of his khaki hat and set it on the bar. "Hi, Nina," he said more softly, with a smile.

"I've been fishing the flats off Sandy Point all week, and I've been seeing fish, but I haven't caught a goddamn thing," said Frank. "Where're you boys looking these days? Are you having any luck?"

"We got a beauty yesterday morning. Ricky's hooked a few off Wreath Cay and in Turtle Creek. The fishing will improve once the full moon passes. They're feeding at night and not too interested in what we're throwing at them during the day," said Ted. He looked at Nina.

"I thought we might try dinner again next weekend after your conference is over. Somewhere down-island where there's less chance of being ambushed by well-wishers. There's a nice little place on the water in Lank's Cove." He thought for a second. "Problem is, it's mainly a seafood place, and you're vegetarian, as I recall. I'll call ahead. Linda, the cook, is very accommodating."

"That sounds really nice," said Nina. "I'll look forward to it." She smiled at him.

"Great, I'll give you a call. I've got to get back to the lodge right now. See you soon. Frank. Good luck," he said, and was gone.

Nina sat there for a moment after Ted left, staring at the rows of bottles on the wall behind the bar and wondering if maybe she should have offered to cook for him at her place instead. He'd already gone through a lot of trouble to arrange several outings for her since she'd moved to Pineapple Cay.

On the stool next to her, Frank chuckled into his beer.

"Oh boy," he said under his breath.

"What's so funny, Frank?" she asked. "No, wait. I don't think I need any more advice, thanks. I can take care of myself."

"It's not you I'm worried about, sunshine. It's that poor schmuck. He doesn't know what's hit him. He's had a pretty good thing going here. Fishing every day, doing his own thing. Steak and beer for dinner every night if he wanted. Living a quiet life. Pretty much the ideal, if you ask me. Then you landed on-island. Boom!" He mimed an explosion with his hands, fingers splayed. He grabbed a handful of peanuts from the bowl on the bar and tossed them into his mouth.

"I don't know what you're implying, Frank. I like a quiet life, too, as we have just been discussing," said Nina.

"Let me see. The last time I saw you, you were in a holding cell in the police station—stoned, as I recall. The time before that—just one day earlier—you were being escorted through town in a police cruiser. But maybe that's what passes for a quiet life in New York City." He chuckled again.

"And how exactly do you know I'm from New York?" Nina asked indignantly. "I never told you that."

"Please," he said.

"Well, it's been nice chatting with you, Frank. Ciao," she said, standing and grabbing her bag off the bar.

"Bye, Veronica!" she called to the end of the bar.

"Sure, see you around, kid. Play fair," Frank said.

Nina decided to leave via the deck and walk home along the beach. But before she could start down the steps to the sand, she saw a young woman sitting alone looking out at the sea. It was Philip's fan from the banquet. Nina went over and sat down across from her. She was young and pretty, with fluffy blonde hair and heavy eye makeup.

"Hi. I recognize you from the conference. I'm Nina," she said, putting out her hand.

The girl startled. She looked at Nina for a second and then cautiously shook her hand.

"I'm Samantha." No smile. Was it fear Nina detected?

"So . . . pet vacations," said Nina. "Did you have a good talk with Philip Putzel?"

Samantha looked distinctly uncomfortable now. She glanced around, apparently studying a couple of seagulls hopping along in the surf below the pier, pecking at the sand.

"Samantha, just wondering, were you still talking to Philip in the hotel bar around ten o'clock the night he was attacked?" Nina asked, trying to keep her tone light. Nina was curious who Philip had been speaking to in the bar that night. Whoever it was had been just out of her sight.

"Yes, I was. I already told the police that," Samantha said quickly. "He talked my ear off for over an hour, and I finally got away at ten fifteen. I know it was precisely ten fifteen because I kept looking at my watch."

"Sometimes it's better not to meet the people you've admired from afar, eh?" said Nina.

Samantha shrugged and looked down at the table, then out at the water.

"Samantha, is there something bothering you?" Nina asked gently.

Samantha looked up at her. There was a pleading look in her eyes. "I think I've done something really bad," she said.

Nina didn't react. She just held Samantha's gaze and waited for her to continue.

Samantha took a deep breath. "A couple of hours before the banquet, I was upstairs in my room getting ready. Someone slipped a note under my door. By the time I opened the door to see who left it, there was no one there."

She opened the straw bag sitting beside her on the bench and pulled out a white envelope and a copy of Philip's book on catering to the pet-owning traveler. She pushed them across the table to Nina. Nina didn't reach for the book or the note, thinking they might be evidence. She didn't want to leave fingerprints.

"What did the note say, Samantha?" Nina asked.

"It said that if I got Dr. Putzel to sign his book on pet vacations and then arranged to meet him at his bungalow at midnight, I'd get two hundred dollars. I didn't have to actually show up, just leave the signed book outside my door by ten thirty as proof I'd arranged it. I figured it was just someone trying to make a fool of him. It seemed like an easy way to make two hundred dollars and take that pompous windbag down a peg in the process. He's such a lecherous snob." She looked back down at the table, then up at Nina again.

Nina stayed quiet, waiting for her to continue.

"Pet vacations aren't even my area," said Samantha. "I run a travel agency that caters to history buffs. You know, 'the Dread Pirate Blackbeard slept here,' that kind of thing . . ." Her voice trailed off. She took a sip of her lemonade, then focused on a sailboat tacking across the harbor toward Star Cay.

"So, did you get the two hundred dollars?" asked Nina.

"Yes!" said Samantha, looking Nina directly in the eye again. "Someone slipped it under my door in the middle of the night while I was asleep. I thought it was all a big joke! I walked into town to have breakfast at the bakery, then spent it all on a dress and a pair of earrings I'd had my eye on. When I got back to the inn, the police were there, and Dr. Putzel's bungalow was surrounded by crime tape!"

"Samantha, did you tell the police about the note?" asked Nina.

"No! I was ashamed by what I'd done. I just thought it was funny and kind of exciting, and I wanted the two hundred dollars. And I'd already spent the money! I convinced myself that telling the police wouldn't help them find the attacker, anyway. I never saw or talked to anyone, and the note is typewritten. But then Sylvia Putzel-Cross was attacked! I'm probably an accomplice to one crime, and by not telling the police about the note, I maybe allowed the attacker to strike again. I'm in big trouble, and I don't know what to do." She looked miserable.

"Samantha, listen to me, you've got to go to the police station right now and tell them everything. I don't think you're in as much trouble as you think you are. You didn't try to kill Philip or Sylvia, after all," said Nina. *At least, I don't think you did.* "But if you don't tell them everything you know, you *will* be in trouble. The station is right over there." She pointed to the imposing blue building a few doors down.

Samantha twisted a paper napkin without speaking. Finally, she said, "All right."

Nina stood and waited for Samantha to follow her. They walked down the wooden stairs to the beach together, and then Nina watched the young woman walk slowly down the beach toward the police station.

As Nina turned to leave, movement on the wooden walkway at the marina caught her eye. It was Les again! He was moving stealthily and seemed to be looking for something or someone. He peered surreptitiously at the stern of each boat, where their names and registration numbers were displayed. He must have found what he was looking for, because he stopped in front of a midsize powerboat and scribbled something in a notebook he took from his breast pocket. Then he snapped a photo with his phone before tucking it in his back pocket. He looked around as though trying to determine if he was being watched. When he saw Nina, he fixed her with a stare. She pretended not to see him and turned quickly up the beach toward her house. She forced herself not to look back to see if he was still watching her.

What is he up to? she wondered, yet again. *Maybe he does have more going on than playing video games and drinking beer all day. Well, one crime at a time.* Danish and Pansy were coming over to pick her up so that they could go down to The Pirate's Wake to check out Philip's alibi. The sooner any aspiring murderers were caught, the sooner her life would return to normal. Philip's conference and all the bad vibes that seemed to surround it had sideswiped her easy-living-in-the-islands plan.

Danish and Pansy were waiting on the veranda when she got home. Danish was drinking a beer.

"Sorry, sorry," Nina said. "I'm ready. Let's go."

"No worries," said Danish. "Thanks for the beer."

He went inside and put the empty bottle on her kitchen counter; then they all climbed into Pansy's golf cart and headed south. A mile or so south of Coconut Cove, Pansy turned off the two-lane Queen's Highway onto the dirt road that led to The Pirate's Wake. It was a seedy watering hole on the waterfront that catered mainly to local men of leisure. It held a pool table and not much else. A younger crowd looking for cheap booze after The Redoubt closed occupied seats at the bar most nights, and on Thursday nights the joint was jumping for the two-for-one watered-down rum punches. There was no beach, but a rickety dock out back had room for a few patrons to tie up.

As Pansy slowly picked her way around the deep potholes that pockmarked the narrow dirt lane, the shiny red truck Nina had seen on the beach earlier that day roared toward them from the direction of the bar, swerving around the golf cart without slowing down. Nina turned around in her seat to watch him bounce along over the bumps in the road like a bucking bronco.

"Who is that guy?" Nina asked.

"I don't know," said Pansy. "I've never seen that truck before."

Nina watched the truck until it made a right-hand turn onto the Queen's Highway heading south. It disappeared from view.

They parked in front of the windowless building and went in through the side door. The front of the building opened to the water, but The Pirate's Wake was still cool and dark in the middle of the afternoon. As her eyes adjusted to the dim interior, Nina could see two men playing a slow game of pool on the covered cement patio out front. She was pretty sure they were the same two guys she'd seen playing pool the last time she, Pansy, and Danish were there. She glanced around. Every square inch of the walls and ceiling was covered with women's underwear, giving the room an almost cozy, upholstered feel, if you didn't look too closely. There was a bartender behind the bar. In front of him at the bar sat a guy with a beer. Nina was pretty sure they were the same two men she'd seen at the bar the last time. They stared at Nina, Pansy, and Danish.

Danish strode purposefully over to the bar. "Howdy, fellas. Got a question for you. Did you see a short, pudgy fella in a Hawaiian shirt in here Wednesday night? An out-of-towner?" He looked from the bartender to the patron, then back again. The customer just lifted his bottle of beer to his mouth and drank, keeping his eyes on Danish.

"Sure, I saw him," said the bartender. "Kind of overly interested in the decor, if you know what I mean. We get 'em in here once in a while. The fetishists. In fact, I'm seriously considering redecorating. Maybe something with a nautical theme. Or maybe some shabby chic. I'm reading the magazines. Keeping a file. We'll see. I just need to figure out how to work in the pool table. We have a certain casual vibe here I'd like to keep."

Nina looked around. A sand floor, three bare light bulbs over the bar, the smell of burned french-fry grease from the kitchen, and talk radio from the main island blaring from the speaker perched on top of the fridge behind the bartender. *Casual* was one description for the vibe.

"What time did he get here?" asked Pansy. "And when did he leave?"

"Boy, you're a curious bunch, but OK," said the bartender. "He was here all night. Had supper at the bar. Grilled me and Maurice here for a couple of hours about the underwear. I coaxed Shirley-Anne into dancing with him for a while so I could get a little break. He was really into it. It was a sight to see. He stayed until we closed at one o'clock. I called him a cab."

"So, he was telling the truth," said Danish.

"Thanks," Nina said to the bartender, who shrugged. "One more thing, if you don't mind," she said. "Who was that guy who just left? They guy in the red truck?"

She could feel the sudden tension in the air. The man on the stool got up and walked away.

"Never saw him before," said the bartender tersely. "Can I get you something?"

"No, thanks, man. We've got to go," said Danish. The bartender grabbed a couple of empty bottles off the bar and disappeared into the kitchen without another word.

"That was weird," said Pansy.

"Mmm," said Nina. She walked outside and looked down at the rickety dock. A man with a gray ponytail under a ball cap was sitting in a lawn chair on the deck of a rundown tub of a boat tied to the dock. His dog was lying on the deck beside him in the shade of an opened umbrella. Rusty and Rusty. The dog got up and wagged his tail when he saw Nina approach. He barked a friendly greeting. Rusty the man looked up from the newspaper he was reading.

"Hi, Rusty," called Nina with a wave. Rusty the man responded by raising the newspaper in front of his face to block her view of him and his view of her. Rusty wasn't overly fond of visitors.

Nina took the hint, and they left. Pansy dropped Danish off at the inn and Nina at her cottage before hurrying to pick her kids up from playgroup.

10

The next morning, the conference delegates were beginning to show signs of stress after looking over their shoulders for a murderer for the last several days. At the scheduled midmorning break, they hovered in small groups on the side veranda. A refreshment table was piled with baskets of freshly baked muffins and chilled pitchers of fruit juice and iced tea. The delegates eyed one another warily and chatted dutifully about the presentation they had just attended on the comparative density of vacationers on French and Italian beaches.

Nina approached a clutch of delegates in time to hear Bridget guffaw and say, "I mean, I just don't get France. What's the big deal? I went to the beach there once. There wasn't even any sand! Why do people pay all that money to lay out on a rock ledge or on a stony beach with a half-naked stranger sitting two feet away from them? I mean, Fort Lauderdale has about twenty-five miles of sandy beaches to choose from."

"Good morning!" Nina said with more enthusiasm than she felt. "Bubba and Nancy Delancy have invited anyone who is interested to join them on their boat for a trip over to Delancy's Island. We're meeting on the dock in an hour. Don't forget your bathing suits!"

She smiled and moved on to the next group. To her surprise, Danish was standing there with a heaping plate of fruit salad in one hand and a frosted glass of iced coffee in the other. There was a ring of smiling admirers listening to him hold court.

"Yeah, Gerry. You facilitated the hell out of that small group discussion, man. I took a course in change leadership at Boulder College of the Healing Arts, and your performance was textbook," he said. A short man in pressed Bermuda shorts and Birkenstock sandals grinned widely in response.

"Hi, everyone," said Nina. "If you're up for an outing today, we're leaving at noon from the dock. Otherwise, enjoy the afternoon by the pool here."

The crowd began to disperse.

"Danish, what are you doing here?" said Nina, grabbing his elbow. He turned to face her.

"Well, good morning, Nina. I ran into Gerry and Mike at The Redoubt last night, and they were pretty interested in my insights into the cruise-ship industry based on my employment as a yoga instructor and gentleman dance host for Supersun Cruise Line. We had a few cocktails, and they invited me to come share my thoughts with the gang this morning. I won't lie and say it's been the most riveting two hours of my life, but I appreciate the invitation. Say yes when you might say no, that's my motto."

"Didn't your cruise-ship career only last about nine days until you were put off the ship in Nassau?" said Nina.

"Sad but true," said Danish. "But those were nine jam-packed days. I saw *a lot*. Behind-the-scenes stuff, you know. You wouldn't believe it if I told you." He tilted his head back to drain the last of his iced coffee, then set the empty glass on a table behind him and popped a wedge of pineapple into his mouth.

"Uh-huh. Well, I'll look forward to that. Excuse me, I've got to get going," said Nina, heading for the door.

"Okeydokey," he called after her. "Catch you later. I've got some details regarding our project to share with you ASAP."

She pretended not to hear him. She walked briskly home, changed into her bathing suit, and pulled on a pair of shorts and a T-shirt. She stuffed some sunscreen, a towel, and a hat into her straw bag, then headed back to the inn. A small crowd was milling about on the dock beside the Delancys' enormous gleaming white yacht.

They were all there—Philip in his huaraches and a Hawaiian shirt, Sylvia looking cool and chic while chatting to a handsome ship steward at the foot of the gangway, Bridget eagerly clutching her giant canvas satchel and grinning at anyone who glanced her way, and Victor, standing aside with his hands in his trouser pockets observing them all, his eyes obscured behind tortoiseshell shades. Even Razor Hudson had turned up in his voluminous swimming trunks, although he had also brought his laptop.

They made their way onboard, and the steward led them up onto the forward deck.

"Hey, Nina! Isn't this cool? This is the life, man." It was Danish. He was reclining in the hot tub with a fruity beverage in his hand.

"Ah, hello, Danish," she said.

"Yeah, Gerry and Mike opted to catch some shut-eye due to last night's slight overindulgence, so they bailed, but Nancy invited me to come with."

"Of course!" said Nancy, who was lying on a sleek padded chaise longue, wearing a frilly beach cover-up and a wide-brimmed straw hat. She waved her long magenta fingernails casually as she spoke. "The more the merrier. Danish was just giving me the lowdown on what happened to poor Sylvia the other night. You poor thing!" she said to Sylvia, who was leaning back onto the chaise longue beside her. "Never a dull moment around here, it seems."

"Hey, man, what's with the computer?" Danish asked Razor. "Maybe you didn't get the memo, but this is a recreational outing."

"Oh, my interest here is purely professional. I've heard about these places. Day camps for adults. This is a stellar opportunity to see what your average person will do when the constraints and responsibilities of everyday life have been removed, and all they have to do is indulge their hedonistic desires. Thank you very much for the invitation, Mrs. Delancy."

"Call me Nancy, please, darlin'. You are most welcome," said Nancy, giving Razor a curious look.

"Admirable, Razor, I'm sure, but I don't know that you'll find anyone aboard this particular vessel who considers themselves *average*," drawled Sylvia. She opened her beach tote, withdrew a bottle, and began applying a coat of suntan lotion.

"OK, man, type away, but if I catch you having any fun, I'm going to have to report you to the authorities," said Danish. "Have a beverage. It's good cover." He lifted himself out of the hot tub and tossed Razor a bottle of beer from the cooler on deck. Then he stretched out on a padded bench running along the railing and put a towel over his face.

"What a lovely shade of nail polish, Sylvia. Sit right down here, Nina, and tell me all about yourself," said Nancy with a big smile, patting the chair on her other side. "How did you end up here on Pineapple Cay?"

She interrupted herself to speak to the steward in a crisp white uniform standing at a discreet distance behind her. "Jimmy, bring us a few of your killer banana daiquiris, will you? I think the sun's gone over the yardarm, don't you?"

"Yes, ma'am," he said, and disappeared.

Nina wasn't too keen on going into the whole story about walking in on her husband shagging his paralegal and then buying a cottage on a Caribbean Island she'd never heard of in the middle of the night at the moment, so she sidestepped the question.

"This is great, Nancy. It's so nice of you to invite us out for the day." She paused briefly. "Are you and Bubba down here cruising through the islands for a while? That sounds idyllic."

"Yeah, it's great for a week or so, and then I get antsy. Bubba likes to go fishing with his buddies, and I usually have a gal pal or two along. Most nights we go ashore in some port or another for dinner. I sure can't complain, but I'm a city girl at heart. Atlanta, born and raised. If I hadn't crossed paths with Bubba way back when, I'd still be there, most likely running my father's clothing store."

"So, how did you and Bubba meet?" asked Nina. Was she being too nosy? But Nancy didn't seem to mind.

"Well, as a matter of fact, I was working as manager of guest services at the Sweetwater Hotel, and Bubba kept calling the front desk asking for ice. So, after five or six of these calls, I went up to his room to see what the heck he was doing with all that ice. Turns out he had a dead swordfish in the tub. He'd just flown in from Bimini. We had words. Then he invited me out for dinner and dancing, and we fell in love before the sun came up. That was thirty years ago." She sighed contentedly and took a sip of her daiquiri.

"I was born Nancy Weston, and my mama raised me to be an independent woman, but I just couldn't resist the opportunity to become Nancy Delancy." She threw her head back and laughed. "Of course, the hundred mil didn't hurt. Besides which, me and Bubba, we both like to have a good time."

Victor had strolled down the length of the boat, and Nina could see him leaning on the railing, looking out at the water. Philip glanced over at Sylvia, then wandered off to the wheelhouse to seek out Bubba. Nina watched them through the glass. Philip was talking and gesticulating with his hands while Bubba puffed on a fat cigar and nodded distractedly now and then, his eyes focused on the horizon.

Nancy turned to talk to Sylvia about places they both knew in Atlanta, and Nina took advantage of the opportunity to watch the scenery. The yacht had slipped its moorings and was cutting a wide arc through the brightly colored water, heading out to the channel. A warm breeze tugged at her sun hat, so Nina pulled it off and sat back in the thickly upholstered chaise longue. They were heading northwest, out past Star Cay, the low hump of white-sand beach and lush green coconut palms that sat about a mile offshore from the village of Coconut Cove. There were a couple of sailboats crisscrossing the harbor between Star Cay and the bustling marina on Pineapple Cay, their white sails billowing.

On the back side of Star Cay was another, larger island, about a mile farther offshore. This was their destination. As they rounded the tip of Star Cay, an enormous five-story cruise ship came into view. It was anchored near the second island in a shallow cove of pristine turquoise water. It dwarfed both the island and Bubba's yacht, which until that moment Nina had thought of as colossal.

"That's what we now call Delancy's Island—it's trademarked," said Nancy with a laugh. "Bubba bought it a few years ago and made a deal with a couple of cruise lines to stop here and give their passengers a day at the beach without the hassle of clearing customs. The deal is they can have any cocktail they want, as long as it's Delancy's rum." She laughed. "On some days, this is the most populous island for miles around."

The *Take-a-Chancy* tied up to a mooring, and the crew sprang into action, lowering the tender into the water and helping the passengers aboard for the quick zip over to the beach dock.

"Have a nice day, kids!" said Nancy, waving goodbye to them and sinking back into her chaise longue, a fresh banana daiquiri in her elegantly manicured hand and Jimmy standing attentively behind her. Bubba had gone belowdecks.

From the dinghy, Nina heard music wafting out across the water. Bouncy Caribbean steel drums. On the dock, they were greeted with a cheery "Welcome to Delancy's Island!" from a smiling young man and woman in blue-and-white-flowered batik shirts who were handing out tropical cocktails with paper umbrellas in them. Nina followed the group up the dock onto the long strand of white-sand beach.

Holy cow, she thought as she looked around. She stole a look at the group from the *Take-a-Chancy*. Most of them looked as dumbfounded as she was. Razor was furiously taking notes in his little Moleskine book. Danish was dancing, his hands in the air.

Delancy's Island™ certainly delivered on the tropical beach daydream. Big-fronded coconut palms arched gracefully over the sand, just like in a postcard. The pure-white sand was so soft it felt like it had been sifted. The beach was packed with several hundred greased-up holidaymakers in their bathing suits, lounging in beach chairs under thatched sun umbrellas or cavorting in the water. Others paddled around in bright-orange and green kayaks, and there was a noisy, laughing bunch playing beach volleyball. A flotilla of buzzing Jet Skis zipped back and forth, weaving around water skiers and banana boats. Nearby, on a giant inflatable trampoline, kids and adults bounced like popcorn. Brightly colored hammocks hung between picturesquely bowed palm trees, waiting for their chance to make it to Instagram. Several were heavily freighted with dozing day-trippers.

Dozens of tourists were seated at tables in the beachfront restaurant, from which the aroma of deep-fried everything wafted through the air. And at the thatch-roofed beach bar, the cruise-ship passengers were three deep. A small army of bartenders in blue-and-white-flowered batik shirts were shaking cocktails in time to the music. Delancy's fine rum appeared to be flowing like a river. A limbo contest was under way on the sand in front of the bar, and a circle of onlookers stood clapping their hands to the beat as a young woman bent backward and slithered under the stick. At the other end of the long white-sand beach, a straw market was doing a brisk business in Delancy's Island™ souvenir T-shirts, key chains, and straw bags. Nina estimated there must have been a thousand people on the long swath of beach.

Behind the fringe of palms that lined the beach, the vegetation was thick. A wide sandy path led into the jungle. It was framed by a rustic wooden arch thatched with palm fronds. A wooden sign hung from the top of the arch with **DELANCY'S ISLAND**™ painted on it. Under the arch a man in—what else—a blue-and-white-flowered batik shirt danced and punched the air with one fist. In his other hand, he held a megaphone.

"Woo-hoo! YES!" he shouted into the megaphone. Nina jumped involuntarily. "Welcome, all you party animals to Delancy's Island. Just pile all your psychological baggage, preconceptions, and inhibitions right there under that coconut tree. You can pick them up on your way out. You won't be needing them here, *DARR-LINGS!*" He strutted back and forth in front of the small group that had disembarked from the *Take-a-Chancy*, eyeing them.

"My name is Brad," he shouted into the megaphone. "My job title is Official Party Starter. The name of the game here today is Let the Good Times Roll. *Are you ready to have a good time?*" He held his hand to his ear, apparently assuming they were the type of crowd who would be good sports and play along.

Oh boy, thought Nina, glancing around at the others. This was the opposite of her own tropical daydream—which did feature a hammock, but was accompanied by a good book and the gentle *shush* of the surf in the background rather than a thousand other people and a deejay.

"Cool," said Danish, who had sidled up beside Nina.

"Yes, I am! Woo-hoo!" yelled Bridget, clapping her hands.

"Right ON!" yelled Danish at the same time.

An awkward silence followed. Philip huffed and crossed his arms across his chest, sending Nina a hard look.

"Maybe the rest of you didn't hear me. I said, *Are you ready for a good time?*" Brad called out again.

There was a sputter of uncoordinated, halfhearted applause.

"All right, all right," said Brad, nodding his head and grinning encouragingly. "I can see we have some serious unwinding to do here. Let me assure you, you have come to the right place, my friends. Delancy's specializes in good times and sweet memories that pack a little punch. No worries. No time to waste, so let's go waste some time!"

He swung his arm up over his head and pointed forward, dancing up the path at the head of the group, which shuffled after him somewhat uncertainly, with the exception of Danish and Bridget, who did their own interpretive dances up the path into the jungle.

The path came to an end in a clearing just out of sight of the beach and the thousand lolling vacationers but still within earshot of the steel drums. In the clearing sat rows of shiny golf carts, like strings of brightly colored beads.

"Now, listen up!" shouted Brad, although no one else was saying anything. "Here is the plan. Grab yourself a partner and a map." He started circulating through the small crowd, handing out glossy maps of the island. Nina held hers in two hands, trying to orient herself to her surroundings.

"X marks the spot, babies," said Brad. "We are now at location X on your map, otherwise known as Party HQ."

Nina heard Philip exhale angrily nearby.

Brad continued. "Your task is to get to Y on the map."

Nina looked down at the map in her hands. Y was marked near a deep semicircular cove on the far side of the island. A track ran along the coast all the way around the small island. *Easy enough,* thought Nina.

"Now here is the important part," said Brad, wagging his finger at them with mock seriousness. "Under no circumstances are you to go in a straight line from X to Y. Where is the fun in that? If you come to a fork in the road, *take it!*" He waited for a laugh or some sign of life, but none came. Danish had wandered away and was busy securing his backpack to a tomato-red golf cart.

Brad tried again. "No, seriously, we'll follow the scenic coastal road to the Pink Lagoon. Along the way, we'll pass several sites of interest, at which I encourage you to stop, get out, and have a look around. I'll be around to give you a hand if you need anything. At the Pink Lagoon, we'll enjoy a delightful tropical lunch on the beach, followed by some *shenanigans!* Are you ready? Ladies and gentlemen, start your engines!"

Nina felt sorry for him. She whistled and clapped her hands encouragingly. Bridget joined in. The rest just looked on suspiciously.

Sylvia and Victor were standing together, and after glancing at each other, they proceeded toward a baby-blue cart.

"Hey, Philip! Over here!" called Bridget. "I've got this green one." She appeared to have forgiven him.

Old habits die hard, thought Nina.

Philip looked over at his tall, gangly assistant waving to him frantically in a nearly deserted jungle clearing and proceeded to march purposefully toward the red cart at the front of the queue, sliding his bulk behind the steering wheel and turning the ignition before he replied. "I will take this time in private contemplation. It's so rare I get the chance to hear myself think." He sped off solo down the track and was soon out of sight.

"What a pleasure that must be to hear the innermost thoughts of the great Philip Putzel," muttered Razor Hudson. "I'll drive with you, Bridget," he said, and headed over to where she was still standing by the green cart.

Brad looked uncomfortable. He must have been told that these were Mr. Delancy's personal guests and to show them a good time. Nina caught his eye and smiled encouragingly at him.

187

"Hey, Nina!" called Danish. "Just like old time times, eh? You and me on the open road in a golf cart. What do you say?"

"All right," she replied, "but I'll drive this time, if you don't mind." She and Danish climbed into the last cart in the queue. When everyone was settled, the golf-cart convoy moved out slowly, bumping gently over the grass of the clearing and onto the single lane of smooth black tarmac that, according to the map, circled the island.

Away from the crowded beach, the island was like a cartoon version of a tropical island. The paved golf-cart path curved attractively toward the water and then veered slightly away again, winding around aesthetically pleasing groupings of boulders and clumps of spiky aloe vera and buttonwood. Groves of soaring coconut palms had been planted all along the path on both sides, and their smooth gray trunks curved gracefully this way and that in a pleasing tableau. The spectacular turquoise sea was always within view.

At the spot on the map marked with a giant ice cream cone, Nina and Danish came upon a thatched ice cream stand with a cheery yellow-and-blue sign: ISLAND ICE CREAM STAND. Three employees in blue-and-white-flowered shirts scooped coconut, pineapple, or key lime ice cream cones for a swarm of excited kids and their parents, all wearing yellow wristbands that identified them as cruise-ship passengers. A fleet of golf carts was parked in the designated parking area beside the ice cream stand.

"Cool," said Danish. "Want to stop for a cone?"

"Sure, why not," she said, pulling into the lot. She sat on a bench while Danish ordered and ate a triple-scoop cone.

A little farther on, at the spot on the map marked with a skull and crossbones, they came to a giant replica pirate ship crawling with kids. They were climbing up thick nets hanging from the mast like spider webs, looking through telescopes in the crow's nest, and whacking at one another with toy swords down on the beach. Delancy's Island™

employees dressed in pirate costumes wandered around the ship and the beach saying *"Arrr matey"* to the kids, who shrieked and laughed and whacked at them with their toy swords. Nina put her foot on the accelerator.

"Hey!" said Danish, "You heard what Brad said. Stop and smell the roses. That looks like fun. I wanted to try it."

With a sigh, she pulled into the parking area. Danish collected his toy sword and eye patch from the teenager at the concession stand and joined the fray, taking on a gang of ten-year-old pirates. She watched as they chased him up the ropes of the ship, then up and down the beach until he ran to where Nina was sitting on a bench in the shade. He collapsed on his back at her feet.

"That was great!" he said.

The band of miniature pirates surrounded his fallen form.

"Is that your mom?" one of them asked.

Nina and Danish got back in the golf cart and drove on, past a sign for the BOTANICAL GARDENS on their left and then a cheery yellow-and-blue sign for LOVER'S BEACH on their right, marking a wooden staircase down to a secluded cove. There were five golf carts in the designated parking area. At the top of the stairs, a woman in a blue-and-white-flowered shirt minded a thatch-roofed stand that loaned out towels and sold "lover's picnic baskets." According to the sign, the baskets—which could be charged to your cabin—included two bottles of Delancy's ready-to-drink piña coladas, chocolate-dipped fruit, and various creole-style amuse-bouches to feed each another. Offshore, Nina could see a glass-bottomed boat bobbing in the waves and a dozen passengers with their heads bowed.

"Yo, Mrs. Robinson, *qué pasa?*" called Danish to a woman pounding cassava in a large stone mortar in the front yard of a wooden chattel house painted a festive lime green. The sign in front proclaimed it A TRADITIONAL ISLAND HOMESTEAD. Another woman sat on a wooden bench in front of the house, weaving a basket from strips of palmetto palm leaves. A shelf of straw bags with Delancy's Island™ embroidered on them with colored straw stood beside her. Nina rolled to a stop.

"Oh, it's just you," Mrs. Robinson said to Danish, halting her pounding and leaning against the big stick she was using as a pestle. "We were told there was a group of VIPs coming around this afternoon and to look sharp."

Nina smiled. She knew what Mrs. Robinson meant. They were local. Mrs. Robinson brought a travel coffee mug out from the folds of her peasant skirt and took a slug.

"Danish, where is my order from Williams Sonoma? My daughter is getting married in one month, and I still don't have the William Morris antique floral dinner serviettes I ordered for her wedding breakfast. I can see on the Internet that the package was delivered to the post office last week. It says *out for delivery*. That means you."

"Sorry, Mrs. R. I only see what they put in my delivery bag. I'll look under Doris's desk tomorrow a.m. That's where we found Bernadette's three-pack of Spanx. Oops. I wasn't supposed to talk about that. How's tricks, Mrs. Johnson?" he called to the woman weaving in the shade of the house. She just nodded and waved.

"Well, we'd better get going. Have a great day, ladies," said Danish. Mrs. Robinson waved goodbye wearily and strolled over to sit with her friend and drink her coffee.

"Right on," said Danish after they'd driven across a scenic wooden bridge over a creek that meandered photogenically on its way to the sea a short distance away. "I knew that would sort itself out. I may have accidentally thrown a wet towel on top of that package after my midroute swim break and dissolved the address label. But no harm done. Now I know where it goes. Life has a way of sorting itself out, doesn't it?"

"I'll let you know. So, you just fabricated a story about packages getting lost under Doris's desk?" said Nina.

"No, that's true. Bernadette's package was under Doris's desk for about a month. In the meantime, Bernadette dumped Claude, cut out the french fries, and started working out, so she didn't really need the special form-shaping undergarments by the time Doris found them, anyway. And who knows? Maybe Mrs. R's package *is* under Doris's desk, and the package in my cart is something else."

They drove past neatly kept beds of bright tropical flowers and rows of royal palms, signs leading to a petting zoo and a miniature golf course, and a spun-sugar beach with a row of striped umbrellas shading pairs of beach chairs, most of which were occupied by sunbathers. A line of golf carts painted in primary colors filled the parking area. Nina and Danish passed a few couples cruising along the smooth, flat pavement on bicycles, snorkel gear in their baskets. Just a few miles offshore, Delancy Island™ was a whole world away from Pineapple Cay.

Nina and Danish rounded a bend, and in front of them was a lovely, horseshoe-shaped cove, accessible by a flight of wooden stairs. In the parking area at the top of the stairs, Philip was standing beside his cart, stretching his back. Nina pulled in beside him.

"Hello, Philip," she said.

"Yes, hello," he said. "I see the others are already here. I stopped at the botanical gardens myself. It was surprisingly pleasant strolling along in the shade. I quite lost track of the time."

Nina looked over the edge of the dune down onto the beach. She could see Sylvia and Victor already comfortably ensconced in two of the low-slung beach chairs set on the sand facing the water. They had rum punches in hand. Razor Hudson was a ways down the beach, walking purposefully along in the surf, head down, his knapsack slung over his shoulder. Bridget was standing beside a thatch-roofed bar between two palm trees and talking to a guy with long dreadlocks tied back in a ponytail. The cheery wooden sign above his head read, IT'S FIVE O'CLOCK SOMEWHERE.

"Isn't that your friend Warren?" Nina asked Danish.

"Yeah. There's Fuzz, too. They work out here sometimes," said Danish.

Nina looked around and saw Fuzz sitting in the shade of a coconut tree, laying out a tray of sliced fruit and cheese. Beside him something sizzled away on a barbecue made out of an oil drum cut in half. Their official party starter, Brad, chatted with some of the other conference delegates. Philip started down the stairs and strode toward the group, with Nina and Danish following him.

"Now gather 'round, people," Warren called out. "I'm going to prepare a special island treat for you using only fresh, local, organic ingredients and the finest Delancy's rum."

Warren had a green coconut in one hand and a machete in the other. He lopped the ends off the nut, then hacked away the stray coarse fibers with a couple of practiced chops of the blade. Fuzz wandered over with the platter of sliced fruit he'd been preparing and set it on the picnic table beside Warren.

"Here in the islands, we live on nature's bounty. We eat the fish from the sea and the beautiful fruits that grow on our island. Oranges, mangoes, pineapples. Coconuts grow everywhere, as you can see. We grate the flesh and use it to make coconut bread and pies—you can buy them in the market. We eat the coconut jelly and drink the coconut water inside—see?" He held out the coconut so that the bunch of conference-goers gathered around the rustic bar could see the clear juice inside the hollow green globe of the coconut.

"Now, listen carefully. This is the important part," said Warren. "I'm going to show you the best way to drink coconut water." He took a bottle of Delancy's fine Caribbean rum from behind the counter and poured a generous dollop from a dramatic height, so that it looked like a miniature waterfall of amber elixir as it gurgled into the open top of the coconut. When he was done, Fuzz garnished it with a tiny pink paper umbrella and a red-and-white-striped straw and handed it to Bridget, who was standing in front.

"Come on, try it, sister," Fuzz urged.

She giggled and took a sip. "Yum!" she said.

"Yeah!" Fuzz said enthusiastically. "Coconut is the wonder fruit. Fix everything. Make you feel like a lottery winner at an all-you-can-eat buffet on a full moon night. Nature's Viagra."

Nina broke away from the group and plopped down in a beach chair to read. After a while, they had a picnic lunch of barbecued chicken, shrimp, vegetable rotis, and fresh fruit while reclining on beach blankets spread on the sand under blue-and-white-striped umbrellas. Brad regaled the group with ribald pirate jokes and then somehow rallied the group for a tug-of-war in the sand and a limbo contest, which Sylvia won. Danish and Bridget joined in the games. Then some of the group peeled down to their swimsuits and splashed around in the lagoon. Victor went to sleep stretched out on a beach blanket with his hat over his face. Philip sat upright in a beach chair in the shade of an umbrella and ostentatiously read a thick academic tome he'd brought with him.

Razor typed away on his laptop until the battery died. From her beach chair, Nina watched him curse and then walk down to the water and slowly make his way along the surf with his head down. Danish was playing Frisbee with Bridget and a couple of others nearby. He glanced over at Razor as he passed, and gestured for him to join the game. When Razor shook his head, Danish broke away from the circle and walked along the shore with Razor. Danish was talking. Razor nodded once in a while. Finally, they stopped, and Razor unbuttoned the long-sleeve plaid shirt he'd been wearing over his voluminous surf jams. He waded into the water after Danish, who ran into the surf and dove under with a whoop. Good old Danish.

Nina got up and walked quickly down to the water. She stood with the waves washing over her toes, watching Danish and Razor dive and thrash around in the water like a pair of dolphins. When Razor finally emerged from the water, he was smiling for the first time since he'd arrived. Nina felt guilty for what she'd been thinking, but she did get the answer to the question that was bugging her. Razor didn't have any angry red scratches on his arms or torso. If he had dragged himself over the broken glass embedded along the top of the back wall of Sylvia's bungalow, tearing his clothes in the process, he'd somehow managed to do it without hurting himself.

"Time to head back to your boat!" Brad yelled. "Whoever makes it back to the dock first will get a fabulous prize to take home. You know you want it! On your marks, get set, go!"

"Come on, Razor!" Bridget yelled at her driving companion as she headed for the stairs, her beach satchel banging against her legs as she ran. "We can do it!"

Razor gathered his things and walked briskly after her, but he did not run to catch up. Nina could see the wheels turning in his ever-analyzing mind. He liked Bridget and wanted to please her, but he didn't want to appear too eager to win Brad's silly contest.

"Let's go, Nina. I never win anything. I'm due," said Danish, grabbing her bag and taking the stairs two at a time. She sighed and jogged after him. She'd be happy to get home. In the parking area at the top of the stairs, everyone was piling into their golf carts. Danish had the motor running, and the red cart was positioned at the front of the line out onto the paved lane.

"Let's go! Hop in, Nina! Time is money!" Danish shouted. As she climbed in beside him, he peeled away from the pack and floored it.

"Jeez, Danish!" she said.

"It's uphill most of the way back," he said. "Let's hope this baby has some juice."

"You know, the prize is probably a Delancy's T-shirt or something," said Nina.

"So?" said Danish. "I like T-shirts. I also like having a good time, and you guys are a bunch of party poopers. Where's Bridget? Is she gaining on us?" He glanced back over his shoulder.

"Just watch the road in front of us, Danish, please!" said Nina. She gripped the metal bar supporting the roof and turned her head to look behind them.

"They're way back. You're king of the road," she said.

"Woo-*hoo!*" he shouted, raising both arms in the air. Nina grabbed the steering wheel as the cart veered toward a roadside flower bed.

"Seriously, Danish!" she said. He took the wheel again, and Nina pulled the map Brad had given them out of her bag. The road back to the dock and the waiting yacht was shorter and less winding than the trip to the Pink Lagoon. She sat back to try to enjoy the scenery while Danish kept the pedal to the metal. Nina could hear the little engine strain against the gradual incline and the pressure of Danish's foot on the accelerator. They zoomed through a grove of coconut palms and past another cheery yellow-and-blue sign marking the island aviary.

"Ah, that would have been cool," said Danish.

They rounded the last bend, and the dock, Bubba's yacht, and the bars, restaurants, and shops along the beach appeared in the distance ahead of them.

"It's in the bag!" yelled Danish. The clearing with its neat rows of golf carts lay a hundred yards in front of them, at the bottom of the slope. It looked like all the cruise-ship passengers had gathered at Party HQ and were now preparing to return to the ship for the evening. Maybe to have a shower, put on some fancy clothes, and have a multicourse dinner in the dining room. Afterward, they'd catch a variety show or try their hand at blackjack.

"I can't stop!" shouted Danish suddenly.

"What?" cried Nina.

Danish was pumping the brakes frantically. "The brakes aren't working! Nothing!"

Nina looked at the path ahead of them. They were quickly closing in on the golf-cart lot. There were several people milling around among the carts, and Nina and Danish were seconds from plowing into them. Danish pumped the brakes again and again. Nothing. They couldn't jump out, Nina realized. They were going too fast, and the cart was going straight into the crowd. She looked around frantically. The wide sandy path down to the boat dock was just ahead on the right.

"Turn right! Turn right, Danish!" yelled Nina, grabbing for the wheel. She yanked it to the right, and the cart bumped off the paved path and onto the sandy track that led down to the dock. The cart gathered speed as it headed down the slope. Out of the corner of her eye, she saw the group of people gathered around the golf carts watching openmouthed as Nina and Danish careened past.

"Get out of the way! Off the path!" she yelled. People loaded down with beach bags and cameras scattered as the runaway cart barreled toward them.

"Drive it right off the end of the wharf, and then jump clear!" she said, holding on to the bars of the cart with both hands and looking over at his panicked face.

"I think I can safely predict we're going off the end of the wharf!" he said, holding the steering wheel steady and bracing himself against the seat with his back. Nina looked straight ahead at the wharf in front of them. It was empty of people, thank God.

"Runaway cart! Get out of the way! Watch out!" Danish shouted.

"Stand back!" Nina yelled. *"Ahhhhhh!"*

They bounced over the boards of the wharf and right off the end. The cart began to fall away beneath them.

"Jump, Danish!" Nina yelled. She swung her body out of the cart and pushed off the running board with her feet. A fraction of a second later, she plunged into the sea. The water closed over her head. She closed her eyes and held her breath and kicked to the surface in time to see the roof of the golf cart disappear.

"Nina!" She heard Danish's voice and looked around for him. He was swimming toward her. They swam together to the dock, and he boosted her up the ladder. Brad was pounding down the dock, asking if they were all right. Assorted conference delegates and bystanders trailed after him, watching with concerned looks on their faces. Nina looked back at the water where the golf cart had gone in. She could see it now, resting upright on the sandy bottom in ten feet of clear water. She looked at Danish.

"Are you all right?" she asked.

Water streamed off her clothes, ran down her legs, and pooled in her sandals. Danish's dark hair was plastered to his head, and his vintage T-shirt with I AM NOT A TARGET MARKET written across the chest clung to his frame.

"Yeah, I'm fine. What the hell? Those brakes were fine on the way out."

"Nina! Danish! Are you all right?" asked Sylvia, squeezing her way through the crowd to where they stood dripping.

"No damage done to the *cuerpo*, Sylvia. Don't worry," said Danish. "Faulty brakes, that's all."

"This is preposterous!" It was Philip, pushing his way to the front to stare at Nina and Danish and then glare at poor Brad, who was standing off to the side, making a call on his ship-to-shore radio. Nina assumed he was notifying Bubba or the police or maybe both.

"It's just one thing after another!" Philip said.

"We're fine, thank you, man," said Danish.

"Stand down, Philip," said Victor, walking up behind him. "First things first. Dry clothes, dry land, and a cocktail to soothe jangling nerves for these two, I should think."

Razor and Bridget stood beside him, both looking concerned. Bridget, wide-eyed, had her hands clasped to her chest; Razor was watching them silently beneath slightly knitted brows.

Brad rejoined the group. "The police cutter is on its way out from Pineapple Cay. Mrs. Delancy is waiting for you all onboard the *Take-a-Chancy*. She'll take care of you until the deputy superintendent gets here."

"Well, there you go. There *is* a silver lining to every cloud," said Sylvia. "The dashing deputy superintendent is coming out to interrogate us over cocktails aboard the yacht. How exciting."

"Why would he interrogate us?" asked Bridget. "Is it a crime to drive a golf cart into the ocean?"

"Well, Bridget, my dear, perhaps he thinks someone tried to murder Nina. Under the circumstances, it is not out of the question," said Victor.

"Hey, what about me? I was *driving* the golf cart," said Danish with some indignation.

"No offense, Danish, my sweet. You know I think the world of you, but why would anyone want to kill you?" said Sylvia.

"Why would anyone want to kill *me*?!" said Nina. She looked around at their faces. Victor, Bridget, Sylvia, Razor, and Philip, off to the side, glowering away with his arms crossed. It was a ridiculous idea. The small crowd of bystanders from the *Take-a-Chancy* expedition started to move slowly back up the dock to make room for the sunburned groups of yellow-wristbanded cruise-ship passengers now heading toward the row of tenders arriving from the enormous ship anchored out in deeper water.

Nina, Danish, and Victor hung back, waiting for the crowd to thin. Victor took off his linen blazer and put it over Nina's shoulders.

"So, make any complaints to the police against anyone lately, Nina? Another neighbor, perchance?" asked Danish meaningfully. "Maybe Les is out to get you. Maybe it's old Philip, the supreme grouch. He doesn't seem too happy with this conference you've organized. Remember? He said it was a black mark on his record, and he blamed you for it."

"Who's Les?" asked Victor.

"No one," said Nina firmly. "Why would anyone want to kill me? I can sort of see someone wanting to get rid of Philip. He can be very obnoxious. Even Sylvia, I suppose. She's a big personality. I guess she could get under someone's skin—most certainly, Philip's. But me? Am I really that irritating?"

"Nobody's perfect. Don't be so hard on yourself," said Danish.

"Of course not, Nina, darling," said Victor, putting his arm around her. "It was just an accident, I'm sure. A coincidence."

～

As it turned out, it wasn't just an accident.

"The brakes were cut," said Blue a while later. He looked tired.

They were onboard the *Take-a-Chancy*, still anchored off Delancy's Island™. Blue and Nina were sitting across from each other at a teak table on the private upper deck, untouched glasses of iced tea in front of them. On the deck below, Danish was back in the hot tub, along with Bridget and a merry assortment of other passengers enjoying the cocktail hour. The golf cart had been pulled ashore and examined by the police.

"Are you sure?" said Nina, profoundly shocked.

"Yes," said Blue. "Was the cart out of your sight at any point while you were on the island?"

"Yes, Danish and I stopped a couple of times on the way to the beach where we all had lunch, but there were lots of people around at both the ice cream stand and the pirate ship. Someone would have noticed a person with wire cutters fooling around with a cart, surely. And, anyway, we stopped again after that, to talk to some people along the road, and the brakes worked fine."

"Anywhere else?" asked Blue.

"At the beach, we parked our cart at the top of the cliff and went down to the shore. We were there for a couple of hours." She thought back, trying to remember anything out of the ordinary.

"Danish and I were the last to arrive. Philip was still in the parking lot when we got there, and we went down the stairs together," she said. "We all left at the same time. I don't remember anyone missing from the beach."

Blue sighed. "All right. I'll be in touch. Right now, I've got about a thousand cruise-ship passengers to process before I can let them go."

"OK, Blue. Thanks. And I'm . . . sorry," Nina said.

He nodded. She watched him go.

"Well, my goodness!" exclaimed Nancy as Nina rejoined the group by the hot tub. "It is never a dull moment with this crowd. I told Bubba we might just have to stick around a few days to see what else happens. Of course, I am so glad to hear that you and the young man are none the worse for wear. That dress fits you well, Nina. I can see that green is your color. You must keep it as a souvenir of this occasion. It's not every day a lady drives off a pier in a golf cart!" Nancy threw her head back and laughed.

It was the tail end of the afternoon by the time they got back to the inn. Everyone was exhausted. Nina said her goodbyes and walked slowly home. She took a shower and put on her new slinky black swimsuit under her shorts and T-shirt, thinking she might take a refreshing dip before the sun went down. Jumping into the water fully clothed from a moving golf cart didn't count as swimming. She made a cup of tea and wandered outside.

"Honky Tonk Woman" by the Rolling Stones wafted through the palm trees from the direction of Les's back deck. She could live with that. So. He was home. Good. Perhaps she could solve at least one mystery. She wanted to get to the bottom of what she saw from the top of Lime Tree Hill. She put her cup down and headed through the trees to Les's deck.

He was tinkering with his barbecue, and he was wearing his swim trunks. Bonus.

"Les, I want to talk to you," she said.

"Do you?" Les replied, glancing up at her briefly and then turning his attention back to his barbecue.

"Yes," said Nina. "I want to know why the guy in the red truck is so interesting to you that you're skulking around taking pictures of him and his pals."

"Do you now?" said Les, still not making eye contact with her. She waited. He glanced at her before turning away again to close the lid of the grill and take a gulp from the beer bottle resting on the deck railing beside him. He watched her out of the corner of his eye as he drank. He turned to face her.

"OK. We can powwow if you want, but it's going to be in the hot tub," he said.

"Absolutely not. No way," said Nina.

"Yes way. And I'll tell you what. Just to show you what a gent I am, because I know you're a little squeamish, I'll keep my trunks on. Although, I've got to tell you that trunked or trunkless, it's still going to be Les-and-Nina soup with all the seasonings, baby."

Nina gagged. "Oh God. That's disgusting. You are truly disgusting."

Les got into the hot tub carefully, holding his bottle of beer aloft. He slouched down on the underwater bench with a sigh.

"Well, I guess you'll have to decide how badly you want to know what I know about Mr. X, the owner of the red truck. Note, I said *want* to know rather than *need* to know, just so we're both clear that you're being a busybody, and not acting in any official capacity whatsoever."

Nina stood there uncertainly for a moment, weighing her options. The prospect of a Les-and-Nina soup was nauseating. On the other hand, she *really* wanted to know what the deal was with Red Truck Man. She was pretty sure he was up to no good. She sighed, then shuffled off her flip-flops and wiggled out of her shorts. She left her T-shirt on over her bikini top and climbed in, perching stiffly on the edge of the underwater bench.

"Now we're talkin'," said Les, sliding his eyes over her as she sat down. "Care for a beer, milady?"

Nina wasn't a big beer drinker. She bought it mainly for guests. Mainly for Danish, but it occurred to her that it might take the edge off the situation.

"All right, sure," she replied. Les reached back over his shoulder into the Styrofoam cooler on the table beside the tub and withdrew a bottle. He screwed off the cap with one hand and passed the bottle to her.

"A toast," he said, holding his bottle up like a torch. "Here's to being single and drinking double."

Nina rolled her eyes and took a sip. Les gulped half the bottle, his Adam's apple bobbing in his thin neck. Then he leaned back and closed his eyes.

"OK, Les," she said. "Let's hear it."

"All in good time, all in good time. I think we should take a moment to appreciate the sunset. Isn't it lovely?" he said, opening his eyes and gesturing to the spectacular panorama of the pink-, purple-, and orange-streaked sky before them.

"Yeah, it's great," said Nina, her eyes flitting briefly to the big orange ball of the sun sinking into the sea, then back to Les. "Start talking. I have things to do."

A figure coming down the beach toward them caught her eye. It was Ted. He stopped in front of Nina's cottage for a moment, then turned around and started slowly back toward his lodge. There were no lights on in the cottage, and the sun had begun its rapid descent while she was at Les's. She gave a small, involuntary squeak. Mistake. Les swiveled his head around to see what had startled her, then looked back at her through narrowed eyes, like a shark on the hunt.

"Ah, Mr. Ted Matthews. Cover boy for *Boring Fishing Story Monthly*. Your cup of tea, is he? We should say hello. Hey! Matthews! Care to join us in the hot tub for a beer?" Les yelled to Ted, then grinned at Nina wickedly.

Ted turned around again, looking for the source of the invitation, and Les waved him over.

"Welcome, welcome. The more the merrier. Nina and I were just chillin', shooting the breeze. Being neighborly. You know Nina, don't you?" said Les as Ted approached.

"Evening, Nina. Les." Ted nodded at her as he spoke. He held her gaze, a slightly puzzled look flitting across his face before his features returned to a neutral expression. No smile.

Nina wanted to disappear. She could only imagine what Ted might be thinking, finding her cozied up with Les, drinking beer in his hot tub as the sun set. She stood up.

"I was just leaving," she said, climbing awkwardly over the side of the hot tub, still holding the bottle of beer. She stood dripping in her bikini with her T-shirt clinging to her. She couldn't even articulate a reasonable explanation for why she was there. Somehow, she didn't think her desire to get dirt on the guy who drove the shiny red truck would make Ted think more highly of her.

"I heard you were in an accident," Ted said to Nina. "Are you all right?"

"Yes, I'm fine, thanks. Just a couple of scratches," she answered.

"Good. Well, I don't want to break up the party," said Ted, already beginning to walk away. "I just wanted to see if you were OK. Thanks for the invitation, Les, but I've got to get back to the lodge. Good night, Nina. Les." He gave her another look in the eye, then turned away to walk back up the beach along the shore. Nina watched him go.

"Oh dear. I hope he didn't get the wrong idea," said a smirking Les.

"You're a jerk," said Nina irritably. "What is your problem?"

"Oh, calm down. Can't two neighbors have a friendly drink together? If Golden Boy Matthews's ego can't take it, that's his problem. Now, are you interested in what the guy in the red truck is up to or not? Because I've got things to do—or perhaps I should say someone to do—very shortly. Not you, just to clarify, so don't get your hopes up."

"You're a pig. Just say what you've got to say, and I'll gladly be on my way," said Nina. Way up the beach, Ted was now just a dark shape against the pale sand. The lights in the guest cabins below the main fishing lodge were visible through the trees. Nina sighed quietly and returned her attention to Les, who was leaning back in the hot tub with his arms stretched out along the rim and a knowing grin on his face.

Nina crossed her arms.

"Well?" she said. "We had a deal, Les. I saw you skulking around the dunes yesterday where Red Truck Man was up to something. And I saw you sneaking around the marina last night. What're you up to?"

"Well, now, that's not the question I agreed to answer. The question I agreed to answer is 'What is your so-called Red Truck Man up to?' Let's call him Jimbo. I'll tell you this much: Jimbo's been a bad boy. He's taken something that doesn't belong to him."

"What's he taken that doesn't belong to him?"

Les took a long pull on his beer before speaking. "Well, I'm pretty much done with him, and he's not getting off this island anytime soon, so I'll tell ya, just because I feel the tiniest bit of remorse about pouring cold water on your budding romance with Matthews. So sad. Sand."

"Sand," said Nina, letting his comment about Ted pass.

"Yessiree. Piles and piles of soft white sand. Jimbo and his mates cruise in on a barge and suck it up with a vacuum pump when no one's looking, then sell it for a hundred dollars a yard to a middleman who can get twice that from hotel owners who don't ask too many questions about where it comes from. The trick is to take just a little bit here and there so no one notices it's missing."

"Why would anyone want to buy sand?" asked Nina. "This place is literally covered in sand."

"Not here, obviously," Les said. "But everyone wants a nice white-sand beach and palm trees on their Caribbean vacation. Problem is, half the islands in the Caribbean are volcanic or are missing a few beaches. Black sand, rough brown sand, or no sand. Florida, too, for that matter. No one dreams about sipping cocktails on a black-sand beach. The hotels import white sand and spread it like a blanket over their rocky, mud-colored shores. The schoolteachers gone wild from Akron don't know the difference. It takes about a hundred yards of sand to cover your average beach volleyball court, and it's got to be done every year or so. It's a lucrative business."

"If this sand stealing is a regular practice, why I am just now seeing Jimbo and his shiny red truck everywhere? And why are you so interested in him?" asked Nina.

"Well, Jimbo's been a greedy boy. And he's getting cocky. Instead of concentrating his business on the uninhabited cays around here, he's cutting corners, taking sand off Pineapple Cay. It isn't his usual hunting grounds, but he's sold enough recently to buy himself a brand-new truck, get it shipped over here on the mail boat, and drive it back and forth through the middle of town ten times a day. That's attracted the attention of various onlookers. Moron. He should have stuck to his legit job at the distillery. He deserves what's coming to him."

"And how do you know all this?" asked Nina. "What does it have to do with you?"

"Nope. You've used up your one wish. Let's talk about something else," said Les. "My turn to ask a question. Do you wear your hair like that because you think it looks sexy, or because you don't own a hairbrush?"

"Good night, Les. It's been a real pleasure, as usual," said Nina, heading toward her cottage.

11

Nina woke up the next day determined to set things right with Ted. She spent the morning over at the inn dutifully attending conference sessions, including "How to Market Polar Bear Dips As Tourism Products in Northern Climates" and "Promoting Road-Hockey Tournaments to Expatriate Snowbirds at Beach Resorts." It was the last full day of the conference, and mercifully, the delegates were due to start heading home that evening. The regularly scheduled twenty-seater couldn't handle them all at once, so they were shipping out in batches. With any luck, no more of them would be picked off before they were safely off the island. Nina was looking forward to putting the whole week behind her and getting back to normal. Preoccupied with thoughts about her encounter with Ted the previous night, the recent attempt on her life, and the guy in the red truck, she declined Victor's invitation to join him and a few others for lunch.

"Let's meet up at The Redoubt for dinner later," she suggested instead.

Nina walked home through the village. As she passed Les's house, she noticed his car was gone, and the air was blissfully Guns N' Roses–free.

She wondered what he was up to as she opened her own white picket gate and went up the path to her front door. She inspected her window boxes. Her flowers were perking up—looking quite pretty, in fact. Blue had been right in his diagnosis and suggested treatment. Passing through her tiny cottage with a brief detour into the kitchen, she pushed open the screen door onto the veranda and leaned against a post sipping a glass of iced tea. She looked up the beach to the point. No sign of activity. All the fishing skiffs were pulled up onto the sand in front of the lodge. Strange. Usually at this time of day, the guides were out on the flats with clients. She remembered Ted's battered wide-brimmed hat, still sitting on her kitchen counter. Now might be a good time to walk it over to him.

She gazed out at the gorgeous white-sand and turquoise-water vista that served as her backyard and smiled to herself. Despite her recent near-death experience, she still couldn't quite believe her good luck in landing in such a beautiful place. It was serendipity. Victor was wrong. Our life stories aren't written in advance by our genetic codes or our hormones. Or even by our pasts. Along with whatever blows life delivers—like a philandering husband—there is room for the delightfully unexpected and for charting our own courses.

The sun was at full strength and the water enticing, so Nina decided to take a quick swim before heading up to the fishing lodge. She went inside and peeled off her clothes, slipped on her swimsuit, and padded barefoot down to the shore and into the surf. The water was crystal clear and just cool enough to be refreshing. Schools of tiny fish darted around her ankles as she waded out across the soft, sandy bottom. When it was deep enough, she dove under, then floated on her back with her hair trailing in the water like seaweed, feeling the sun on her face. The saltwater stung her scratches.

In such an idyllic setting, it was hard to believe that someone had really tried to kill her and Danish yesterday. It had to have been an accident. Brakes wear out. A tear could look like a cut, couldn't it? She didn't have a clue what brakes looked like or how they worked. And the break-in at Sylvia's could easily have been a petty thief who thought the bungalow was empty. But what about Philip? That was definitely not an accident. Someone very angry had tried very hard to kill him. And if that was true, were the other two incidents possibly unrelated? She just didn't know.

She swam a few lengths back and forth in front of her cottage, then splashed back to the shore. She glanced over at Les's bungalow as she walked up the path. Still no sign of him or his bare bum. Very curious.

~

Showered and freshly dressed in a clean white T-shirt and cutoffs, Nina headed up the beach to the lodge with Ted's hat in her hand. She felt invigorated. As she approached, however, she realized something had changed since she'd gone inside for her shower. There was now a bikini-clad woman reclining on a beach lounger and reading a magazine in front of the guest cottages. She glanced up as Nina approached.

"Hello!" the woman said. "You're the first person I've seen on this beach since I arrived. How do you do? May I help you?"

She was about Nina's age, Nina guessed. Maybe a little younger. She was stunningly beautiful, her ruby fingernails and toenails manicured to perfection, with just the right hint of matching lip gloss framing her perfect toothy smile. *Friendly,* thought Nina, *but who is she, and what is she doing at Ted's fishing lodge wearing a bikini?*

"Hi," Nina said. "I'm the neighbor. I just wanted to return Ted's hat. He left it at the bar."

"Oh, he's up there," said the woman, gesturing up toward the main clubhouse. "He said he had some paperwork to do. I thought I'd enjoy this lovely beach today. Would you like me to give it to him?"

It was like a shock of cold water sluicing through her chest. Nina hadn't seen this coming. Ted had a girlfriend visiting. New, old, occasional, it didn't matter. There was someone else.

"Ah, thanks. That's all right. I'll get it to him later. Thanks. Enjoy your holiday," Nina said, and swiftly turned and headed back toward her cottage still clutching Ted's hat, suddenly downhearted.

Nina changed her clothes and went back to the inn. She sat through the remainder of the conference discussions in a bit of a daze. Victor was right about one thing. The waterslide and lazy-river proponents did get into a heated argument with the wilderness canoeing and white-water-rafting advocates. The points of contention seemed to be which type of activity created more jobs, which was more fun, and whether or not it mattered if we had any natural rivers left. Nina was thankful for the distraction. After the meeting adjourned, some delegates migrated to the bar and eventually into the dining room. Nina climbed in a van that was headed for The Redoubt.

The bar was jumping. Veronica had brought in a blues musician for the evening, and he was playing a searing slide guitar on the raised stage in the corner when Nina followed after the group from the conference. Patrons were two deep at the bar, and most of the tables inside and out on the deck were full of noisy patrons. Candles were lit on all the tables, and the servers moved briskly from table to table and to and from the kitchen. Nina hung back by the door, not eager to wade into the crowd. She watched the group she'd arrived with colonize a picnic table on the waterside deck.

"Hiya, Nina!" It was Bridget with her perennially sunny smile. She was wearing a new batik sundress and a pair of Pansy's sea-glass earrings. Her nose and shoulders were sunburned.

"Bridget, how are you doing?" said Nina.

"I'm great!" said Bridget with a huge smile. "Guess what? Philip came over to me this morning and told me he called someone he knows at the research institute I want to work for and got me an interview next week! Isn't that amazing? I'm so excited! And I'm meeting Les here later for dinner. He's so great, don't you think? I'm having such an amazing time!"

So, Philip had come through for Bridget. Maybe his trip to Pineapple Cay had been transformational for him, after all. John Steinbeck would approve, thought Nina.

"That's such good news about the job, Bridget. I'm very happy for you," said Nina, avoiding comment on Les's greatness. She looked around. "Where's Philip tonight?"

"I don't know," said Bridget. "I stopped by his bungalow on the way over here to see if he wanted to come along, but he wasn't there. Sylvia was on her porch having cocktails with Nancy Delancy. She said she hadn't seen or heard from him since the last session ended. I guess he's tired, with all that's happened."

"Yes, I imagine so," said Nina. "I'll see you at the inn to say goodbye tomorrow morning, Bridget. Have fun tonight."

She leaned against the bar and scanned the crowded room again, looking for Victor. He'd skipped the last session at the conference. She saw the solo traveler Victor had ambushed with a bottle of wine. He was seated in a booth with the two women he'd shared the wine with, along with a couple of other people. They were eating and laughing. They looked like they were having a good time.

"Good evening, Nina." Victor had come up beside her.

"Victor!" she said with a smile, genuinely pleased to see him. "You look great! The jogging must be paying off."

He smiled and took a sip of his drink. Veronica's fresh-squeezed lemonade with a sprig of mint, Nina noted.

"So, you and Veronica seem to have hit it off," she said, pleased but slightly puzzled. Maybe she had assumed the wrong thing about him.

"Yes. She's marvelous. A bracing draft of fresh air. We've had a few good talks in here this week," he said, looking down the bar at Veronica. They shared a private smile.

"Well, that's nice. Veronica is great," said Nina, still puzzled, but pleased. "Now, Victor, I'm sorry to bring this up, but it looks like you've lost our bet," she said, changing the subject. "Look over there," she said, pointing her chin at the lonely male traveler, now surrounded by new friends. "And the mysterious lady with the same taste in reading material is nowhere to be seen."

"Well, actually, Nina, maybe it is a tie," said Victor—a bit bashfully, Nina thought. "Half of our mysterious pair may have found a bit of romance in the moonlight. You see, Steve is quite a nice guy, actually," said Victor, gesturing at the man. "He's on some kind of sabbatical from Silicon Valley and is sailing around the world. He's invited me to tag along for a bit, and I think I might, at least as far as Guadeloupe or maybe even Curaçao. You've set an example. I'm going to take a few risks and see what happens. It's quite thrilling, really. Veronica has been plying me with salad and jogging and stern talking-tos, and I think I like feeling the blood course through my veins again."

He gave Nina a cautious smile.

Aha, thought Nina.

"That's great, Victor," Nina said. "It sounds like a grand adventure. Send me a postcard, all right?"

"Of course," said Victor. "We're leaving tomorrow as soon as the provisions are stowed, but Steve has invited some people out for a moonlight sail tonight. Will you join us?"

Nina thought for a moment.

"Thanks, Victor, but I think I'll have to give dinner a pass, if you'll forgive me. I'm a little tired. I think I need an early night. I'd better say goodbye now." She decided not to mention her own emotional state or the fact that a few days ago Victor had suggested Steve might be a psychopathic murderer. "See you soon, Victor."

She reached up and gave him a big hug. He hugged her back and kissed her cheek.

"Righto, then. I like your handsome man, by the way. He's a keeper, I'd say. Take care, Nina."

Nina watched him walk over to Steve's table and join the group of laughing vacationers. Then she turned back to the bar, looking for

Veronica. The restaurant owner was standing a short distance away, also watching Victor.

"Veronica," said Nina, "thank you for whatever you did." She leaned across the bar and gave Veronica a hug.

"He's a good man. Just a little sad. But Pineapple Cay has worked some magic on him. He'll be all right," said Veronica. She smiled and rapped her knuckles on the bar, then went down to the other end to serve some thirsty customers.

Nina slid onto a stool and looked around, thinking she might just go home. She wasn't really in the mood for a crowd of happy revelers tonight.

"Nina. Jeez, I'm late. But guess what I found out?" It was Danish, walking rapidly behind the bar and tying an apron around his waist. He glanced over at Veronica, who gave him a stern look, and then he leaned down until his face was close to Nina's.

"I was over on the wharf, shooting the breeze with the guys while they cleaned their catch. Warren happened to mention that he took a woman over to Delancy's Island in his boat yesterday, i.e., the day we plummeted into the sea in a faulty golf cart."

"Really? Who?" said Nina. "Sylvia and Bridget were on the *Take-a-Chancy*. They didn't need a lift over to try to kill you or me. And if it's a woman, that means it wasn't Razor, either. Who else is there?"

"She didn't give a name. Paid him a hundred dollars cash."

"What time?" she said.

"Morning, he said. She asked him to come back at five o'clock to get her, down-island a ways from the main dock. He thought she was a craft vendor or something. They travel back and forth from Pineapple Cay every day. She had a bag with her."

"What did she look like?" Nina asked.

"Warren was a little light on details. He said brown hair about this long," he gestured to his neck. "Average size. Not too fat. Not too thin."

"That could be just about anyone," said Nina. "Let's see. Maybe Sylvia tried to kill Philip, then Philip tried to kill Sylvia, or Razor tried to kill Philip, then Philip tried to kill Sylvia, thinking she had tried to kill him. Except Philip has an alibi for the night at Sylvia's. So, maybe Razor accidentally broke into Sylvia's bungalow thinking it was Philip's, and ran away when he realized it wasn't. Then someone else decided to get in on the action . . . I don't know."

"I've got to get to work. The boss is giving me the evil eye," said Danish, grabbing a tray and heading out onto the floor to clear some tables.

Nina was stumped. Everyone seemed to have a motive to kill Philip. And the means to do so seemed to be easily accessible—poison apples, crab cakes, feather pillows for smothering, and shears to cut the brake cable on a golf cart. Fewer people on the list of suspects had the opportunity. Everyone had an alibi for at least one of the three murder attempts, which meant that either there was a murderous team at work or it was a series of inept murder attempts by two or three different people. Or it was someone Nina, Danish, and Pansy—and maybe the police—hadn't considered. Nina sighed heavily and headed for home. She had a shower and crawled into bed, trying not to think about how Ted might be spending his evening just a few hundred yards away.

~

Nina dawdled around home the next morning. The remaining conference delegates had the morning to themselves to pack and enjoy a last few hours on the beach. Philip, Bridget, and Razor were all booked on the same flight off the island in the late afternoon. Sylvia had decided to stay on an extra few days as a guest of Nancy Delancy. Nina sat on her veranda with her coffee for a long time. She could hear Les's voice and Bridget's distinctive laugh coming from the direction of his hot tub.

This morning he was playing "Roxanne" by the Police at a slightly lower volume. She could live with it.

Nina wrote a light, newsy e-mail to her parents in Maine, and a more revealing one to her best friend, Louise, in New York. Then she weeded the flower beds along the path to her front door, attempted to cut the grass with the machete she'd bought at the hardware store, and watered her window boxes. After spending an hour at her kitchen table planning her lessons for the online courses she was due to start teaching in a couple of months, she made herself a grilled cheese sandwich for lunch. After lunch, she read for a while. She had just sat down on the edge of the veranda, her back against a post, to have a cup of tea and listen to the waves when she heard a knock at the front door. It was not followed by the sound of heavy footsteps through her house, so that ruled out Danish. It was Pansy.

"Hi, Nina," Pansy said when she opened the door. Pansy had a look of concern on her face.

Who said what to whom? Who told Pansy, "Nina's feeling blue"? Nina wondered. The Pineapple Cay bush telegraph was a more effective means of communication than fiber-optic cable.

"I just finished showing a few houses in The Enclave, and I have a little while before I need to pick up the kids up from their playdate. I thought I'd stop by and see how you're doing."

"I'm fine, Pansy," Nina said, smiling to prove it. "I was just having a cup of tea before going to the inn to see off the last batch of delegates and settle up with Michel. Do you think you could give me a lift?"

"Sure," said Pansy with a reassuring smile. They climbed into her turquoise golf cart. When they got to the inn, the remaining conference delegates were milling around the lobby between piles of luggage waiting to be shuttled to the airport. Bridget was standing by the door checking off names on a clipboard. Razor Hudson was over in the corner typing furiously on his laptop. Sylvia was chatting with Michel in another corner. She must have come up to say goodbye to the other delegates. Philip was nowhere to be seen. Nina went over to Bridget.

"Bridget, where's Philip?" she asked. "He should be here by now. The flight leaves in an hour."

"I know," said Bridget. "I haven't seen him. I knocked on his door on the way over here, but there was no answer. I had to get down here, so I couldn't wait. I figured he'd gone for a last walk on the beach before we leave."

That sounds more like something Bridget would do than Philip, thought Nina. She was starting to get alarmed.

She turned to Pansy. "I don't think anyone has seen Philip since the conference ended yesterday at around five o'clock. I'm going to run down to his bungalow and see if he's there."

"I'll go with you," said Pansy.

They walked quickly down the front steps and across the lawn to the row of bungalows. Nina took the stairs up to Philip's door two at a time. She knocked. There was no answer. She tried the doorknob. The door opened easily. She and Pansy stepped inside.

"Philip!" called Nina. No answer. His room was neat, the bed was made, and his laptop stood open on the desk. A pair of trousers and a white shirt were folded over the back of a chair. He had not packed yet.

The hairs stood up on the back of Nina's neck. She crossed the room and pushed open the door to the walled-in garden shower, afraid of what she might see. But it was empty. It looked like it had been recently cleaned by the housekeeping staff. A freshly folded towel and a wrapped bar of soap sat on a teak stool by the taps. There was no sign of a struggle. Maybe he had gone AWOL for his own reasons.

She studied the papers on his desk without touching them, looking for a clue as to his whereabouts, but they were just notes for his article on The Pirate's Wake, as far as she could tell.

"He's not here," Nina said. "Let's go back to the lobby and see if Sylvia or Razor has seen him today."

They walked quickly back to the inn's main building. As they entered the lobby, they could hear a frantic conversation at the front desk. It was Steve, Victor's new friend. He was talking to Josie, the front desk manager. He seemed alarmed about something. He was holding the same paperback novel Victor and Nina had seen him reading the first day on the beach. The thriller with the lurid red-and-black cover.

"I was packing to leave," he was saying urgently. "I picked up my book to put it into the bookshelf on my boat, and these fell out of it."

He held up a conference brochure and spread a couple of other sheets of paper on the desk in front of Josie. Nina and Pansy leaned in to see. One sheet was a map of the Plantation Inn grounds, with Philip and Sylvia's bungalow marked with an X. The brochure was also marked up. All of Philip's presentations and the sessions he was moderating were circled. The third piece of paper was a printed page from the Internet on bush medicine. There was a picture of a manchineel tree and a summary of its poisonous properties. Nina and Pansy looked at each other.

"Excuse me, Steve, where did you get this?" asked Nina.

"I don't remember getting it anywhere. I thought it was my book until this stuff fell out of it a little while ago. My boat's moored out in the cove," he said, gesturing outside. Nina could see Victor tying up a tender to the dock, then walking quickly across the lawn and into the lobby to join Steve.

"Victor says this is the guy someone tried to kill," Steve said, tapping Philip's name with his finger. "I thought I'd better let someone know, so you can pass it on to the police, if it's relevant."

"Victor," said Nina. "Do you remember? This is the same book our mystery woman was reading. It's her! She's the one who tried to kill Philip. But who is she?"

Victor shook his head. "I've never seen her before in my life," he said.

Nina searched her mind frantically, then spun around to face Pansy.

"Pansy! She was wearing earrings I'm pretty sure you made. Did you sell a pair of green sea-glass earrings to a dark-haired woman in the last week or so? She was by herself. Did she tell you where she was staying or anything else?" said Nina.

"I sold a few pairs. Let's see. Bridget came in to the shop and bought some white glass ones yesterday. Some women over from Orlando for a girls' weekend a week ago. Probably not them. Some yachties, but they had a couple of husbands trailing after them. A young woman came in a few days ago, but she had blonde hair. Oh, there was Susan. She arrived a while ago, almost a week before your conference began. Dark hair. She's traveling on her own. Just wanted some solitude by the sea, she said. Doing some bird-watching. She said she was recently divorced. I rented a villa to her, down near the salt ponds. That's where the birders like to go. No one for miles around. She bought the earrings when she came into the office to pay for the rental. Come to think of it, she paid in cash. Sometimes people do, to avoid the credit-card fees on foreign exchange." She and Nina locked eyes.

Nina walked quickly across the lobby to where Sylvia sat with Michel, drinking tea.

"Excuse me, Sylvia," Nina said. "What is Philip's second wife's name?"

Sylvia looked with surprise from Nina to Pansy to Victor and Steve, who were all hanging on her answer.

"It's Suzanne. Suzanne Lafontaine."

"What does she look like?" asked Pansy.

"Like a silly young girl. A ponytail and a tight sweater," said Sylvia.

"I'm guessing she has changed a bit since then," said Nina. "Sylvia, have you seen Philip today?"

"No, not since yesterday afternoon," said Sylvia. "Why? What's the matter?"

Josie came out from behind her desk. "Would everyone leaving on the five forty-five flight please collect your hand luggage and proceed to the vans out front? We're sorry to see you leave, but it's time to go. Safe travels, and please come back and see us again soon!" she said with a smile.

All around them, guests started to gather their belongings and make their way outside to the vans.

"I won't be sorry to see them go," said Nina under her breath, running over to where Razor was packing up his laptop.

"Razor, have you seen Philip today?" Nina asked him.

"No, I haven't. Hopefully, I'll never see him again. Thank you for everything, Nina, but I won't be at the conference next year. I'm putting in for a six-week stay at the research station in Antarctica. Or maybe I'll replicate that study by the guy who lived alone on an island for a year to see what effect it had on him. I'd do the biosphere, but I think they shut that down. I've also heard of this project up in Canada where volunteers live like nineteenth-century pioneers for a year. Time travel. I'm mulling over lots of ideas." He stuck out his hand, and Nina shook it.

"Well, have a safe trip, Razor, and good luck with everything." She jogged back over to where Michel and Sylvia were now standing.

"Michel," said Nina, "Philip Putzel is missing. We think he might have been abducted or maybe killed by his second ex-wife, Suzanne Lafontaine. She's rented a house down near the salt ponds—Pansy, where is it exactly?"

"It's the old foreman's house overlooking the pans," said Pansy.

"Oh my," said Sylvia.

"Right," said Nina turning back to Michel. "Michel, could you please call the police and tell them we think that's where she is and that she probably has Philip?"

"Of course," he said, walking as quickly as Nina had ever seen him move over to the phone at the reception desk. Nina and Pansy were sprinting across the driveway to Pansy's golf cart when Danish came strolling leisurely across the lawn from his quarters.

"Whoa, whoa, whoa, *mujeres*. Where's the fire?" he said, intercepting Pansy and Nina.

"Get out of the way or get in, Danish. We've got a situation," said Nina.

"It's Philip Putzel," said Pansy. "We think his ex-wife is trying to kill him, if she hasn't already!"

"*Sylvia?*" said Danish.

"No. His other ex-wife," said Nina.

All three of them sprinted toward Pansy's golf cart and threw themselves in. Nina gripped the dashboard as Pansy peeled away from the curb. Danish sprawled across the back seat and struggled to right himself. Nina turned all the way around in her seat to talk to the other two.

"I'm pretty sure the woman I saw on the beach at the inn and then having dinner here is Philip's second wife! Only Philip and Sylvia would recognize her, but her plan would be spoiled if either saw her. That's why she tried to keep such a low profile, wearing a big hat and sunglasses on the beach and disappearing when Victor sent a bottle of wine to her table. She didn't want to be noticed, but she wanted to keep track of Philip's movements."

"Why would she try to kill Sylvia?" asked Pansy.

"Jealousy?" suggested Danish.

"I don't think so," said Nina. "I think maybe she just got the rooms mixed up. Philip shared the bungalow with Sylvia, and the outdoor showers were side by side."

"So, the brakes on the golf cart were also meant for Philip?" said Danish.

"I think so," said Nina. "If you remember, both Philip and you and I were driving red golf carts. We were parked side by side at our last stop. Maybe we took his cart or he took ours by accident, or she cut the cable on the wrong cart. Philip was the target all along. During all this, we forgot about the other significant person in his life who might have a serious grudge against him. Philip has a reputation for collecting adoring young women and then unceremoniously shedding them that goes all the way back to Sylvia."

"Oh Lord. I've got to call Andrew and have him pick up the kids. Here, Nina, take the wheel for a minute," said Pansy, letting go of the steering wheel and digging in her purse for her phone. Nina grabbed for the wheel as the cart lurched sideways. Pansy had a hurried conversation with Andrew, then slipped the phone back into her purse and took control of the steering wheel again.

The sun was beginning to set. It would be dark by the time they reached the salt ponds.

"I know this island is only six miles long," said Nina. "but every once in a while, a vehicle that can go faster than fifteen miles per hour would come in handy."

"Too bad you decided to cheat on Ted with your neighbor the nudist. Ted could have driven us," said Danish from the back seat.

Nina turned around in her seat to face Danish.

"I did not cheat on Ted with Les. Please, give me some credit. For the record, Ted and I have never successfully completed a single date, so cheating would be technically impossible. Anyway, he seems to be making out just fine. And how do you know anything about this, anyway?"

"Whatever you say," replied Danish. "All I know is, he was at The Redoubt with his head hanging low on Saturday night, and the next day he picked up what appeared to be a supermodel at the airport and installed her at Fortress Matthews. You do the math. Les filled me in. Ted called me over there to give his lady friend a private yoga session. She's pretty hot."

"Danish, what gives you the idea that I would be in any way interested in your opinion of how hot someone is?" said Nina testily.

"Just saying," he mumbled.

Pansy glanced over at Nina with a look of concern on her face, but she didn't say anything.

"Should we call Blue just to make sure he got the message?" Pansy asked a few seconds later.

"Let's see if our hunch is right. Then, if he hasn't shown up, we can call him," said Nina. "If we're wrong and we get him out here for no reason, I might have to move back to New York. Michel can handle Blue's disapproval better than I can."

A few miles later, Pansy turned off onto an unpaved road. They bounced along until the dry, scrubby brush gradually thinned out into salt-stained hardpan studded with clumps of stubby grass. Up ahead, Nina could see water shimmering on both sides of the narrow road. The sun was low in the sky, and the surface of the water was golden, reflecting the last rays of the sun. Pansy rolled to a stop, maneuvering the golf cart into the lee of a lone, crouching silver-top palm and pocketing the key.

12

"We should go on foot from here. The house is up there on a narrow ridge between the ponds and the beach. If we drive right up, she'll see us coming," said Pansy, pointing to a weathered clapboard house perched on a ridge on the far side of the ponds, about one thousand yards away. There was a faint light glowing from a downstairs window but no other sign of life. Single file, they started walking toward the house up a narrow gravel causeway that bisected a vast grid of water. The salt ponds. In the fading light, she could see the ponds stretching away into the distance on both sides of the narrow road, and a network of gravel ridges cutting across the watery expanse at right angles as far as she could see, dividing it into squares of pinkish-tinted water. The causeway itself sat just a couple of feet above the surface of the water. It was an eerie, treeless moonscape teeming with wildlife. As the sun set, a cacophonous din of hundreds of birds squawking and honking rose from the ponds. Peering into the growing gloom, Nina could see the dark silhouettes of flocks of large birds stalking through the shallow water in the middle of the pond to her right. Herons? Flamingos? Much closer by, just a few feet away, she could hear—but not see—a bird or animal of some kind splashing in the water close to where it lapped against the road.

"Where are we?" she asked, shivering a little.

"These are salt ponds. The old Pineapple Cay Salt Works," said Pansy. "They're no longer in use. This area's now a protected bird sanctuary. The working ponds are farther south, near Sandy Point, although there's still a storage facility here, over that way." She gestured vaguely with her hand.

"It's kind of creepy," said Nina.

"Maybe it's because we're here, in the dark, all alone, looking for a *murderer*," said Danish.

"Thank you, Danish," said Nina. "Let's get up there and see what's going on. I swear to God, after tonight, I am never going to leave my house. I'm going to keep my nose out of other people's business and take up a safer hobby like golf or knitting."

"Yeah, you might want to rethink that. My buddy Murray is a caddie at the golf club, and some of the stuff he tells me goes on there, you wouldn't believe," said Danish. "Like this one day this old lady shows up with the ashes of her dead husband in a peanut-butter jar and asks Murray to take her out to the thirteenth hole. Well, they had the lid off the jar and were shaking things out around the tee, when the wind came up and it started to rain—"

Nina broke into a jog. Danish and Pansy hurried to catch up.

The beach house was in darkness except for a single bulb burning over the back door, and light from a window on the main floor. The three of them crept up onto the wooden wraparound porch, Danish leading the way. Nina could hear the waves crashing against the rocks on the other side of the house. They were very near the ocean. They inched closer to the lit window. It was open. The sun had set now, and they had to feel their way in the growing gloom. There was a sudden, rapid movement to Nina's left, from a dark recess directly beside her. She could make out the shape of an empty chair. She jumped, clutching her hand to her chest.

"Aahhh!" she whispered. Pansy and Danish spun around.

"What's wrong?" Pansy whispered frantically.

"There's someone on the porch!" hissed Nina.

"Yeah, a man-eating gecko," drawled Danish, pointing to the flip-flop-length lizard that had sought shelter under the railing and was staring at them with its little eyes glittering in the porch light.

"It sounded a lot bigger," said Nina.

They stood still for a moment, listening for sounds from inside the house. A woman's voice wafted out the window. Suzanne, presumably. Danish dropped to his knees and crawled under the glass, then sprang silently to his feet on the other side. They stood on either side of the opening and peered into the room.

The interior of the beach house was large and open—the kitchen, dining area, and sitting area were all one big room. A wall of glass doors faced the ocean, a black void now that night had fallen. Suzanne was standing in the kitchen with a gun in her hands. It was pointed at Philip, who was on his hands and knees in front of her. She had a white gauze bandage wrapped around one hand.

"She did break into Sylvia's! She cut her hand on the glass along the top of the wall," whispered Nina.

Philip had a scrub brush in his hand, which he plunged into a bucket beside him, then slopped onto the floor, pushing it around in frantic circular motions. He was still dressed in the seersucker suit he'd worn at the conference the day before, dark circles of perspiration under his arms and on his back. The night air was humid, heavy with sea salt.

"She's got a gun!" said Pansy. "Where are the police?" She looked back over her shoulder. There was no sign of a police car.

"We'd better call Blue again right now," said Pansy. They looked at one another. Nobody wanted to be the one to call Blue.

"I vote for you," said Nina, looking at Danish. "He hates you already."

"Why me?" hissed Danish. "He explicitly told me after the thing at Sylvia's that he didn't want to see my face for the next six months. I assume that included phone calls."

Junie Coffey

"It's just so painful," said Nina. "Hello, Blue, remember how you told me not to get involved in police matters? Well, guess where we are?" She cringed.

"I'll do it," said Pansy. "Once you've given birth in a room full of strangers, including first-year medical students who can't quite keep the shock and horror off their faces, nothing really fazes you ever again." She crept soundlessly off the porch and out of earshot. Nina and Danish turned their attention back to what was going on inside the beach house.

"That's it," said Suzanne. "Oh, wait. You missed a spot over here." She reached behind her with one hand to grab a bottle off the counter. She upended it, emptying the contents—ketchup—on the floor.

"What a mess! Clean it up!" she said sharply, wiggling the gun at Philip. He whimpered and shuffled over to the mess on his hands and knees, scrubbing at it ineffectually, swirling the ketchup and soap into a bubble soup on the floor.

"Yes, it's not as easy as it looks, is it, Philip?" Suzanne said nastily. "If you don't mind a bit of advice, I think you are going to need a mop for that. But where, oh where, do we keep the mop?" she said, putting her hand to her cheek in mock wonder. "You wouldn't know, would you, Philip? Don't stop! I'll shoot you right here and now!"

She took several long strides over to the living room, never turning her back on him. He watched her progress anxiously, clearly wondering what else she had in store for him. His suit was now smeared with ketchup, which looked disturbingly like blood.

Pansy was back, her head next to Nina's at the edge of the window.

"What did Blue say?" whispered Nina.

Pansy was silent for half a moment. "Um. He said he's on his way," she said. "He also said not to do anything stupid."

There was a heaping laundry basket on the sofa. Still with her eyes on Philip, Suzanne reached into the basket and pulled out a sock, which she threw into the middle of the room. It landed on the coffee table.

226

She reached in and grabbed another sock, then another and another, scattering them around the room—on the floor, on top of a lampshade, and in a trail across the dining room table.

"*La-de-da-de-da!*" she sang. "All right, Philip," she said sternly. "Get over here and clean up this mess. This place is a disaster! What do you do all day? All you have to do is keep this house clean. I do everything else. Come on now!"

She marched over to the crouching, whimpering Philip and prodded him in the backside with her foot. He stood and scurried over to the living room, where he collected the socks and stuffed them back in the laundry basket.

"You're insane!" he shouted contemptuously. "You're not going to get away with this! My absence will be noted!"

"Oh, maybe," replied Suzanne casually. "But by then I will be long gone. And so will you!"

Bing bing bing! The timer on the stove started beeping insistently.

"Oh, Philip. Dinner's done. Quick! Get it out of the oven before it burns!" snapped Suzanne.

She marched him over to the stove, the barrel of the gun nestled between his shoulder blades. With fumbling hands, he pulled on flowered oven mitts, bent down, and heaved a large pan of lasagna up onto the top of the stove. His forehead was slick with sweat.

"What?" said Suzanne. "Lasagna *again*! Anyway, never mind. I already ate in town on my way home." She grabbed an edge of the pan with one hand and flipped the lasagna onto the floor. It made a huge, messy splat of tomato, cheese, and noodles. Philip stared down at it.

"Oh, I'm sorry, Philip. Were you hungry? Oh dear, I am sorry. Sometimes I forget you are a human being." She laughed. "Never mind. Well, that isn't going to clean itself up, is it? Let's go. You have about ten thousand hours of unpaid domestic labor to work off before I make a final decision as to what to do with you."

She shoved a dustpan and a roll of paper towels at him, then climbed onto a stool next to the kitchen island. From her perch, she watched him slop the paper towels around in the lasagna for a little while, her mouth twisted into a satisfied half smile. Then she hopped off the stool and took a few steps over into the living area of the large room, all while keeping her eyes and the gun trained on Philip. She paced the floor.

"OK now, Philip. In case you haven't fully grasped the situation here, we are playing a game. It's called Retribution. The object is to see if you've learned anything useful since our interlude together. To determine if you meet the basic minimum standard to be allowed to live, and perhaps, God forbid, even reproduce again. If you successfully complete the tasks you are given, you will earn redemption points. If you don't, well, then . . . Not good news for you, I'm afraid." She grimaced mockingly. "As you told me many times, it's survival of the fittest out here in the real world, and some people—I think you were referring to me—just can't take it."

Suzanne paced in front of Philip, wiggling the gun at him periodically.

"Now, Philip, I am sorry to report that you failed—*disastrously*—the first test you were given: fidelity. You have received an *F* in fidelity. Your new wife wasn't very pleased with the photo I sent to her of you and the lovely Samantha snuggled up in the corner of the hotel bar, your hand on Samantha's knee. Yes, I knew Samantha would be a good test. A test you failed. On the upside, your wife *did* like the photo I sent to her a few hours later of you stuffing your mouth with mini crab quiches. I knew you couldn't resist them, either. Self-control is not your forte, is it, Philip?"

"Suzanne, the police can trace everything you've done, you know. You're screwed," said Philip from his kneeling position on the kitchen floor.

"Can you say *burner phone*, Philip?" Suzanne said sarcastically. "Don't you even watch television? Oh, that's right. As you love to tell people, the only things you ever watch on TV are the news and educational documentaries—oh, and every reality show ever made, you big phony!"

Suzanne stopped pacing and stood in front of a flip chart in the middle of the room. From the little aluminum tray that ran along the bottom of it, she picked up a pointer. She whacked the flip chart smartly.

"So *that's* where that flip chart got to," whispered Nina. "Josie and I couldn't figure it out. We were one short for the session on public sanitation at waterfront music festivals."

"Now get over here, Philip. Sit down," snapped Suzanne. Philip hustled over at her command and sat on the sofa in front of her. He crossed his arms defiantly.

"Our next event is called What's the Difference? Pay attention! Big points are riding on your answer." She flipped back the top sheet of the chart to reveal two large photographs. They were head shots of the same woman.

"Man, if I had to take a wild guess, I'd say this crime was premeditated. She's got visual aids and everything," said Danish.

"So, Philip," Suzanne was saying, "what's the difference between these two photographs? Answer carefully, now."

"I've never seen that woman in my life!" said Philip.

"That wasn't the question, Philip! Keep up! What. Is. The. Difference. Between. These. Two. Photographs?"

Nina and Danish both leaned forward a bit and squinted to get a better look at the photos. From where Nina stood, they looked identical.

"I don't know, you maniac," said Philip. "They're exactly the same!"

Suzanne blew a raspberry. "Come on now, Philip. This is *Sesame Street* stuff. A preschooler could do this! Hairdo. HAIR. DO. In the second photo, she's had her hair done!"

Suzanne traced swooping lines through the woman's hair with the pointer.

"Highlights. Blonde here. Auburn here and here. Two hours in a salon and at least a hundred dollars. All the time and money I wasted on trying to look nice for you. *You never even noticed!* Doofus."

She dropped the pointer and started pacing the room again.

"Zero points for that round. Let's move on. Now, here's an oldie but goodie. I'll give you a hypothetical scenario, and you give me the correct response. Question one. A husband and wife are in the kitchen of their rented house in Middle of Nowhere, USA, where the husband has moved them after being run out of his department for what he told her—and she believed, fool—were fabricated charges of sexual harassment. They only have the one car, so the wife, who gave up her job to stand by her man, is now stuck in the suburbs all day, alone. As she loads the last dirty dish into the dishwasher, she says to him, 'Would you like to go see a movie tonight?' Now, what is the correct response?"

"She is crazy!" whispered Danish. "How could he possibly answer that right without knowing what's playing?"

"That was always the problem with you, Suzanne!" Philip shouted from the sofa. "That's the problem with women, period. All the mind games. You all become so bitter, so fast! If you want to go to the movies, why don't you just *say*, 'Let's go to the movies,' instead of giving me a pop quiz on the murky contents of your pretty little head?"

"Oh boy," said Nina.

"Wrong answer!" snapped Suzanne, striding toward him with the gun pointed straight at his forehead.

When it was two inches from him, she leaned down until her face was close to his. He sat absolutely still, his eyes crossed as he stared at the barrel of the gun. Then she said in almost a whisper, "Here's an easy one, sport. Are women really that complicated, or are some men just deliberately obtuse?"

She stepped back abruptly and started pacing again.

"Never mind. No longer interested," she said in a brisk, business-like tone.

She stopped and looked at him and then shook her head slowly, with exaggerated fake concern.

"I've got to say, Philip, that you are not doing as well as I might have hoped."

Suzanne circled around the room again and stopped in front of a side table where she plucked up a cloth napkin to reveal an open bottle of red wine. She poured a generous glassful and took a drink, keeping her eyes and the gun trained on Philip. He watched her warily from the couch.

"*Mmm.* So nice of you to bring a bottle for dinner, Philip. It's divine. The 2006 Screaming Eagle cabernet sauvignon. The same vintage you ordered that night you took me out to dinner in Boston, remember? Back in the good old days, before you ruined my whole life!" she said.

"What?" squeaked Philip. "Is that mine? Where did you get that? It cost a fortune!"

"Oh, come on, Philip. It wasn't a fortune. It was less than the diamond ring you bought that tart you left me for." She took another sip and started pacing again.

"Although, as it turns out, Amber and I really hit it off when I stopped in to visit her on my way down here. In fact, she gave me the wine as a parting gift. Yes, we had a very nice chat over a couple of dusty old bottles of Italian red we found in your climate-controlled wine cellar."

Philip squeaked again.

"Yes, it went down like a dream. Turns out we have a lot in common, me and Amber. A word to the wise. Don't count on your keys working in the lock on your front door when you get back. But, of course, you won't be needing them, anyway. I've decided. This is the end of the line for you, Philip. If you want to know, it's that ridiculous seersucker suit that tipped the scale. A piece of fashion advice for the afterlife: just because they sell it doesn't mean you have to buy it. Now. Time to pay the toll on the road to hell!"

She stopped and faced him directly. She raised the gun in front of her and held it with both hands. It was aimed straight at his chest.

"She's going to shoot him!" hissed Nina. She, Pansy, and Danish all whipped their heads around, searching for the headlights of even one police car on the causeway. Nothing. Just the silent, darkened ponds.

"Oh no, oh no, oh no!" chanted Pansy, covering her face with her hands.

"We can't wait for Blue," said Nina frantically. "Suzanne is going to kill him any second! We've got to stall her, get the gun away from her. Something!"

"I'm on it," said Danish, rising to his full height and striding over to the back door. He rang the bell repeatedly.

"Yoo-hoo! Suzanne. Can I talk to you for a second? It'll only take a minute," he sang out.

Startled, Suzanne almost dropped the gun. She recovered and stood staring at the solid aluminum door, unsure what to do. Nina hopped up and down silently.

"What are you doing, Danish? Want to let us in on the plan?" she hissed.

"Help!" yelled Philip. "She's got a gun. She's going to kill me! Do something!"

"Shut up!" screamed Suzanne. She motioned Philip to his feet with the gun. "Get up. We're going for a boat ride. Don't they say spontaneity is the key to keeping a relationship fresh?"

She marched him over to the patio doors.

"Open the door," she ordered him.

"They're going down to the beach!" said Pansy. She and Nina stood peering through the window at the scene unfolding in the living room. Danish was jiggling the doorknob, trying to get inside. It was locked.

"She must have a boat down there," said Nina.

"I'll go this way, you go that way!" said Danish, running away from them and around the corner of the porch toward the ocean. Nina and Pansy sprinted around the other side. They were too late to catch them on the deck. When Nina, Pansy, and Danish met on the other side of the house, Philip and Suzanne were already scrambling down a stony path to the beach. Suzanne followed Philip with the gun pointed at his back. Nina could see a dual-engine powerboat bobbing in the dark water close to shore.

"Run after them!" Nina shouted. "She's got a boat!"

Philip and Suzanne were on the beach now, moving swiftly toward the boat. Philip stumbled through the sand, but Suzanne prodded him in the back with the gun. Nina, Pansy, and Danish ran down the rocky path, slipping and sliding on loose stones as they went. Danish was the first to reach the beach. He sprinted after Suzanne, bringing her down in a football tackle.

"Aahhh!" she yelped as Danish sat on her back, pinning her to the sand. Pansy ran swiftly up behind them and put her foot on Suzanne's arm, then reached down and pried the gun out of her grip. She wound up and threw the gun as hard as she could into the sea. It disappeared with a splash about fifty feet offshore.

"Good arm, Pansy," said Danish from his perch on Suzanne's back as Nina reached them.

"You can still get fingerprints off a gun that's been in the water, can't you?" asked Pansy with concern.

"Philip, are you all right?" Nina jogged over to Philip, who was kneeling in the sand near the boat, his head down, breathing hard.

In that instant, Suzanne heaved Danish off her back and sprinted toward the boat. She splashed through the water and was halfway up the swim ladder when Danish pulled her off. They floundered around in the surf for a few seconds until Suzanne managed to free herself again.

"*Aargh*! She scratched me with her claws!" Danish yelled. His face was bleeding.

"Who are you people?" screamed Suzanne over her shoulder as she took off running down the beach.

"I don't think so!" said Nina through gritted teeth, running after her. Nina stumbled, then scrambled to her feet again. She could hear Danish pounding across the wet sand beside her. Pansy was on her knees beside Philip, her arm around him. Suzanne glanced back over her shoulder again. Nina and Danish were gaining on her. She veered left toward the dunes, scrambling up and over and out of sight. Nina and Danish sprinted after her, reaching the top of the dune seconds after Suzanne. They scanned the vista in front of them for her. It was dark, and the only light on the salt ponds came from the moon and the stars. Everything was in shadow. The causeway and the stone ridges between the ponds were pale lines crisscrossing a grid of black squares. In the distance, Nina could make out huge mountains of what looked like snow. The salt mounds. The birds had fallen silent.

"There she is!" said Danish, pointing down at the watery grid. Suzanne was running along the causeway, heading in the direction of Pansy's golf cart. They hurried down the slope after her. Suzanne looked back over her shoulder again, and suddenly she veered off onto one of the narrow stone ridges that separated the ponds, heading toward the looming, pale mountains and the dark bushland behind them.

"You take the causeway in case she doubles back. I'll try to cut her off," said Nina, turning off onto a narrow stone ridge between the ponds and trying to close the distance between herself and Suzanne. The footing was rough and loose, and she stubbed her toe on the coarse stones. Nina whimpered in pain as she tumbled off the ridge into the shallow, dark water. God only knew what creatures were lurking there. She scrambled to her feet and back up onto the ridge. Now she was soaking wet with a throbbing toe, but she kept moving after Suzanne's dark figure, now silhouetted again the looming white mountains of salt.

Nina guessed they were headed toward the storage facility Pansy had mentioned. She looked back over her shoulder. Danish was running along a ridge toward her.

When Nina reached the edge of the salt ponds, the footing underneath solidified into hard-packed sand. It was crisscrossed with the tire marks of heavy trucks. She was standing next to a giant mountain of salt several stories high. Two huge yellow bulldozers were parked a short distance away. Nina thought for a moment that Suzanne might have climbed into one, but the cabs were empty. No sign of Suzanne. Nina jogged around the base of the salt pile and saw Suzanne running through a valley between three or four similar colossal piles of salt. Suzanne looked back and saw Nina, then looked frantically from side to side. She had walked into a salt canyon. The only way out was back toward Nina or over a high salt ridge directly in front of her. To Nina's surprise, Suzanne chose the ridge. She charged up its steep face, the salt breaking away beneath her feet and tumbling down the side of the pile. Nina sprinted after Suzanne, scrambling up the mountain of salt, grabbing for a handhold only to have it run through her fingers. She lost her balance and pitched headfirst into the white mass. The salt filled her sandals and got into the open cut on her toe; she sucked in her breath at the sting. The salt stuck to her wet skin and clothing.

Nina summited the salt mountain, her quad muscles throbbing from exertion. She was breathing hard. Suzanne was stumbling along the ridgeline of the salt massif, just out of Nina's reach. Beyond her, Nina could see the vast grid of moonlit ponds, the darkened ocean, and the surrounding flat scrubland. Down below, a line of three police Jeeps screamed up the access road, sirens wailing and lights flashing.

Nina balanced herself in the salt and then stepped carefully toward Suzanne.

Suzanne backed away from her. "Who are you? Why don't you just leave me alone?"

"I'm sorry, Suzanne. I understand Philip was a lousy husband, totally unqualified for the job. I feel your pain for spending years with him, but killing him is a bit extreme, don't you think? Do you really think it would make you feel any better?"

"Yes!" shouted Suzanne. Nina glanced down at the road. The police cars were still at least a few minutes away. Her best bet was to keep Suzanne talking until they arrived.

"OK, well, so did you try to kill him with a mini crab quiche the other day?" she asked conversationally. "That was clever. Everyone would have assumed it was an accident. Except that you wrote on his chest with a Sharpie."

"I wanted everyone to know that someone had finally got the best of him. Me. Oh! I can't believe he actually brought his EpiPen! He always left it to me to take care of those little details, and I really didn't think his new tootsie roll had it in her to plan that far ahead. If she did, she wouldn't have married him! Turns out there's more to her than I thought." Suzanne glanced over Nina's shoulder. The sirens were growing louder.

"You called the police!" Suzanne said angrily. She lunged at Nina, and Nina jumped back.

"Suzanne! Suzanne, tell me about Philip," said Nina, struggling to regain her balance. "What did he do to you to make you so angry?"

"Oh, the usual," said Suzanne bitterly as she continued to swipe at Nina. They shuffled around an ungainly circle until they had shifted places. Nina could see the line of police cars advancing toward them. Suzanne had her back to them.

"I thought I was finally rid of him!" Suzanne was saying angrily. "But the shellfish didn't do the trick, so I had to improvise. Plan B. The manchineel tree. I was pleased with myself for coming up with that. Nicely hideous and painful. He's so vain. A good warm-up to the main event. Until you and your friends ruined it all!"

"You're right. I'm sorry about that," said Nina, raising her hands, hoping to placate Suzanne. "Philip's awful, but why attack Sylvia?" She wondered if Suzanne was so delusional she'd confess to it all right there on the salt mountain.

"That was a mistake. I thought it was Philip's shower. Why would I want to hurt Sylvia?" said Suzanne. "I never had anything against her. When Philip left her to move in with me, she was quite civilized about it. No hard feelings."

"*Hmm.* And the golf cart. You thought it was Philip's, too?" asked Nina casually.

"Yes, of course," said Suzanne irritably. "I don't even know you or that stoner guy. I didn't come all the way down here to kill you!"

"Good point," said Nina. The police cars had stopped about a hundred yards away, blocking the road. Two officers took up positions behind the open doors of their vehicles. Four others drew their weapons and fanned out, moving to surround the salt pile. They moved silently.

"Suzanne," said Nina, "I think things would go a lot better for you if you were to turn yourself in to the police and tell them everything you just told me. You'd feel a lot better if you just got it off your chest."

"Are you crazy?" said Suzanne, pulling a tiny gold pistol from her bra and pointing it at Nina. "I'm not going to jail for that jerk! Not while he gets to wake up and go snorkeling tomorrow morning! Or maybe have a pedicure. I didn't tell you all of this because I want to confess. I told you because you're never going to get the chance to tell anyone else! Someone should know how perfect this plan was, even if you won't have the memory to cherish for very long. Sorry, but that's what you get for butting in where you have no business."

Suzanne's face seemed to harden, and she cocked the gun. They were only about ten feet apart. Nina didn't know much about guns, but she was pretty sure you could do some real harm to someone by shooting them at close range. Her mind whirred with possibilities, but she only came up with two: getting out of Suzanne's way or getting the gun from her.

She stared at the gun and counted silently to five, then dove at Suzanne's feet. She felt Suzanne fly through the air and sensed that she was trying to keep the little gun trained on her. Suzanne grabbed at Nina's waist, but Nina caught her wrists and forced the hand gripping the gun over her head. Now they were both rolling down the salt slope. Nina and Suzanne tumbled, locked together, as Nina struggled to keep the gun pointed away from her while Suzanne tried to maneuver the muzzle toward her. Nina closed her eyes to keep the salt out, feeling increasingly dizzy, and they rolled over and over, gathering speed.

Nina shrieked with pain as she and Suzanne landed with a thud on the hard-packed sand at the foot of the salt pile and rolled to a stop inches from the toes of Blue Roker's boots. The little gold gun skittered away across the sand and was quickly scooped up by a police officer.

Blue looked down at Nina and Suzanne in amazement.

"Nina!" shouted Pansy, running toward her. "Are you hurt? Are you shot?"

"It's the salt! I shaved my legs this morning! It burns!" said Nina, scrambling to her feet in front of the police chief. She hopped from foot to foot, frantically trying to brush off the coarse grains of sea salt that coated her legs and arms.

Danish snickered. "You look like a life-size human pretzel," he said.

"It's her! She tried to kill Philip!" Nina pointed at Suzanne. Her clothes were still wet from splashing through the ponds, and her hair was full of salt.

"Mandy!" said Blue in a loud voice, still staring at Nina. An officer stepped forward.

"Cuff the one in the skirt," said Blue. The officer moved swiftly toward Suzanne, and in one motion, lifted her to her feet and hand-cuffed her. He led her away to the police car.

Blue stood with his hands on his hips, looking from Nina to Danish to Pansy and back to Nina again. The radio at his hip crackled. Another officer stepped forward and whispered something in his ear; Blue waved him away.

He raised his eyebrows. "A loaded gun. No, two loaded guns. A dangerously mentally ill woman. A man's life at stake. And you thought it was a good idea for you three to come out here alone because . . . ?" he asked them.

"We couldn't wait," said Danish. "We had a hunch, and—"

"Don't. Say. Another. Word," said Blue in a deadly quiet voice. He was pointing at Danish but looking at Nina and Pansy.

"I know this looks . . . bad, Blue," said Nina. "However, I would like to point out that we did, in fact, inform the police as soon as we thought Suzanne might be involved. And if we hadn't been here, Philip would likely be dead now." She suddenly remembered Philip. "Philip! Where's Philip?" she looked around frantically.

"I'm right here," said Philip. He was sitting on the ground. His suit was stained and tattered, and his eyeglasses were bent. He cleared his throat and said, "In defense of these three brave individuals, I would like to say that if they hadn't arrived, I would most surely be dead. I know Suzanne. She once flushed a live goldfish down the toilet without batting an eyelash. Nina, you can expect a letter of commendation to be appended to your employment file."

Blue stared at all of them for a moment longer, then sighed and turned away.

"Let's go, Mandy," he called to his deputy. "The rest of you stay here and secure the scene. The house, too. I'll be back as soon as I can. Dr. Putzel, Officer Mandel will escort you back to town, take a statement, and call a doctor to check you out, if you will come with us now, please."

Philip scrambled to his feet and allowed himself to be bundled into a police Jeep by the deputy.

"Um, Blue," said Pansy tentatively, "do you think you could give us a ride back to town? The solar batteries on my cart seem to have run down . . ."

Blue looked back at them, then gestured impatiently for them to get in his car. They drove in silence all the way back to Coconut Cove. When the convoy pulled up in front of the police station, Nina stepped stiffly out onto the sidewalk. She ached all over.

With surprise, she noticed that there was a police van in front and several Defence Force officers walking briskly up the lane from the police dock wearing full gear.

I guess we weren't the only ones to have an exciting night, thought Nina.

She got another surprise when she saw Sylvia and Nancy walking up the lane from the public dock, each carrying an enormous crayfish in her hands. They were giggling uncontrollably. It appeared they'd been out fishing and were perhaps three sheets to the wind.

They stopped and took in the scene. "Well, what have we here?" Nancy said, looking from Suzanne, who was handcuffed between Blue and another officer, to Philip, his clothes covered in mud and ketchup and his hair standing straight up, to Nina, who was still covered in white patches of coarse sea salt.

"Suzanne?" said Sylvia incredulously. "Is that you? What on earth is going on? Philip. You look insane."

"*I* look insane?" shouted Philip. "That psychopath tried to kill me!" He pointed at Suzanne. "Not once, but *four times*! I'll be leaving on the first flight tomorrow morning."

Suzanne struggled to shake off the officer's grip, her eyes blazing.

"You deserve it after what you did to me!" she spat. "He cheated and he lied and he used up the best years of my life. Then he dumped me for some student and had a *baby* with her. *That's* criminal! When I heard he was headed to a fancy hotel on a tropical island for a weeklong 'business' trip, it was too much. He was getting away with it! All of it! *Not if I could help it!*

Sylvia shook her head slowly. "Oh, honey," she said sadly. "Didn't anyone ever tell you? The best revenge is living well. He isn't worth it."

"I don't recall anyone asking your opinion, Sylvia," said Philip indignantly.

Sylvia shrugged.

"Come on, Philip. We'll give you a ride back to the inn," said Nancy. Philip looked at Blue.

"Go on home, Dr. Putzel. It's been a long day. We've got enough going on here tonight to keep us occupied. Mandy will be over to see you in the morning," Blue said.

Nancy, Sylvia, and Philip climbed into Nancy's golf cart, which was parked in the lane. Philip sat stiffly on the back bench as they drove away.

Blue gestured for his officers to take Suzanne into the station. When they were gone, he walked slowly over to where Nina, Pansy, and Danish had gathered. He stood in front of them with his hands on his hips. He looked first at them and then across the street at the row of dark shops on Water Street. Finally, he looked back at the trio of self-styled investigators.

"I would thank you for your assistance in capturing the suspect," he said slowly, "but I don't want to encourage such behavior in the future. Can we come to an understanding that you'll stay out of police matters from now on?"

"Yes, sir!" said Nina, Pansy, and Danish in unison.

I really mean it this time, Nina told herself.

She looked down and saw that Danish had crossed his fingers.

Oh boy, she thought.

"All right, then, we've got a deal," Blue said. "Thank you, and have a good night. I'll be in touch. We'll need to get your statements tomorrow, but for tonight, let's just all get a good night's sleep."

He nodded to them and went into the station, his head bowed. As she watched him go, Nina felt a bit sorry for him. He'd be up all night processing Suzanne. Did he ever get to let loose while someone else was the heavy?

"I vote we head to The Redoubt for a celebratory drink," said Danish.

"Good idea," said Pansy.

"I'm in," said Nina. "Just let me get this salt off first."

13

Nina cleaned herself off with a garden hose at the marina, then stood in front of the electric hand dryer in the public washroom drying out her T-shirt and shorts. She thought about how drastically her life had changed since she and her friend Louise used to meet up at a chic downtown wine bar after work, dressed in tailored suits and heels.

She pulled her damp and salty hair into a ponytail with a rubber band and rejoined her friends. "I think I'm good to go," she said.

The Redoubt was at full capacity when they arrived. A reggae band was playing, and the crowd on the impromptu dance floor pulsed to the beat. The tables were full of locals and tourists.

When a booth at the back became vacant, they made a beeline for it.

"I'll get the drinks," said Nina, weaving back through the crowd to the bar. While she stood waiting for their Goombay Smashes, she scanned the evening crowd, looking for Ted. He wasn't there.

"Howdy, neighbor," said a voice in her left ear. It was Les.

"Looking for someone?" he asked, his eyebrows raised. "Of course, I don't know who that might be, but I did see Ted Matthews drive by on my stroll down here. He had a lady friend with him. Come to think of it, I saw them last night, too. Dressed to the nines. Very chic.

A candlelit dinner at the Plantation Inn would be my guess. That's his signature move."

Nina's heart sank.

Les took a pull on his beer, his eyes pinned on her. He seemed to be waiting for some kind of reaction.

"Buzz off, Les," she said, and turned away.

He laughed. "Actually, I'm just in here blowing off a little steam after settling the sand-man case. It was a big win for the agency," he said.

"And what agency might that be?" asked Nina. She was intrigued, although she didn't want to show it. She turned slightly back toward him.

"The Ministry of Natural Resources. I'm a freelance conservation agent on special assignment to the government," he replied with casual self-importance. "Yeah, we were executing the sting when your friend called Roker about some situation you'd gotten yourself into. Roker doesn't lose his cool very often, but there were some fireworks tonight. You might want to think about minding your own business for a while."

So that's what took Blue so long, thought Nina.

"I thought you were a professional gambler. Now you're an undercover conservation agent? Whoever heard of an undercover conservation agent? Whoever heard of a *freelance* undercover conservation agent? Even if it's true, I think you screwed up on the *undercover* part. You're the least covered person I've ever met. You're pretty much always naked. You're not exactly keeping a low profile, are you?"

"Ever hear the expression 'hiding in plain sight'? Fooled you, didn't I? And actually, I *am* a professional card player. I'm also a private investigator specializing in marine cases. Roker hired me on contract to gather evidence on the sand man because he's been a little busy." He smiled at Nina. "I am a man of many talents."

"Sort of a poor man's James Bond."

"Call it whatever you want, if it makes you happy. I'm living the dream." Les turned to look out the open doors at the water and took a long pull on the bottle of beer that always seemed to be in his hand.

A glimmer of hope dawned in Nina. "So, is that really your house or just part of your cover?"

"Oh, it's all mine, baby, and boy, I can't wait to get back there and unwind a little. Or a lot. I think I'm in a James Brown mood tonight. I wonder what your pal Bridget's up to. Still waters run deep, my friend. That's all I can say about that."

"Bridget left this afternoon," Nina said.

Les shrugged. "Probably for the best. She was getting too attached."

Nina snorted. "Don't flatter yourself, playboy. She was laughing when I saw her leave for the airport."

Nina's drinks arrived, and she carried them back to their booth. Les followed her and slid in beside Pansy. He gave her a slimy grin, and she rolled her eyes.

"Are we celebrating something?" Les asked as Nina distributed the drinks.

"You betcha," said Danish, providing a rapid-fire account of Suzanne's abduction of Philip and the high-stakes parlor game she'd played with him in the isolated house by the salt ponds.

"Yeah, she's totally nuts," said Danish. "One of the questions she asked him was, 'If a woman asks a man if he wants to go to the movies, what's the right answer?' How was he supposed to answer that without knowing all the pertinent facts, like what's playing at the movies and what's on TV? Apparently his answer was wrong, because she freaked out."

"Oh, that hoary old chestnut," said Les.

Nina ignored him and looked at Danish.

"She freaked out because she's gone off the deep end, but also because the only correct answer to that question is *yes*. She isn't asking if *he* wants to go to the movies. She's telling him *she does*," said Nina.

"Um, I beg to differ," said Les, pausing to take another swig of his beer.

"Oh, really?" said Nina, waiting for him to continue.

"Yes." He looked Danish in the eye. "For future reference, man, you have three viable options in this situation. Option A, you can call her bluff and say no, then just tune out the fallout. You're a man and you have rights. Option B, you can make her happy and say, 'Sure, let's go to a movie.' Your call. But the thing is, what she's really asking is, 'Do you care enough about me to want to spend quality time with me?' So, if you don't want to go the movies, you can go with option C and say, 'I don't really feel like a movie tonight, babe, but I really do want to spend some quality time with you. How about a soak in the hot tub or a sunset sail?' Chicks *love* that. Or you could go for broke and say, 'I'd like to be alone with you. Why don't we curl up together on the sofa and watch the game?' You see, by demonstrating that you're aware of her emotional needs, you've avoided an argument, gotten out of going to a chick flick, and managed to watch the game in the comfort of your own home. Meanwhile, your chances of getting lucky are still strong."

"Don't take advice on women from him, Danish," said Nina. "He's a misogynist pig."

"True, but he's also sort of right about the first part, don't you think?" said Pansy, wincing. "That's exactly what that question means, sometimes."

"Genius, man. I'm putting it in the toolbox," Danish said admiringly, and high-fived Les across the table.

"Oh, I'm sorry," said Nina. "Please, I yield the floor to someone who knows more about women than I, a woman, could possibly know."

"I'll accept that," said Les. "Of course, you're an expert on *one* woman. You. I, on the other hand, have gathered my expertise from many and varied sources."

Danish laughed but stopped abruptly when Nina glared at him.

"Go away, Les!" said Nina. "This is a private party!"

"I was just leaving," Les said as he stood, a filthy smirk on his face.

When it was just the three of them, Danish lifted his glass. "I'd like to propose a toast to us," he said. "We're awesome."

"I guess I can drink to that," said Nina.

"To us," said Pansy. They clinked glasses and drank in unison.

"Poor Suzanne," said Pansy. "How unhappy she must be, to follow Philip all the way down here and try to kill him."

"She couldn't be more different from Sylvia," said Nina. "Sylvia should patent her approach to getting over a cheating husband. I wonder if Philip has learned anything from this."

"Well, I've learned one thing. Don't ever get married," said Danish. "I really feel like I dodged a bullet!"

"Oh, Danish. Marriage isn't always like that. Sometimes it's pretty nice," said Pansy.

Nina didn't say anything.

"C'mon, let's dance," Pansy said, grabbing Nina's hand. They joined the crowd in front of the stage and danced until the band took a break.

Pansy looked at her watch.

"It's nine o'clock! I told Andrew I'd be home by eight at the latest."

"Relax. My cart is in front of the post office. I'll give you a lift home," said Danish. "You want a ride, Nina?

"No, I think I'll walk, thanks."

"Night, Nina!" said Pansy, giving her a hug. "I'll call you tomorrow."

"Don't forget, we still haven't had a chance to talk about my fantastic business idea!" said Danish as they headed for the door. "I'll be in touch."

Danish's business idea. Right. With any luck, he'd forget about it before Nina saw him next. But when did Danish ever forget about anything? She had a feeling she was going to have to sit through this pitch eventually. She sighed and waved goodbye.

Nina walked home along the beach, splashing through the surf in her bare feet and thinking about Suzanne and Sylvia and the very different directions their lives had taken. At home, she took a hot shower and put on fresh, salt-free clothes, then sat on the veranda with a cup of tea. It had been one strange day.

She glanced up toward the point. The lights from the guest cottages were twinkling through the trees. She wondered what Ted was doing. Had he really found himself another woman already? Was he actually bothered by her kibitzing with Les? Or maybe it was her detention in the local jail that had put him off?

She shook her head with impatience at herself. The adult thing to do would be to go see him, say hi, and clear the air. If he had company, she'd just give him his hat and go home. It would be a perfectly normal thing to do, returning his beloved hat. She went back inside, got a bottle of wine out of the cupboard, grabbed his hat off the table and a flashlight from a drawer, and headed up the beach to the lodge.

The path from the beach to the main lodge climbed a slight incline up through a grove of feathery casuarina pines, passing by the dim shapes of guest cottages on either side, their windows glowing with rectangles of yellow light, curtains drawn. Nina emerged into a small clearing where the main lodge stood. Its wraparound veranda was shadowy and vacant, and the lodge was dark, except for the porch light over the door and the faint glow of one reading lamp in a corner inside. Nina tiptoed up the steps and peeked in. There was no one there.

She continued up a steep path through the trees to Ted's cottage on its secluded perch above the lodge. She emerged from the trees a few feet from his front step. Like the lodge, it was a wooden clapboard cabin stained a soft gray-brown that blended into its surroundings. Golden light spilled out of the windows onto the veranda. He must still be up. Nina started up the steps. Twangy country music wafted out of the open windows, along with the aroma of rich, spicy food. Patsy Cline. Torch music.

He's not alone, thought Nina with sudden alarm. *Of course not.* She retreated swiftly down the steps, lighting the path through the trees with her flashlight.

Nina heard the screen door open behind her, and she looked back. Ted was on the porch, bare-chested and barefoot, wearing only his all-purpose khaki fishing shorts.

Oh, thought Nina. *He does have company, and he's half-dressed.* A stab to the heart.

"Nina," Ted said with surprise. His eyes dropped to the bottle of wine in her hand, then returned to her eyes. She wanted to disappear. Instead, she turned to face him.

"Hi, Ted. I thought I'd come by and say hi and return your hat. But it's late. You're busy. I'm so sorry. I'll see you later." She forced a weak smile, then turned and started quickly down the path again, still clutching his hat and holding her chin up, trying to maintain some dignity.

"Nina! Wait!" he called, running down the steps after her. "Where are you going? Come on in."

She hesitated for a moment, then walked slowly back toward him. "OK," she said.

"I just got back a little while ago. We were fishing down south around Wreath Cay today, then I had to make a run to the airport. I was just getting around to making some supper," he said as they walked back up the steps onto the porch. He held the screen door open for her. He smelled fresh from the shower.

"Are you hungry?" he asked. "I know you're vegetarian, so you wouldn't be interested in chili, but I can make you an omelet. Have a seat. I'll be right back."

Ted disappeared through a doorway, and Nina glanced around the cabin. There was no visible sign that a woman had recently been there. The cabin's living area was one big room. From the front door where she stood, she could see into the kitchen in the far back corner, separated from the seating area by a kitchen island. Dishes were stacked neatly on open shelves, and a few pots and pans hung from hooks on the wall. In the front corner of the cabin, opposite where she stood, a blue twill sofa and chair sat beneath a bank of windows. In daylight, the room must have a view of the water and the coastline in three directions. Light from a reading lamp on a table by the sofa cast a warm honey glow on the varnished pine-board walls and floor.

Nina placed Ted's hat on a coat hook by the door and took a few steps into the living room, still looking around. A guitar leaned against the wall, and a floor-to-ceiling bookcase stood between the windows. It was crammed with books, objects, and a couple of framed photographs. Nina leaned in to peer at them. A recent picture of Ted with three smiling blonde women, then another with the same women, an older couple, and assorted small children. They all looked alike. *His parents, sisters, nieces, and nephews,* thought Nina. Next to the bookcase was a fly-tying table with a little bundle of brightly colored feathers wrapped in silver thread pinched in a clamp under a large magnifying glass. The room was neat and clean.

A book lay open on the arm of the chair, spine up. Nina turned her head sideways to read the title. *The Old Man and the Sea* by Ernest Hemingway.

He really must think about fishing all the time, thought Nina. It was an early-edition hardback with an illustrated dust jacket. She picked it up to have a closer look. A card fell out from between the pages and fluttered to the floor. She bent down to pick it up, glancing at it as she tucked back in between the pages of the book. It was a birthday card.

Happy 40th Birthday, Ted. Watch out you don't end up like this guy. Love, Sandy xo

"My sister sent me that book a while ago. I'm just getting around to reading it," said Ted from behind Nina. She turned to look at him, the book still in her hand. He was pulling a white T-shirt on over his tanned torso. She looked away.

"Oh, that's nice," she said.

"Yeah, I think I read it in school, but I can't remember the particulars. It's not looking good for Santiago at this point. May I pour you a glass of wine?"

He gestured to the bottle she'd brought. It was now standing on the floor at her feet where she'd set it down to pick up the card.

"That would be nice, thanks," said Nina, bending down to pick up the bottle at the same time he reached for it. Their heads bumped.

"Ow, sorry," said Nina.

"That's all right," he said, looking into her eyes at close range. His brown eyes were warm beneath their fringe of long blond lashes. He gave her a smile and headed for the kitchen with the bottle, digging around in a drawer for a corkscrew. If he was bothered by Les and the hot tub, he gave no indication of it. He came back and handed her a glass.

"Cheers," he said.

"Cheers," said Nina.

They both took a sip of wine and then stood for a moment facing each other, neither speaking. Outside, the cicadas hummed loudly in the dense bush behind the cabin.

"Come keep me company in the kitchen while I make your omelet," Ted finally said. So, they weren't going to jump right into discussing the supermodel or Les's hot tub, thought Nina. Good.

She relaxed a little. She sat on a stool at the island sipping her wine and watching him expertly whip a couple of eggs, chop some spinach and onions, and sauté the lot with butter in a cast-iron frying pan. He turned it out onto a plate and set it down in front of her, along with a knife, fork and napkin. Then he dished up a bowl of chili for himself from the stove.

"Thank you. It looks great," she said.

"My pleasure," he answered, pulling a stool up to the counter and sitting across from her.

"So, it's been a while since I've seen you. What's new?" he said, taking a bite.

"Well, I guess you could say a lot has happened," she said. She recounted the evening's events, culminating in Suzanne's arrest by Blue and his officers at the salt-storage depot. He listened to the story with a combination of amusement and amazement. When she was done, he gave a low whistle.

"Boy, you've sure livened up Blue's days. I'm guessing his project cataloging seaweed has ground to a halt since you blew into town."

"Pardon me?" said Nina.

"Blue's got this idea that the seaweed growing off the west coast of Pineapple Cay could be harvested for fertilizer. A new industry for the island. Good jobs for young people so they can stay if they want. In his spare time, he's been cataloging the types of seaweed and where they're found. He used to have a fair amount of spare time, in between the odd drunk and disorderly at The Pirate's Wake and patrolling the cays for petty smugglers and poachers. But it sounds like he's got his hands full these days."

So Blue does have some kind of a life outside supervising Pineapple Cayers and working in his garden, thought Nina.

Ted chuckled and looked at her with . . . fondness . . . admiration? She wasn't sure. The silence lengthened, and Nina decided to plunge in headfirst.

"So, has your friend gone home?"

"Pardon?" he said.

"Your lady friend," she said brazenly.

"Oh, her," he said. He took a drink of his wine before he spoke. "She's an attorney," he said. "She came to a fishing show I was at about six months ago, in New York. She booked the whole lodge for three days. I assumed she was bringing a group with her. As I recall, she had a boyfriend in tow at the show. I took the van to the airport to pick them up, and it was just her. She said she booked the trip because she needed some peace and quiet. I guess she must be a very successful attorney, to buy this much peace and quiet."

"You must have made a real impression on her in New York," said Nina.

He shrugged.

"She's very attractive," said Nina. *Oh, Nina, really,* she chastised herself.

"Yes, I guess she is, in a certain kind of way," said Ted. "But she wasn't all that interested in fishing, as it turns out." He said it like that voided any other charms she might have had.

"I think she'd read an article in some magazine, or maybe she just liked the gear and got it in her head that fly-fishing was for her," he said. "Turns out she liked the idea of fishing in the abstract but not in the execution. I think she found it boring."

He said this in a mystified tone, as if she'd confessed to him that she believed in fairies.

"Anyway, I took her out the first morning, and she fished for about half an hour. Then she said she just wanted to go for a boat ride and look at the scenery. Fine. I asked Ricky to take her out for the afternoon session, but she insisted that she'd booked the head guide—me. Dinner in the empty lodge was a bit awkward, especially with Cheryl giggling in the kitchen. Day two, she decided to spend her time sunbathing on the beach. I stayed out of the way, up here. I even got Danish Jensen over here to give her a private yoga lesson while I caught up on some paperwork. She asked several times where the nightlife was. I told her there was none, but she wasn't buying it, so I took her to dinner at the inn last night. By the time I put her on the plane tonight, I was wrung out. Turns out I don't have that much to talk about with an attorney from Manhattan."

Good, thought Nina. "Me neither," she said aloud, referring to her philandering soon-to-be ex-husband Darren, a lawyer. Although in a roundabout way, she guessed a New York lawyer was responsible for Nina's move from New York to Pineapple Cay.

Ted chuckled. "Thank God I've just got a group of refinery workers from Texas to deal with tomorrow morning."

They sat looking at each other, and the silence grew between them again. Patsy Cline had finished singing. Nina waited for him to ask about Les and the hot-tubbing at sunset, but Ted obviously had more restraint than she did. Or maybe he just didn't care that much. Easy come, easy go. He no doubt had his share of female admirers. If one woman proved to be too much work, another one would be along shortly. In the meantime, he was courteous and polite.

She sighed quietly and looked around the room for a topic of conversation. Her eyes landed on the guitar in the corner.

"Do you play?" she asked.

"Poorly," he said.

"Will you play something?" she asked.

"I suppose I could, if you'll make allowances," he said, and rose from his chair, holding his hand out to her. "Let's sit on the sofa awhile."

She took his hand, and he squeezed hers gently. He held on to her hand as he guided her over to the sofa, where she sank back against the cushions, feeling a bit light-headed. He picked up the guitar and sat facing her. He strummed a few chords, then played an old Hank Williams melody, slow and melancholy, his fingers moving up and down the frets.

He can cook, he can fix a boat engine, and he plays the guitar, thought Nina. *I wonder what else he can do?* She had a pretty good idea.

By the time he finished playing, her eyes were open wide, and her heart was beating fast in her chest.

"That was beautiful," she said.

He laid the guitar gently on the floor beside him and moved closer to her, holding her gaze. He leaned toward her and kissed her. A long, tender kiss. Nina felt the room begin to spin.

"You smell nice," he said softly in her ear.

"So do you," she murmured.

"Should I look behind the sofa to see if Danish Jensen or Philip Putzel is there?" he whispered. She smiled.

He pulled her to him, wrapping his arms around her, and grazed her neck with his lips. Then he kissed her mouth again, more deeply. She kissed him back. She could feel both their hearts pounding as she put her hand on his chest, her fingers tracing his muscles and taking in the heat of his body through the thin cotton of his T-shirt. His hand slipped under the fabric of her shirt and slid across her bare skin to the small of her back. He pressed her to him. They were headed somewhere fast.

"When I was sitting across from you at dinner the other night, listening to Sylvia talk about her trip to England, this is what I was thinking about," Ted murmured. He kissed her again. Nina felt light-headed. Was she ready for this? She felt a sudden panic set in, and her body stiffened. He sat back and looked at her questioningly.

"Are you all right? Is this OK?" he asked.

She struggled to answer. He waited for a moment, watching her, then pulled gently away, holding her hands in his.

"How about a cup of tea?" he asked. She nodded. He gave her a small, reassuring smile and squeezed her hand, then stood and walked slowly to the kitchen. He rubbed his hand over his face and through his hair while he filled the kettle. Nina sat on the edge of the sofa and watched him. A few minutes later he came back holding two cups of tea. He handed one to her, then sat beside her on the sofa.

"Nina, it's all right," said Ted, looking her in the eye. "I think I've got a pretty good idea of where you're at. You're recently divorced, just finding your feet, enjoying a new adventure. Look, I've been there, I understand," he said. "I think my feelings are pretty clear. I'd like to get to know you better. But I'm a patient man. It's a job requirement in my line of work. And I want you to be sure of what you want." He smiled and breathed deeply, in and out.

She smiled back tentatively and relaxed. Man, he was really good at this.

Eat your heart out, Les. This is how a real man talks about his feelings, she thought.

"I like you a lot, Ted. Really. A lot," said Nina, finally finding her voice. She chose not to elaborate on how her whole body was electrified when he touched her arm or the number of hours she had already lost thinking about his beautiful eyes and charmingly old-fashioned manners.

"It's just too fast," she said. "Not because I have doubts, but because it's new and strange and overwhelming."

"So we'll take it slow," he said softly.

In a brisker tone, Ted said, "Let's get some fresh air." He stood and pulled her to her feet. "On quiet nights like this when the sky is clear, I like to take a blanket down to the beach and lie there looking at the stars. Are you up for it?"

"That sounds perfect," said Nina.

Ted grabbed a folded quilt off the arm of the sofa, and still holding hands, they walked down the path to the beach. Ted spread the quilt on the sand and patted the spot beside him. They lay back together, her head on his shoulder and his arm wrapped around her. The velvet-black sky was full of stars. The steady, quiet *shush* of the surf was the only sound.

"Let's just see where the stars lead us, shall we?" said Ted.

"That sounds perfect," said Nina with a smile.

ACKNOWLEDGMENTS

My deep thanks to the team at Lake Union Publishing for the wonderful experience of publishing my novel with them and for contributing their substantial expertise to the project. I am indebted to editor Miriam Juskowicz for calling me out of the blue one day to ask if I'd like to publish my book with Lake Union, and for her kind words of encouragement along the way. Thank you to editorial director Danielle Marshall for keeping me on track with *Beachbound*, to Devan Hanna and the marketing department for helping readers find this book, and to Gabe Dumpit for answering my questions along the way.

I would like to thank Kristin Mehus-Roe for her sensitive and astute edit of the manuscript. She has made me sound more literate than I am, and her contributions have improved the story. My sincere thanks also to copy editor Sarah Engel, proofreader Jill Kramer, and production editors Nicole Pomeroy and Elise Marton. If you compared the first draft of *Beachbound* with the book you are now holding, their efforts would be immediately apparent. I am grateful to book designer Danielle Christopher for the beautiful cover. It was an honor to work with you all.

Finally, thank you to all the readers who took the time to write to me and post book reviews online. It is always great to hear from you.

ABOUT THE AUTHOR

Junie Coffey lives with Fisherman Fred and Hurricane Annie in a little town north of forty-five degrees latitude, which got two hundred inches of snow last winter. She has worked as a travel writer, and has both lived and vacationed throughout the Bahamas and the Caribbean, spending time in the islands every chance she gets. To learn more about the author and her work, visit www.pineapplecay.com.

52361162R00166

Made in the USA
San Bernardino, CA
18 August 2017